The
Crying
Out

The
Crying
Out

DIANE KEATING

EXILE
editions
Fiction, Poetry, Translation, Drama and Nonfiction

Library and Archives Canada Cataloguing in Publication

Keating, Diane, author
The crying out : a novel / Diane Keating.

Issued in print and electronic formats.
ISBN 978-1-55096-429-5 (pbk.).--ISBN 978-1-55096-430-1(epub).--
ISBN 978-1-55096-431-8 (mobi).--ISBN 978-1-55096-432-5 (pdf)

I. Title.

PS8571.E38C79 2014   C813'.54   C2014-904189-6
                                              C2014-904190-X

Tesx Design and Composition by Mishi Uroboros
Typeset in Fairfield and Dakota Handwriting fonts at Moons of Jupiter Studios

Published by Exile Editions Ltd ~ www.ExileEditions.com
144483 Southgate Road 14-GD, Holstein, Ontario, N0G 2A0
Printed and Bound in Canada in 2014, by Imprimerie Gauvin

We gratefully acknowledge, for their support toward our publishing activities,
the Canada Council for the Arts, the Government of Canada through
the Canada Book Fund (CBF), the Ontario Arts Council,
and the Ontario Media Development Corporation.

Canadian Sales: The Canadian Manda Group, 165 Dufferin Street,
Toronto ON M6K 3H6 www.mandagroup.com 416 516 0911

North American and International Distribution, and U.S. Sales:
Independent Publishers Group, 814 North Franklin Street,
Chicago IL 60610 www.ipgbook.com toll free: 1 800 888 4741

For Robert Gardner
who held the boat steady
on my night sea voyages

"Who if I cried out, would hear me among the angels'
hierarchies? And even if one of them pressed me
suddenly against his heart: I would be consumed
in that overwhelming existence."

—RAINER MARIA RILKE

❧ PROLOGUE ☙

September 22nd, 1691

The Spring

Two fields beyond the Parsonage theres a littel streem where Mama, Tituba & I gather plants to make into medicines. Abbie cann't come. She giggel'd when a flie landed on Papas nose during morning prayers so now she must scour the chamber potts.

We be picking bunches of watercress & liverwort & marsh marigold when Tituba glimps't the blotchie toadstools that ressembel the shrunk'n heads of Fairies. She claims they will make a potent drink against Witchcraft – speshelly if they stink like they sprung from the dead while being brewed.

Much time passes as we follow the trickeling water of the streem to its source. Here in a hollowe of pussie willows we squat & drink from our cupp'd handes. 'Cept for the water bubbeling up between mossie stones everythinge be still. It seems the world holds its breath. Waiting.

Holy as the well of Bethlehem wispers Mama.

We look quietlie upon each other. Thats when I hast the thought – as below the rock there be water so below what we be, we be somethinge else.

The light be long, Tituba warns, let us make haste. 'Tis the houre when the dogg becomes the wolfe.

On the way home we join hands. Me in the middel.

The
Gateless
Garden

❧ DAY ONE ❧

I remember as a child sitting beside Mama at this same kitchen table, watching her unwrap the Bible with such care it might have been the preserved heart of a saint. I remember the sharp lavender smell of the shawl and the feel of the disintegrating leather cover. Like old flesh. Although I could touch, I was not allowed to turn the transparent yellowing pages. One thousand four hundred and ten of them, Mama would say while opening the last four pages. "Family Record" was scrolled across the top, the red and gold lettering faded to rust brown.

Our branch of the family tree, as recorded in the Bible, began in 1772 with the seed of George James Robinson having been planted in Elizabeth Ruth Perkins. Mama and I counted forty-seven names. Eleven of them are Witherspoons born in this once grand, now dilapidated, old house. Mine is the last – Sibyl Elizabeth Witherspoon. The same as my mother and my grandmother and my great-grandmother. Four generations of Sibyls, our roots deeper than the giant oak creaking in the wind outside the kitchen window as I am slowly making these words.

Each of us is an only child of an only child. Once, while thumbing through a school encyclopedia, I happened upon my name and discovered that, in pagan times, sibyls were priestesses dwelling in sacred caves that were thought to be entrances to the underworld. Since they could summon up spirits of the dead for consultation, they were brought to Rome, and a powerful cult developed around them. Later, under Christianity, the word *sibyl* referred to a prophetess or a fortuneteller or a witch. Maybe that's the reason why folks around here find us strange.

Mama told me that we Sibyls are not like a branch that sprouts twigs and leaves. Our lineage is straight and strong, one linked to another, like rungs on a ladder. There's no need to fear falling, she added – glancing over her shoulder at the trapdoor to the cellar – with a ladder you can climb out of any hole.

The word hole, having no edges when it comes out of one's mouth, engulfed me. Like sleep engulfed me at night, my mattress disappearing into an open trapdoor. Endlessly falling through the dark, I could hear a voice crying way back in my brain – God help me. God help me. Unborn words. You have to beware of words in your head. They can take hold – possess you – if you are not careful. Like unwritten letters to the Papa I've never seen. Of whom Mama seldom spoke.

Whenever I tried to say them out loud my brain would go weak as water. It still does.

I find it hard to believe that after a three-year absence I am back in my ancestral home overlooking New Salem – a village so small it can't be found on most Ontario road maps. I never understood why there were so many places named Salem or New Salem or Old Salem in North America. People are always searching for peace it seems. *Peace* – an odd word – unlike *hole* with no edges, it sounds sharp, pointed as a unicorn's horn.

For most of the afternoon since my arrival I've been sitting here at the kitchen table, pen in hand, staring at the blank first page of this journal. Then the fingertips of my left hand, as though acting on their own behalf, left off drumming the edge of the table and began to smooth across the perfect whiteness of the paper. That's when it came to me. I was once left-handed. A first grade teacher had forced the change.

Now, having switched the pen to my other hand, I've watched the words form. Watched the letters crawl like tracks of an injured beetle with a long way to go…two hundred and twenty pages to be exact. I know. I counted each one in this journal as I marked the upper corner. Always the same. A five-pointed star inside a circle. While drawing, I never lift the pen from the paper, which is why some call it an endless knot.

Mama, who first drew one for me, called it a gateless garden. Eventually she found the way out. Of life, that is.

I carry on her struggle to make the star-circle perfectly. Over the years I must have doodled thousands — from the size of a penny in the margins of notebooks to the size of a dinner plate in the cubicles of public bathrooms. The arms of the star are always elongated or lopsided, the squished circle resembling more the shape of a skull or a Celtic cross or a spider wheel. The summer that Mama disappeared I was ten years old and tried tattooing our secret symbol on my palm — pressing the ballpoint pen so hard the flesh opened, the bright colour of the pain seeming pleasurable because it proved my devotion. I studied the swelling, the purplish skin translucent as an insect's wing. When I squeezed my hand into a fist the pain increased. And so did my hope that Mama would return. Not having the words — they must be specific as bricks — I somehow believed that this wound would be a gate letting out torment. At night, wakened by the throbbing pain and the heat, I was comforted by that thought.

When Gammer (as grandmothers are called in our family) found out, she washed my palm in a tincture made from the red root of peony and then applied a bread poultice which she changed every two hours. The scar still prickles whenever I am introduced to someone and forced to shake hands. Gammer never asked why I did it — just mumbled about my being over-wrought. I said nothing. How could I explain? All I knew was what I felt. To speak, to make each word into external reality – separate from me as the pen in my hand – has always been difficult.

I was barely sixteen when I broke the family curse and escaped on the only paved road with centre lines going through what for me was the Valley of Death, but for others was the Madawaska Valley, salmon fishing capital of northern Ontario. Over the next three years I gradually invented myself as I journeyed south to the Big City. That's what people around here call Toronto, the centre of the world for us teenagers. Only a few brave ones dared the pilgrimage to this Mecca of fame and fortune and even fewer made it – settling along the way at the "little cities" of Kingston or Ottawa. But I reached the shimmering city of my dreams and for the past six months I've been working at Robarts Library – fetching and returning books to its inner sanctum.

The massive building, rising from the heart of the city, is a raw concrete structure with overhanging towers. It exudes the brutal strength of a futuristic palace or prison, which is why I keep my head down as I round the corner of St. George Street at eight each weekday morning.

After pushing through the glass revolving doors into the mammoth lobby, I take an escalator to the second level and then make my way along the narrowing corridors to the windowless cavern at the centre. Here I am safe. The overhead march of fluorescent tubing is so insistent that the most distant corner has no shadow. And not once – even alone on the evening shift – do I have to listen for footsteps approaching.

Yes, here in the sacred core I am safe. Light, order, reason prevails.

Millions of books. Each with a place and each in its place. Solid as bricks. And as silent.

Billions of embalmed words waiting for the eye to raise them from the dead, to grant their creators immortality.

Such vanity, Gammer would snort. She never allows herself wings of hope. Her broad flat feet, pressing so firmly on the ground, can feel the tremors of earthquakes, mine explosions, train derailments from hundreds of miles away – even through the thick-soled black oxfords she always wears. I didn't inherit this ability, but I did grow into her peasant feet and plodding walk.

It makes me feel akin to a dray horse, pulling my grey metal cart loaded with books up and down the regimental rows of shelves. Because of my cart's creaking left front wheel, I've been nicknamed Creaky by the other library assistants, or fetch-and-carry-go-fers as we call ourselves. I don't mind. I hate *Sibyl*. In the future I intend to officially change my name to Cybelle, which sounds exotic – more fitting to who I am now. No, let me correct myself – to the smoke and mirrors I've created.

At school I was nicknamed Silly Sibyl. This was because when concentrating I had the habit of chewing the side of my tongue, and sometimes it would slip out of the corner of my mouth without me noticing. Miss Stewart used to tell me to stop behaving dumb as a cow chewing her cud. The reason I never raised my hand in class was the fear, if I opened my mouth to speak, that my tongue would take over and make the words come out wrong.

I am fond of my job at the library. It is the symmetry of the shelves. The precise order of the thousands of books…each one a solitary universe. Although I seldom open a book for fear of being sucked into it, sometimes my mind will consider the infinite ordering and reordering of twenty-six letters. It always makes me dizzy. Too much…as though attempting to comprehend the cosmos.

Sometimes, pushing my cart along the narrow rows, I daydream about a previous life where I might have been a burrowing rodent – perhaps a muskrat, a gopher's cousin – trapped and killed for its luxurious coat. I do have the same brown richness to my hair, the same large, slightly protruding eyes and the same strong jaw. And I'm most happy when by myself, digging…digging further back…back into my own dark recesses.

Although the other assistants complain about working the evening shift, I enjoy being alone in the sacred core. I give a quick kiss to every book I return or retrieve – just as my ancestors might have kissed their prayer books. Generations of these hardworking pious people, going all the way back to the Loyalists who fled America during its war for independence, are recorded in our family Bible. The oldest book in the house, it lies on the top of the dining room cabinet because there's no space on the shelves crammed with various patterns of china. Each set of china came with a new Witherspoon wife when she moved into the house, but none has been used since Great-Gammer died. The only thing ever laid on the room's mahogany table was a coffin, before it was carried out the back door to the family graveyard up the hill.

Yesterday seems a year ago. I had no inkling of my return to New Salem as I pulled my cart of books through the innermost cave of the Holiest of Holy. Nor was I aware of the sudden shift in weather in the outer realm. The bowlegged security guard, Mr. Poland (Roly Poly they call him behind his back), warned me.

"The warmest May 27th on record," he announced, opening the door. After days of rain the air was steamy and, even at six o'clock, the sun lay hot and heavy on top of my head. As I began my usual fifteen-minute walk home, my eyes were constantly on the pavement in order to avoid the grit and mud and many puddles. For the first time, I grew aware that the heaving and buckling caused by the long hard winter had greatly increased the number of cracks. To avoid stepping on one, while at the same time skirting a dawdler or puddle, required my complete attention. But I was happy. That afternoon, at my six-month review, Miss Slade had given me a raise and said she was pleased with my work. This must have been the reason I reverted back to my childhood, gradually transforming the half-mile length of sidewalk from the library to home into a gigantic hopscotch court.

Years ago I had invented my version of the game to amuse myself as I walked to and from school. Here in the Big City, surrounded by so many people, I refined the process to include a marker – that is, a person about ten paces ahead moving in the same direction. I tried to overtake such a person by walking briskly. A passerby, I imagined, would have the sense of someone on an urgent errand. Any overlap of toe or heel on a crack means instant disqualification, and I have to stop and find a new marker. If I am fast enough to catch up with one person, I must quickly find another.

So the game continued along the snow-bare sidewalk, and I was aware only of my hurtling over the irregular weird cracks to reach the marker who was always retreating. Like Mama in the fragment of a dream who is always walking away. Like Mama on the day I turned ten.

That was nine years ago. School holidays had just begun. We were leaving to pick my favorite fruit. Strawberries. The small sweet wild ones hiding in the fields beyond the Mad, which is what locals call the Madawaska River. As we pulled on our boots,

Gammer came in from the barn. "All the cows are lying down in the pasture," she warned, "and the clouds are low."

"Sibyl, you will have to stay home," Mama said, "so I can hurry and get back before the storm comes. Then you can help whip the cream for your birthday shortcake."

I sat sulking on the porch steps. I had hoped this day would be different, but Mama was walking out of my world – as she so often did – down the road that led to the old stone mill. It had been closed for over a century but now the abandoned building, situated where the river forks, had been sold to a big-city businessman who wanted to convert it into a country inn. Because of her knowledge about local plants and flowers, Mama had been hired to help with the gardens.

As I sat picking at a scab on my knee, I heard the squeaking handle of the tin berry pail, the scrunch of the pebbly lane under her scurrying step – so different from the quicksilver stride of her coming down the hall when I cried out in the night.

The sound stopped. She had turned to look back. Our eyes met. Most times she looked through me as though I was made of glass – a window through which she saw a distant mountain. But this day she seemed to be really seeing me. I froze under her stare…so fierce it almost hurt.

Then a gust of wind blew by me, picking up the long copper curls of her hair so they appeared to be waving goodbye. "So long," she sang out. I was supposed to reply, "God speed you," and then she would say, "Safe home." That was our little ritual whenever she went out, whether it be for an hour or a day. But this time, punishing her for not taking me, I didn't reply. And in the heavy days that followed, as I waited and listened – the way a dog does – for her return, I heard her last words, "So long, so long," echo from the void she'd left inside me.

I'll be twenty on my next birthday…as many years without her as with her. If only she hadn't taken refuge under the bridge during the four-hour deluge, the torrent pouring down the escarpment so powerful it flattened our barn into an arc which drifted downhill a mile. Only one chicken survived. But the worst was the flash flooding. It broke the dam at the Old Mill and turned the toothless babbling of the river into a devouring rage that swept up Mama, grinding her into tiny bits too small to ever be found.

If only I had said goodbye. Even waved my hand. Then I would not have slept every night (until I met Rosie) with my face down and the blankets tucked smooth as water around me – a dead body floating into the future. I would not have wakened every morning drenched by unreachable sorrow at finding her gone.

I did not intend to write these words. To inflict pain on myself. It's not the same as tattooing a pentacle into my palm, as using one pain to diffuse another. According to Gammer, before the invention of anaesthesia, when a horse's tooth was being pulled a nail would be driven into its hoof. The brainless bright pain of the body need not be feared. It's almost as if we need it – like bread, said Gammer – to build stronger lives. What we don't need is unquenchable sorrow.

While staring at the cover of this journal, my mind has been tracing the events of yesterday, starting with the woman who cut across my path and interrupted my hopscotch game. It was the red of her hair – the same colour as Mama's – that forced me into following her. Tall, loose-limbed as a scarecrow, she slipped quickly and easily along in worn jeans and an ill-fitting jacket.

She looked neither left nor right. I became bolder, getting close enough to catch the pungent scent of cheap cologne.

I was absorbed by a kind of excitement I had never felt before. We were alone, walking the rim of the world. The twenty paces between us dissolved into ten. Then three. Then I disappeared right into her. I could feel her stiffness in my neck, the ache of her feet in my boots, her fat on my inner thighs. How could such intimacy be possible? Perhaps because she lacked all knowledge of my existence, I could cease to exist except through her. I felt safe.

Suddenly she swerved into a doorway and, unable to separate myself, I turned too and there we were – face to face. Lowering my head, I plunged past and found myself standing in a small corner store. I dared not look back but reached for the first thing that came into my vision, a painting I recognized – Botticelli's *Birth of Venus* – on a book cover. As I was flipping through the blank pages, a clerk appeared beside me. "We're closing in five minutes," she said, her eyes cold as pebbles. Afraid the woman was waiting outside, I dawdled over the display of journals, trying to decide between Monet's water lilies or a ballerina by Degas. Of course, I bought the one I had first picked up, because Venus had Mama's amber eyes and Mama's coils of golden-red hair. As the clerk counted out my change on the glass counter, the clicking of her long red nails spoke of her disapproval and I dared not ask if there was a back exit.

Fortunately, the woman I was following had vanished. Nothing was familiar. I was standing on a street surrounded by tired, shabby storefronts pressing hard against each other. No one was in sight. A large white cat, sitting motionless as a milk jug on a front step, stared at me with eyes that appeared savage in the dusk. I shivered, having escaped my body even for a short duration had made me feel more alone.

When the streetlights flicked on at exactly the same moment as the bells from a nearby church tower began to chime, I thought of Mama. How she would say it was a sign of God's blessing. Mama! I sensed her presence the way, she used to tell me, one senses the ocean (which she always longed to see) hours before one gets there. I no longer felt alone. The succession of street lamps stringing the city together became my guiding beacons and I began to follow them. I could smell onions frying, hear the distant drone of a radio interrupted by the clatter of dishes. And as I watched the windows – one by one – turning into transparent curtains of yellow light, there came over me a feeling – not so much of happiness but of the rightness of things. The same feeling I experienced as a child, playing in the vast space of my own dark yard, while knowing at any moment I would be called inside to where light and heat and life curled around Gammer cooking supper.

It seemed no time at all that I followed my feet from lamp pole to lamp pole silently chanting the old childhood rhyme, *step on a crack and break your mother's back.* Arriving at the house where I board by the week (in order to save rental money for an apartment), I was about to turn down the unlit lane to the back entrance when, at the far end, I glimpsed a large shadowy figure moving in and out of the darkness. It was him. The panhandler who plays his flute outside the library's main entrance. The one my fellow workers named Pan the Wild Man or Pan the Godman or simply Panman. They all have a crush on him, whispering about his killer eyes and his wicked smile.

He is said to be the brilliant only son of a wealthy Boston family, a Brahmin, who – while attending the University of Toronto – had come unhinged after experimenting with psychedelic drugs and running away to the far North. There, the story goes, he met his native spirit guide and was taken on a long journey to the top of a high plateau where he performed the ancient initiation rite of stalking and killing a mountain goat. Then he cut out the hot quivering heart and devoured it – not because he was starving (which he was), but as a sacrifice...as an ultimate act of love that transformed the two of them into one being. The ritual was completed only after he skinned the animal, scraped off its fur and sewed the hide into a coat.

I don't know how much of this is true, but he always wore a long strangely cut leather coat that clung to his body like flesh...and as such gave the illusion of being alive. The same could be said of his wide-brimmed hat, pulled low on his forehead, which was rumoured to be made from the skin of ravens, their feathers stuck upright around the band. When I arrived for my first day of work he was playing his flute inside the doors of the main entrance. Although I was too nervous to even glance in his direction, the high, hauntingly sweet sound of his music had stayed, and still stays, like a stuck record in my brain.

Perhaps it was due to the warmer spring weather, but often during these past weeks he has hung out in the parkette close to Robarts Library, panhandling his handmade reed flutes to the people sitting on the benches or lining up at the hotdog cart. All the library assistants bought one but only Loose Lou (Louella to her face) was brazen enough to ask for lessons. She and I often took our breaks together. The others found her loud and boastful but I was flattered that she sought out my company.

On this day we were sitting on a bench in the warm noon sun when we saw him coming down the street. She nudged me, "I'm telling you, Creaky, you got to go talk to him – not that he makes much sense, but it sounds as pretty as poetry." Then she whispered because Miss Slade, the head librarian, was walking by us, "Who cares if he's crazy, he has the sexiest eyes. He sees right through your clothes and he likes what he sees."

As my co-workers had claimed, he was exceptionally tall and broad shouldered, but walked with a catlike grace, and like a cat, his energy seemed to move before his body as he picked up a scrap of waste paper. Three times he repeated this odd behaviour. Wondering what solitary game he could be playing, I watched intently while he brushed off each scrap and, after examining both sides, folded it carefully into his bulging pockets.

As the Panman, face hidden by the brim of his hat, grew closer in the deepening dark, I had to get inside before he recognized me. Luckily he was preoccupied with smoothing out a torn page of newspaper plucked from the neighbour's garbage bin as I hurried to the back door of the boarding house. Fumbling through my pockets for keys, I heard him say, "If God is the Word then every word in print is made from His blood and every discarded..."

At that moment Mrs. Janowski, the landlady, opened the inside door. As I squeezed past her butterball torso, I looked over my shoulder, but the Panman had vanished as though he had never been there. I noted Mrs. Janowski must have a visitor because she was wearing her good wig with the yellow shoulder-length hair and thick fringe that fell over her eyebrows. "Your grandmother called this morning," she said sharply. "I asked if there was a message and she said something about 'concern' but I couldn't hear. I told her to speak louder but she hung up."

While I recognized her words, their meaning didn't register. She repeated herself. As I stared at her thin mouth transformed to a cupid's bow by brilliant orange lipstick, she stuck her face up to mine. "What's wrong? Cat got your tongue?"

I shook my head and watched her stomp off on stubby legs that – like a doll's – were attached to the outside of her body. Gammer must be extremely concerned to have called. To her the telephone was a sinful instrument promoting gossip and laziness. When absolutely necessary she would order provisions – flour, tea, sugar, salt – to be delivered, but even then she would be convinced that someone on the party line was listening. For days afterwards she would complain that the entire village was now aware of the contents of her larder.

For the past three years I have hated the thought of going back to New Salem. It takes only a day for my carefully invented self to begin dissolving into the lonesome monster of my childhood. Phoning would be preferable but Gammer won't answer. The circumstances of her birth, followed by the family's misfortunes, have made her into a bitter, fiercely proud woman who trusts no one. This is augmented by the fact that she missed school so can write only her name and read only simple words. In the beginning I wrote to her weekly. And then every two weeks that soon became three. The letters were short, impersonal, mostly about the weather. For some time now, although I keep meaning to write, it never happens. I want to believe I've slipped the noose of my past. That's why whenever her letters arrive, dictated – I suppose – to Aunt Aggie, I throw them unopened into the bottom drawer of my bureau. I always promise myself I will read them later.

As I stood in the hall dialing home, Gammer's dry smell, which lingers like burnt toast, filled my nostrils. The phone rang, three long, one short. I closed my eyes, concentrating on the words my tongue must make. The ringing continued. On the inside of my eyelids appeared the faded wallpaper in the foyer where Gammer's phone hung. The ferns, each the size of a dinner plate, were so clear I could count them. But I didn't. I didn't count the number of weeks since I had written to her, either. It never occurred to me that she would be concerned.

My guilt grew with each unanswered phone call. Around ten o'clock Mrs. Janowski appeared in her nightgown, the same bright yellow as the wig that was no longer on her head. While she ranted about my waking everyone in the house I couldn't stop staring at the nakedness of her scalp glistening through patches of greasy grey hair.

Perhaps that's what brought on the nightmare – the fleshy snake-like creature slipping out from behind the bookshelves in the library. Repulsed, but somehow mesmerized, I was drawn closer. It called urgently in Gammer's voice, "Sibyl, Sibyl, don't leave me alone, don't leave me alone." Somehow I knew I must kiss this pale translucent creature or die from its poisonous bite. Leaning in closer, my lips grazed the undulating body and I pulled back, surprised by its warmth and silkiness.

I was glad to be awakened by the grinding of the garbage truck in the back lane. Although it was barely light I packed a change of clothes and slipped out of the house, leaving a note to tell Mrs. Janowski that I'd been called home and would she please phone to notify the library. I wanted to arrive early at the bus depot (a ten-minute walk away) because there is only one bus a day, departing at eight in the morning, that stops at New Salem – a hamlet of houses clustered like toadstools around a crossroads six hours north of the city.

Our ancestor was one of the original settlers to arrive in the mid-nineteenth century. The village was founded when a saw-mill was built on the rapids of the Madawaska by the McNiece family from Salem who, lacking imagination, named their new home New Salem. As long as the lumber companies flourished so did New Salem. But once the vast stands of virgin pine had been ravaged and the pioneer farmers – discovering the rocky soil could not sustain crops – fled westward, New Salem dwindled to a few dozen families.

Gammer's house – the oldest and the largest and badly in need of repair – sits heavily aloof on the rising hill just outside the village. I asked the bus driver to let me off at the gravel road leading up to the property.

"You live up in that rambling old place?" he asked, opening the bus door.

"No, I'm just visiting."

"I drive this route twice a week and there's never anyone around. Thought it was deserted. Sure is the loneliest-looking house…"

As I stepped from the bus with my suitcase, a cloudburst of needle-sharp rain and wind forced my eyes into slits. As my feet led the way to our lane and closed gate with the No Trespassing sign, I could feel the brooding, accusing stare of the house. Gammer always said that an invisible umbilical cord, strong as a ship's rope, joined the three generations of Sibyls born in this house. "You're a Witherspoon," she had said the day I was packing to go. "You can try to leave but you can't help but circle around and around until you're home again."

The key was hidden in the usual place behind the mossy stone to the right of the steps. As the front door creaked open, I was greeted by the familiar odour of mildew mixed with the lemon oil that had been rubbed for decades into the wood furniture. Instantly time seemed to distort and I called out "Gammer!" with the excitement of a child returning from a first day at school. With my hand still on the doorknob I listened to my voice rippling through the vast stillness. Even before I looked at the grandfather clock standing guard in the front hall I sensed that its ancient heartbeat had stopped.

Then, just as I had been taught, I took off my muddy boots and placed them side by side on the rubber mat next to her thick-soled black oxfords. I hung my wet jacket on the rack between her good black coat and her identical everyday coat. Stealthily, so as not to disturb the unguarded house, I glided in my stocking feet down the narrow hall, passing the stairs of curved oak that led upwards into a deeper gloom, passing the closed curtains to the front room where the overstuffed furniture hunkered down, content as animals in a barn.

At the end of the long hallway where an oval mirror reflected the dim light, I had a flashback – momentary as lightning – of a white cloth being draped over it and Gammer saying, "So Mama's soul will not be held back on its journey," and me snatching the cloth away because I knew Mama's soul had chosen to stay.

Quickly I turned away and, pushing through the swinging door to the kitchen, crossed the worn black-and-white linoleum to the wood stove where Gammer kept a low fire burning the year round. Since only a few live embers remained, I figured Gammer would return soon and I sat down at the table to wait. As a distraction from the growing dread of her anger over my long absence, I reached for the book of blank pages in my bag.

How long have I been writing? My fingers are cramping. It must be late afternoon because dimness, like soot, has smudged the edges of things. All that should be peaceful and orderly has become ominous – the black cast-iron kettle with the chipped spout on the wood stove, the deer's head with the glass eyes hanging on the far wall, the faded gingham tea towel folded on the dish drainer, the round brass handle on the trapdoor leading to the cellar, the rocking chair by the wood stove where Gammer knits through long winter evenings.

And where is Gammer? Probably she was turning the soil in the far garden when the storm forced her to take shelter in the shed. I should force myself to stand up and look out the window to see if the rain has stopped. I should force myself to go out and look for her. I should, at least, force myself to light the fire in the stove and make some tea. But I keep sitting here, turning back to the cover of my journal, focusing my attention on the perfect face of Venus with its expressionless beauty. And as I keep staring into those amber eyes, I am wondering how a face that appears so neutral could radiate such melancholy.

And I remember wanting to touch Mama's face – the face I saw in the mirror as she sat before her dressing table brushing her hair. A hundred strokes every morning while I sat cross-legged on the unmade bed and watched her shoulder blades sliding back and forth under her thin cotton nightgown. To me they seemed more like stubs of wings that still believed they could fly.

Each time the brush unfurled a golden-red strand, I repeated the number after Mama. That's how I learned to count.

The more vigorous the strokes, the more her hair glowed. If people carry their souls in different places of their body, Mama's lived in her hair. The crackle of electricity made it seem alive, sucking light out of the room, sucking life out of her pale face. All the while, she would gaze intently into the mirror, tilting her head this way and that. This had nothing to do with vanity. Mama was not appraising her looks. She was staring through herself into empty space as though hypnotized.

At the stroke of one hundred she laid the brush on the dressing table and, with much effort, pulled back from the mirror. Then, jerking her neck down so her hair leaped over her head wild as a cat on fire, she caught it in both hands and tethered it with an elastic on top of her head. Finally she subdued the unruly ends by twisting them into a topknot which I helped secure with bobby pins.

That's the way Mama is wearing her hair in the photograph on the mantle – except for a few short wisps that struggled free to cling like moth wings around her forehead and temple. It was taken, she had told me, shortly before she met my father. I used to look at the picture and imagine how safe I had been as a tiny egg inside her warm dark womb snuggled by hundreds of siblings. Why did I have to be the chosen one? Why did I have to be the one expelled from paradise?

In the days following her disappearance I was required to greet neighbours and villagers who arrived with condolences and casseroles. They sat stiffly in a circle of hard chairs taken from the dining room to the big front "show room" of the house with its high ceilings, tall windows and carved mahogany fireplace. As soon as I entered Mama looked at me from her photo on the mantle. I felt her eyes, alive as candlelight, following me while I shook each extended hand. But then, before I was halfway round the circle, their light would be extinguished by the cold wind blowing from the visitors' own curious eyes.

Trembling, I leaned against Gammer, who was presiding over the silver tea service on the long side table.

"Why?" I asked, pointing to Mama's photograph.

The force of her breath when she sighed made the lace trim of her collar tremble.

"Why?" I repeated.

"The Lord giveth and the Lord taketh away."

Visitors sighed and nodded.

I didn't understand.

"Why?" I repeated loudly.

"Come, Sibyl," Gammer's voice grew sharp at the edges, "and help me by passing the food."

On the third day, rather than taking the plate of sandwiches, I shouted "Why?" and stamped my foot.

Gammer grabbed me by the shoulders.

"Stop this instant!" She hissed between clenched teeth.

I stared up at her protruding jaw. The slight grinding of her dentures indicated a growing anger. I was familiar with her temper and feared it less than the pity in her eyes. I had to say it. Louder and louder until I was screaming "WHY WHY WHY WHY?" Gammer shook me and the screaming caught in my throat, making me cough and choke.

I was high-strung, Gammer explained to the visitors as she ushered me out of the parlour, because I'd almost suffocated when the umbilical cord had slipped around my neck during my birth. I'd heard the story many times and knew how my face had been blue as a pansy and how Gammer and Mama had taken turns breathing into my mouth.

Soon no one came to visit and the house grew larger, the silence more heavy. Gammer turned Mama's photograph to the wall – as if that would help me. I stared for hours at the blank silver oval of the frame, gleaming like a new moon in the dimness, and prayed for Mama to return. Not once did I cry.

Gammer again said it was nerves when I tried to tattoo the five-pointed star, the secret symbol of Mama and me, into my palm...tried so hard that the point of the pen pierced my skin. I had no words to tell her that I believed that this branding of my flesh would bring me closer to Mama – unknowable beautiful Mama who embodied love like Christ.

Writing these words, I recall the Easter Sunday during my first school year. After I complained that other kids went to church, Mama unwrapped the family Bible and read aloud the story of the Crucifixion. The words hooked so deep in my mind that Golgotha became our Madawaska Valley covered in darkness from the sixth to the ninth hour. It was our home, not the temple, torn asunder. It was the graves in our family cemetery that opened and the bodies of our relatives that rose. I pictured Christ being nailed to Great-Gammer's vine-covered cross. He was dying for my sins. I was responsible...just as a few years later I was responsible when Mama was taken while gathering strawberries for my birthday cake.

That's why I wanted the stigmata. I wanted to see how a nail driven into the palm might feel. That it would end my guilt. It would prove my devotion to Mama. That's why I made imprints of my bloody hand on every door in the house. It soaked into the wood and even after Gammer painted all the doors, the ghostly red print of my palm gradually returned.

I don't recall much else of what happened during the summer after Mama's death. My misery had opened a chasm between myself and everything else. Although I could see people and objects, I couldn't reach them. I couldn't reach Gammer either. Days would pass and she wouldn't speak — not out of grief, I felt, but anger...anger at me.

Locals refer to that summer as "the '78 heat wave." The temperature never dropped below a hundred degrees for six weeks. From my bed, I watched a spider weaving a bigger and bigger web across the open window. A coyote crawled under the shed and lay panting all day. Within seconds after a cow peed, no mark remained on the parched earth. It rained only once for ten minutes. The chirp of the grasshoppers grew so loud I could feel the sound vibrating in my chest. "Hotter than the hinges of Hell," Gammer said.

In our garden, I remember the sunflowers turning to yellow weeds that rattled in the wind, the vines of cucumbers, squashes, pumpkins withering into traps of wire that grabbed my ankles. The Mad, in penance for carrying away Mama, dwindled to a trickle and then into a series of mud holes. In the family graveyard, behind the skeletons of raspberry bushes at the end of the garden, Gammer twisted her ankle when Grandfather's grave caved in.

I was gathering some kindling for the wood stove when I discovered a family of field mice snuggled together under a shrivelled rhubarb leaf. I poked each one with a stick. The four little mice were dead but the big one, who must have been their mother, moved slightly. Picking it up by the tail I counted ten tiny pink teats in the fine white fur of her belly before I laid her on a stump. Then I took a small log from the woodpile and saying, "The Lord giveth and the Lord taketh away," I killed her with a single blow. Frightened by the sight of the squashed bloodied body, I ran to my secret hiding place.

Throughout childhood this place had been under an old dining room table in the bay of the front-room windows. Poorly constructed by one of my forefathers, it was covered by a hand-crocheted tablecloth that hung in fragrant folds to the floor. Here, in this mesh of shadows, I'd felt safe and had created my own world out of the bright slick surfaces of the Eaton's catalogue.

Standing in for the father I had never known, I cut out a man in a blue business suit and white button-down shirt. It didn't matter that one foot was missing – the fault of the price box at the bottom of the page. The cut-out mother, small and smiling in her pleated skirt and cardigan, stayed at home baking cookies for two children – a sturdy boy who carried a baseball glove and a younger girl with curly brown hair. They were Dick and Jane, incarnations from Mama's Grade 1 reader, which was the first book she read to me. Of course I included Baby Sally in a pink knit sweater with matching bonnet and Spot, the dog, who I found on the page that advertised hunting equipment.

While time looped like Great-Gammer's crocheted thread I played house with my paper dolls and mused over the catalogue world of ten thousand things – choosing among the shiny man-ufactured objects that suggested comfort, security and love. Then, with great care, I would cut out a snow blower, a ping-pong table, a barbecue, a dishwasher, a toy box, an electric blan-ket, a popcorn maker, a Japanese kimono. These were all the possessions I wished to own – that I hoped would relieve the foreboding, accumulated by generations of proud cautious ancestors, with lips tight as their purse strings, who had called this drafty old house their home. But who had never been at home in their bones.

And who don't rest even now in the family graveyard behind the scraggily garden, despite R.I.P. etched into the headstones under their names.

And that's why I played house. Not to amuse myself. Not to escape loneliness. Not to be part of something. No. Play was a life-and-death struggle to keep the dead from living. Or to keep my life from dying.

Only on Fridays, when Gammer would neaten the house, did the frail enchantment of my lair under the table yield to her soft yet heavy footsteps. The parlour or the public room as Gammer called it, or the sitting room as Mama called it, was sel-dom used. The three of us never sat together – except to eat at the kitchen table – and never lingered over conversation because Gammer considered it, at best, an indiscretion and, at worst, a dangerous course of action.

The faded burgundy velvet curtain hanging across the door-way was always closed. So were the tall bay windows looking out to the open veranda that wrapped around the house. Even on the hottest August noon the sitting room remained dim and cool. The opaque sheers covering the glass, yellowed with age, dis-tilled the light even more. It seemed to have substance – a grainy glow that settled around me with such accord I felt myself to be in a familiar chapel. Chapel? Why has this word appeared? I have never been inside a church. For me the only place of amnesty was under the round dining room table in the bay window.

Only Gammer shattered this magic circle. Once a week I would hear the squeak of the floorboards, the sudden clattering of the wooden rings along the rod as the curtain opened. Peeking through the eyelets of crocheted web I would watch her worn carpet slippers, ankles almost flowing over the tops, moving along the pine floor. If I bent my head I could see her legs in brown lisle stockings rising, sturdy as tree trunks, into the folds of her house-dress. And if I bent my head slightly more, I could see the apron tied under her large bosoms, accentuating the way they hung – like the ears of a basset hound – over her belly.

Because generations of Witherspoons (according to Gammer) had taken such pride in their home's public room, she took special care with the neatening of it. The ritual would begin with a cloth-covered broom that she used to remove cobwebs from the white plaster trim around the top of the walls. Then she would whack the dust from the Queen Anne sofa and the two wing chairs stuffed with horsehair, and afterwards examine the ancient silk brocade for tiny rips to mend. Next she would flick the feather duster over the sideboard and the three straight chairs with high backs and dainty legs. All the while she accompanied herself with a soft whistling sound created, not by puckering her lips, but by somehow loosening her ill-fitting dentures.

Since Gammer was even more silent after Mama had gone, I paid close attention to her movements. I thought they might reveal something…a kind of signalling like a weather vane on the roof of a house. But all that happened is that her gestures grew slower and stiffer.

"It's rheumatism," she insisted. "Runs in the family and worsens with age. When they laid out your great-grandfather, his back

28

was so bent that his forehead touched his knees. 'Stiff as stone,' the undertaker said. Cost a pretty penny to have a square coffin built."

But it seemed to me after Mama died, it was Gammer's heart that stiffened to stone. I never saw her cry or speak of what happened. And I couldn't speak. There were no words to describe the chasm that had opened between me and everyone else. And no matter how carefully I watched from my mesh of shadows under the table, Gammer remained in the distance.

The focal point of her weekly cleaning was the ornate mahogany fireplace that had been shipped at great expense from Italy by my great-great-grandfather (the first and the last of the wealthy Witherspoons). At the time it was considered the envy of the county, according to Gammer. I imagined its massive form, looming from the empty hole of the hearth, to be a crossbreed of some beast. It invaded the room – mysterious as the Sphinx that knows everything and sees everything but remains aloof and unmoved.

Gammer was its custodian, its interpreter. When her tuneless whistling stopped I knew the final rite was about to begin. Peeking out from the magic of my cave I'd see her standing there, motionless, a cloth in one hand and a bottle of lemon oil in the other, waiting for some unseen signal to begin stroking, kneading, rubbing until the feline monster glowed and seemed about to stretch out and purr.

Then, exchanging the lemon oil for a tin of brass-and-silver polish, she turned her attention to the three sacred objects on the mantlepiece. In the middle was an oil lamp, the oldest possession in the house. Less than a foot high, its ornate hourglass shape etched with interlocking spirals had an awesome presence even though the pewter was dented and the glass shade broken many years before Gammer became its caretaker and high priestess. Although the base was filled with oil and a box of wood matches kept beside it, I don't recall the wick ever being lit. "Too drafty," I can hear Gammer saying, "sure to smoke."

The lamp has always been in the family. Long before the first name appeared in the back of the family Bible. Long before my ancestors wrapped it in cloth and stowed it in the iron trunk that sailed with them from old England to the wilderness of the new world. For over three hundred years the lamp passed through the hands of my female relations. All of them ended up alone, keeping their strong paddle hands busy to stop the past from leaking in…the wordless dark past that grew with the family tree.

The second ritual began when Gammer spat on her forefinger and made the sign of the cross on the lamp – not only to determine how much it had tarnished but also, I knew, to ward off evil.

My nostrils flood with the harsh odour of the polish. Once again I can see her dabbing it on the cloth and then polishing the brass in small circular motions. Once again I can see how the different parts of her body joined in the dance – the loose skin under her arms, the rat-tail of her braid, and the strings of her apron – all swaying in time to her hand movements.

As Gammer rubbed, the lamp grew brighter and brighter. How my heart pounded – so loud I had to wrap my arms tightly around my knees to keep it from leaping out – because I anticipated at any second a whirling pillar of smoke announcing the release of Mama's soul. Mama who loved me too much to be taken by angels to heaven, as Gammer said, but hid in the lamp so she could stay close to me.

When Gammer finished, she replaced the lamp in the exact middle of the mantle and then, stepping back, stared at it with such absolute attention that the world stood still.

I held my breath and so did everything else – the creaking joints of the house, the sparrows bickering in the eaves, the blue-bottle fly trapped between screen and glass of the bay windows. Even the ticking of the grandfather clock grew quiet as a faint heartbeat.

There were only the sheer curtains gently swelling and shifting in the chimney draft, shaping themselves into presences from that other place.

Where I never wanted to go.

So without moving I found myself leaning towards the quiet bulk of Gammer's body. Silence listening to silence. Until at last, giving herself a little shake that started the world turning again, she sighed, "Remember, Sibyl, it's always darkest under the lamp." Each week she repeated the same words. I dared not ask what they meant but could imagine them being whispered through the leaves of the family tree. It was a riddle passing from mother to daughter. Although each of us had to discover her own answer, I knew Mama would help me find mine.

Next Gammer picked up the photograph facing the wall and gently polished the oval silver frame. Holding it with both hands, she opened her mouth and slowly exhaled on the glass – as though her breath could bring Mama's image to life. With their faces a few inches apart she sighed deeply and whispered "poor child." I knew she referred to me hiding behind the lacey folds of the floor-length tablecloth and, wrapping my arms even more tightly around my legs, I watched while Gammer cleaned the glass with the tenderness of a mother wiping the face of a feverish child.

After she returned the photograph to its exact place, facing the wall on the left side of the mantle, the same ritual of polishing was repeated with my great-gammer's photograph kept in an identical oval frame on the right side of the mantle. After its return, Gammer clasped her hands together as if she were about to pray and then, nodding her head in affirmation to a silent question, she sighed, "Poor little mother." But I sensed Gammer was thinking of herself because she had come into the world as her mother was leaving.

Did they happen to meet somewhere in the passageway to and from existence? Can there be an exact moment when life is born or dies?

And, in that space – unknowable as the space between words – did the unstable chemistry of their cells intermingle?

I inherited their awkward bones, broad flat feet, large features that overtake their faces. Except my eyes are pale blue and slightly protruding ("fish eyes" they called me behind the teacher's back) while Gammer's bright darting eyes see everything in a glance. But not things that can't be seen. Not like me.

Take ghosts for instance. When I was young I could see them easily as the nose on someone's face. Not that I would speak of it any more than I would speak of noticing a nose. Gammer's nose became more hooked as she aged. "Runs in the family," she used to say. "You wouldn't be a Witherspoon if you couldn't hang a hat on your nose."

But in the photograph of Great-Gammer she is directly facing the camera so you aren't aware of her nose. It's her skin you notice, looming out of the grainy light, fine and white as an ironed hanky. On the other hand, Gammer's swarthy skin is so wrinkled it reminds me of tree bark. I recall how surprised I was when once – only once – I touched her cheek and found it rippled, soft as water.

When I was young and afraid of falling asleep because of my mattress opening like a trapdoor, Gammer sometimes sat next to me knitting by the light from the hall. "Why are you so wrinkled?" I asked.

"I was born old," she answered.

Gammer didn't talk about her entrance into the world. It was what she didn't say that betrayed family secrets – the trailing sentence, the repeated phrase, the sighs and silences. I collected all these scraps of information the same as I did the cutout images from the mail-order catalogue. At night, afraid of the dark, I played with them inside my head, rearranging them into a story. The more I told myself the story, the more it evolved and the more real it became.

It begins in late fall of the year 1913. A cold drizzly dawn. Under the leaden blanket of the sky, Mars is slipping closer to Venus. In the fields of Flanders, France, blood has not yet bloomed into poppies, but in the gardens around the village of New Salem in northern Ontario their crimson mouths are opening to the rain.

By late morning the rain has stopped. Occasionally a snowflake flits down, big as a feather. In the stone house overlooking the village, my great-grandfather had come back for a scarf and mittens. "The old woman is plucking a goose," he announces to Great-Gammer, who replies, "Winter'll be early this year." She follows him back outside to pick the only flowers still blooming in the garden. After tying the poppies to be dried upside down in the cellar, she puts more wood in the kitchen stove.

Great-Grandfather was only riding to New Salem for the mail and a sack of flour, but she had waited until he left because she wanted to be alone while bathing in the big copper tub pulled close to the heat of the fire. Now its warmth licks at her pebbly skin – a legacy of the smallpox epidemic that carried away both her parents and left her a sickly and shy child with scars over half her skin.

"Like the skin of a nightmare pulled over a broomstick," whispered members of their Baptist congregation when she had stood at the marriage altar six months ago. These days the women pat her waxing cheeks at church socials. "The grey mare makes the better horse," is heard more than once amongst the men.

Her first pains began the night before, but she has said nothing to him because she doesn't know what to say. And he never asks. She doesn't think about it. She has no plans. She accepts not knowing how the life inside her is unfolding, as she accepts not knowing how her own life will unfold.

After her bath it's hot in the kitchen. Great-Gammer wears only a long white cotton slip. Her unbraided hair opens like a fan down her back as she leans over to pull up the trapdoor leading to the cellar. While carrying the armful of poppies down the stairs to hang until their seeds are planted next spring, she catches her foot in the hem of her slip and plummets down ten steps.

The soft earth floor eases her fall but not enough to prevent the fourth vertebrae of her neck from breaking. Another millimeter and her spinal cord would have been severed.

In my story I can never decide how long she remains sprawled there with the stored vegetables and bulbs pressing into her back.

I can never decide how long before the pain explodes like the crimson petals of the strewn poppies.

She doesn't want to open her eyes. But she does. Her vision is thick. She sees the round white mound of her belly. Beyond that are her feet. One shoe missing. She raises her eyes. Stares into the rectangular shaft of grey light falling on her through the open trapdoor. The floating motes of dust she recognizes as angels – angels bringing the knowledge that all flesh must bear. The knowledge of death – death that is life-bearing. The same as any daffodil or crocus or onion, the giant bulb of her body must split open. She must let go. The final push arches her back into a bow. As the life slips out between her wet thighs Great-Gammer slips out of the world. Her spinal cord has severed.

Which of them cries out? I can never decide. But often something at night startles me awake. I strain to listen with a sense of foreboding – a word that has the feeling of a cold knife blade running lightly over my skin. I wonder if Great-Grandfather has the same feeling when he returns. Standing at the back door – stomping the snow from his boots because the flakes are now flurries – he wonders about the cold stove, the open trapdoor, the smallness of his voice when he calls "Sibyl."

Padding across the black-and-white linoleum floor in his stocking feet, he peers down into the cellar. He sees Great-Gammer's white cotton shift looking like a crumpled bedsheet floating in the gloom. In his hurry he slips halfway down and lands on his knees beside her on the soft earth. Picking her up, her bent legs fall apart, and he reels back from the stench. Fecund as a slough in late summer.

At the first glance of the raw glistening flesh in the folds of cotton he thinks her womb has collapsed out between her thighs. But then it moves slightly and he hears a thin mewing. The horror! His heart leaps to his throat imagining a kitten skinned alive.

Great-Grandfather neither marries again, nor attends church services, nor lingers at the general store when he picks up his mail. As season blends into season he leaves his own acreage less and less. The villagers don't know what to make of his behaviour.

Since they love to talk, over the following years the intricate stab-bings of their words as he passes them on the street curve his back so it grows round and stiff as a boulder under his shirt.

"Standoffish."

"Like he's got God Almighty by the toe."

There is a sighing and a shaking of heads by the two old wid-ows who sit on the wood bench outside Wolfitt's General Store. Every fine day they warm their cold bones in the sun, steel nee-dles flashing as their gnarled fingers embroider napkins and pil-lowslips for the church bazaar – while at the same time their tongues embroider the plainness of their lives.

"Shame about his wife."

"Not even a Christian burial."

"The minister was willing."

"Sent old Bea Spicer to lay her out."

"She had no right opening the door in the first place."

"Claims he couldn't hear her knocking."

"Came at her with the hammer raised over his head."

"Couldn't move she said."

"Aah, there wasn't a Spicer born that didn't have a cabbage for a head."

There is a snickering, more like a high whine, trailing into a momentary silence that stops the hands of the old folk in mid-stitch. Then one of them clears her throat and picks up the thread of their conversation.

"He dug the grave on the rise behind the house."

"Where all the other Witherspoons are buried."

"The church cemetery's not good enough for them."

"Yet he married a girl from that queer family."

"Came every summer in a caravan."

"What's their name?"

"Rosenkreux, maybe."

"Strange that nobody in New Salem ever saw them again."

There is a lifting of eyebrows – although neither looks at the other – and, still wielding their needles, both simultaneously stretch out their legs, adjusting brittle bones against the hard wooden slats of the bench.

"The gate to his farm's always padlocked."

"He looks very black upon everything."

"Except for the child."

"Long and thin as a cat's elbow."

"Needs a woman's hand on her."

There is a sighing as one turns slightly to the other, making a half-gesture of embracing the air without missing a stitch of embroidery.

"She's been like a wife to him."

"Even sleeps in a cot beside his bed."

"In the bed they say."

"Do you think she'll bury him next to his wife?"

"I never heard of such a large wood cross."

"Higher than Christ's cross at Calvary."

"It's not fitting."

They are silent for a time, staring down at their motionless hands, veins like knotted threads of the narrative they are embroidering. Then, turning their heads, they look at each other and shrug. In New Salem this is the accepted way of concluding a conversation. It's meant to express indifference. However, what accompanies that shrug – an almost invisible movement of the body from side to side – transforms it into self-satisfaction.

Wolfitt's General Store disappeared long before I was born. Gammer says the village boys set fire to it. The empty lot became a gas station and, a few years later, the red brick church kitty-corner to it was closed for lack of attendance. That was the summer after Mama was taken – the summer of the heat wave when lightning hit the giant wood cross in the family graveyard. Rumour has it that the bolt came out of a clear sky.

But I wouldn't know. I was in my playhouse under the table. I do remember the prickling of the air on my exposed skin, pulling the hairs on my arms so they stood on end. And then the ripping sound of the flash as though the sky was being torn in two. Terrified, I huddled over my paper dolls. Now I huddle over my journal, the weight of the late afternoon pressing down on my pen, listening for Gammer's footsteps. She should be back soon.

I glance over my shoulder at the trapdoor. It hasn't been opened since Great-Gammer fell to her death. I've never stepped on it, of course, but it's so obviously there, in the far corner, between the washroom and the pantry. Since I have been gone, the linoleum has sagged even more where my great-grandfather nailed the metal stripping over the crack around the door. It glows in the gloom, a thin rectangular frame. In the middle the brass ring waits to be pulled.

I regularly asked about the sealed cellar. Many Friday evenings after supper, while I swept the kitchen floor and Gammer scoured the iron frying pan or the soup pot, I started a conversation – a kind of ritual – by tapping the trapdoor with the broom handle.

"What's down there?"

"Just earth."

"Nothing alive?"

"Maybe worms."

"Then why's the door nailed shut?"

"It's always been that way."

"Kids at school say there're no bodies in our graveyard but there's zombies buried alive in our cellar."

"Pshaw," Gammer exhaled, which means this is too ridiculous for words.

"They say you made a pact with the Devil and that lightning struck the cross as a sign of our damn…"

"Swallow your words, Sibyl!" Gammer hissed, clenching her anger as though it were a live coal in her teeth.

Then, heaving herself up with a sigh, she waggled her finger in front of my face and ended our exchange with the order, "Get at your chores if you want hot chocolate and an oatmeal cookie."

And while sweeping the linoleum I gripped the broom handle more tightly because the cold queasy feeling of the words I had swallowed reminded me of worms – the worms I knew were down there – in the cellar – where the family curse was unfolding. The smell of it still festers through the sealed crack between door and floor, and with each breath it distorts our insides, making us different. Misbegotten.

Yes, I've always known why Gammer was born old.

It's the fault of the angels. While bringing her into the world they carved their initials into her face. Although the lines grew deeper as she aged, I never asked what the letters stood for. She who knows the names of fallen angels knows anxiety, fear, sorrow, death.

(How easily these words are coming out. My mind's loosened. Or is it my left hand? The writing slants forward as though I'm pushing words across the page – words that already exist. Like a beetle pushing eggs incubated in its own dung.)

Gammer has a brooch the shape of a beetle ordered from the Birks catalogue. Grandfather gave it to her the evening he proposed – the only gift she ever received, because shortly afterwards he fell from the roof of the house. She called the brooch a scarab and explained that it was an exact replica of the one replacing the mummy's heart in King Tut's tomb. That time when the teacher came to talk about my failing grades I was allowed to take the beetle out of its blue box and pin it to her best dress. "Solid gold," she had said with reverence – although Gammer was not a reverent woman. The only time I heard her make a religious remark was at the mention of some future event when she added, "God willing," as a kind of amen, giving herself a little shivery shake.

It occurs to me, as I watch these words appear from my pen, that Gammer's shivery shake is her way of expressing the unspeakable. Mama (who dreamed of going away to study) claimed that Gammer had no framework for knowledge or faith because she had never attended school or church. Her beliefs, according to Mama, were born from a lifetime of hard work on poor land which she expressed in the sayings passed on by her kin. Her basic concerns for food and shelter have changed little since our Puritan ancestors arrived three hundred years ago. God, and his counterpart the Devil, remain vague but all-powerful...a mystery buried in the everyday world.

Gammer constantly watched for signs. What she glimpsed by chance between earth and sky was a blessing – a falling star at dusk, a hawk silhouetted against the setting sun, light reflecting from a black cloud. Any slight deviation in the order of the world beneath her feet became a warning – a rabbit hopping over Great-Gammer's grave, mouse turds in the flour bin, a double-headed mushroom.

Sometimes a sign foretold a particular occurrence such as a hailstorm or an early frost or a north wind. But most often there was something nameless and foreboding that haunted even her most cheery day.

Certainly my own sense of foreboding has been increasing moment by moment since the middle of the afternoon when I unlocked the front door. Now, as evening creeps through the house, it doesn't help to have the grandfather clock, silent as an upright coffin, in the front hall.

Gammer must have been walking all the way to the crevice caves on the escarpment to gather the first spring lichen that she uses to make her potent poultice to vitalize the liver. I wager she stopped to rest in the hunter's shack and has fallen asleep. She has napped every afternoon for as long as I can remember. To beat the rain she probably left before dawn, forgetting to wind the clock. I don't recall such a thing ever happening, but neither has Gammer ever been so late.

Although I can't see the writing on this page, the pen in my left hand keeps moving, one word flowing into another...like the current of a river carrying me away...but I can't swim and it's deep and dark and cold...

I am shivering. The wind must be shifting to the north. I should pull a sweater out of my suitcase. I should turn on the light. I should eat. My grip on the present is slowly being scraped from the room. Even though I've been gone over three years, I seem to have only pretended to leave.

Not knowing what to do, I stand for a long time at the kitchen window – so high I can rest my elbows on the sill – straining to see Gammer's bulky shape moving towards the house. I think of how she always pulls the curtains or blinds at dusk. She worries that people will peer in. Mama said the only people around were in the family graveyard, just beyond the vegetable garden.

Resting my forehead against the cool glass, I listen to the house sighing and creaking in the wind. I imagine that invisible umbilical cord, which Gammer said was tough as a ship's rope, anchoring me to Mama, to Gammer, to Great-Gammer and further back and back through the generations. There is a secret history carried inside me from birth which will become my fate. I glimpse fragments. I receive warnings in dreams.

But not enough. Not ever enough.

If only I could break the silence that has always kept us apart from the rest of the world. Did the secret begin with Great-Gammer? Or was it already there, hundreds of years ago, stowed in the deepest darkest recesses of my ancestors as they lay on the heaving deck of the Pilgrim ship? Was it there when, falling to their knees on these savage shores, they prayed for help in bringing the Word to the wilderness? The Word – solid as their cast-iron cooking pots and honed as the edge of their axes – could have easily hidden what had never been spoken.

Or did it happen long before names were recorded in the back of the family Bible? When the Word didn't come from a book, but from the body. Those were older darker times when the soul was tied to God. And people heard through the pores of their skin – a kind of awareness of what they already knew.

But perhaps once the Oracles were written down and became truths that could be defined, interpreted, manipulated, then the voices of those ancient ancestors withered into knots in their throats. Perhaps in terror their souls fled their bodies. Perhaps that's when the secret began.

The Dark
Under the
Lamp

❧ DAY TWO ❧

Last night, my worry grew with the darkness. I imagined Gammer falling on the escarpment and lying hurt on its rocky slope or taking refuge in the limestone crevice caves. When I could bear it no longer, I grabbed a few oatmeal cookies from the chipped yellow canister on the counter (only after eating them did I think how odd it was that they were bought, since Gammer always claimed store baking was for lazy city folk), and headed out the back door.

In the summer kitchen, the dampness intensified the profusion of rich earthy odours from the mushrooms and mosses and stringy tangle of lichen drying on the trestle tables. As I pulled her rain poncho over my head and stepped into her rubber boots, it occurred to me that the ugliest, oldest, wildest, most hidden of living things have always revealed their secrets to Gammer, if she lets them.

Once outside, I realized the rain had slowed to a fine drizzle. Looking around in the misty twilight, I realized for the first time how little of the original farm remained. Without a man to do the hard labour, Gammer couldn't generate enough income to pay the rising land tax, so gradually all but ten of the two hundred acres had been sold to the Muellers who owned the neighbouring farm. The clutch of outbuildings had fallen and – besides the vegetable garden, the small apple orchard and the graveyard – there remains only a skimpy bit of pasture and some scrub woods.

I took in a deep breath of the late spring air. The strong odour of manure meant that Gammer must have been turning the soil in preparation for planting. Looking towards the vegetable garden, I was surprised to see neat rows of the first uncurlings of radish and lettuce. I was even more surprised by the noise of the birds coming to perch on the charred cross. It had always been a nightly roosting place for crows, but I had never seen so many, bickering and jostling like people getting on a bus. I wanted to walk up to the graveyard to see what was going on, but there was no time to waste as the crevice caves were an hour's walk and, although the rain had stopped momentarily, storm clouds billowed low as a giant tent over the valley.

Cutting across the Muellers' back fields, I easily found the footpath leading up to the shack used by hunters during the deer shooting season. On the chance that Gammer could have taken refuge here from the rain and fallen asleep I called her name, rattling the latch of the door. This was only the halfway mark and, worried it would soon be pitch black, I put my shoulder to the door and opened it with such force that I hurtled across the tiny room and fell on something soft. I screamed, thinking it was Gammer asleep, but it was a rolled-up sleeping bag in the corner. After that I had to concentrate because the path was becoming more steep and slippery from the rain. Concerned that I would miss Gammer, I called out *Siiibbbylll* every twenty yards. Each time my voice echoed off the limestone face of the escarpment. It felt as though I were answering myself...as though I had slipped out of my body into the near night.

By the time I reached the caves it was so dark that I could barely see my hand in front of my face, and the surrounding bushes reared up in menacing shapes. The narrow openings in the cliff meant that I would have to squeeze through sideways. I stood before one of them and listened. Nothing but the hollow sound of dripping water. I called "Gammer? Gammer?" But the only answer was the scurry of tiny disturbed creatures. Alone and far from the safety of the house, I imagined the icy touch of something dead, or dying, on the back of my neck. I couldn't stop myself from bolting and – sliding, falling, grasping at roots and branches – I ran straight down the steep slope.

Out of the darkness, a large winged creature flew at me hissing and spitting. I cowered, covering my head with my arms, for what seemed a long time and then slowly stood up. All that remained were some half-digested food balls on the ground around me and a stench like an open sewer. I remembered that for years a pair of turkey vultures had lived in a dead tree on one of the wooded ridges near the bottom of the escarpment. I must have disturbed the nest, causing the female to attack to protect her eggs.

My eyes, having adjusted to the dark, allowed me to take the shortcut across the bluff without tripping over rocks or clumps of twitch grass. With the distant yard light of the neighbouring farm as a misty yellow beacon, I walked back unerringly until I reached the barbwire fence of our property. That's when I heard a familiar sound like the plucking of broken banjo strings. It was the bullfrogs in the pond calling for a mate.

It came to me. Spring. Lambing time. The Muellers always fetch Gammer to help. Sometimes, if many of the birthing sheep have complications, she will stay all night applying poultices of slippery elm or greasy salves of moss and cod liver oil. It must have been an emergency, for when I arrived this afternoon there was a full cup of tea and a half-eaten slice of toast on the kitchen table. Gammer never wasted a drop or crumb of anything.

Reassured, I sank into the rocking chair in the corner by the wood stove. This is where Gammer always sits, rocking slightly while she knits or mends. Over the years her ample bottom has moulded its exact shape in the cushion and rattan seat, much like a partridge in its nest of leaves and twigs.

Telling myself I would rest for five minutes before taking off my muddy jeans and phoning the Muellers, I leaned my head back. The next I knew was a voice, powerful but melodious, calling "Sibyl…Sibyl." I struggled to open my eyes…only to find it as pitch black outside as inside my head.

The rocking chair creaked as I forced myself up and lurched towards what seemed the middle of the kitchen. I recall waving my hands in the air in a hopeless attempt to locate the cord hanging from the overhead light, and then, collapsing back into the rocker.

As I become more and more aware of my body, cold and sore from tumbling down the escarpment, the kitchen blind has been washed with the faint grey of dawn. I must have slept because a nightmare still glimmers far back in my brain. It gives me a sick feeling and, telling myself to not think of it, I struggle to my feet. After building a fire in the wood stove and changing out of my dirty clothes, I fill the cast-iron kettle with water. While I wait for it to boil I consider phoning the Muellers who, being farmers, would surely be up, but I don't want to wake the other people on the party line. Especially Mrs. O'Conner, the worst gossip in the village, who Gammer says has a tongue sharp enough to draw blood.

As I sit here at the kitchen table, cupping my hands around a steaming mug of tea to warm them while the room fills with the familiar comforting smell of my wet socks and spot-washed jeans drying over the stove, Toronto seems so far away and long ago. Can it only be yesterday that I began to write in this journal? I have no sense of time. The heart of the house has stopped beating. Only Gammer has the power to bring it to life. Only

Gammer can take the key – worn on a gold chain around her neck – and unlock the little glass door and pull the weighted chains that will release the deadly silence pressing down on me.

Flipping through these pages, I don't recognize the big wide-eyed words looping along. It looks as though they have been written by a child. I won't read them. All this talking, talking to myself – a web of thoughts closing me inside its cocoon, keeping away the unthinkable.

Without hesitation my left hand reaches for the pen. By concentrating on forming each letter, I don't have to think of what I'm saying.

This house is achingly familiar as though I have become the ghost of my own childhood. How odd, those words! But I did see ghosts in my childhood. Somewhere between thinking and daydreaming I wandered through the house snooping in cupboards and drawers, peeking through knotholes into closets. I never knew why. Searching for something. Some answer, I suppose. I know I wasn't afraid.

It always happened when I was alone in a room. I sensed a displacement of air and, looking up from whatever I was doing, there they would be – the ghostly figures – in my peripheral vision. They appeared, more than anything else, like projections from a double-exposed black-and-white film. Unaware of me, or of each other for that matter, they went about daily life – if it could be called that – in a manner similar to Gammer or Mama or me. Sometimes I thought I recognized one of them, but when I tried to bring them into full view they kept slipping into the corners of my sight.

I believed these pale shapes of light belonged to a world running parallel to mine…kind of like the freight train that ran through the valley. Although no train ever stopped in New Salem, it was comforting to hear the whistling and the faint rumbling of the cars loaded with iron ore. Some nights I lay in bed imagining the silver tracks in the moonlight – straight and shiny – with me rushing along them. I would be leaving the village and the valley forever. But then the nightmare started again. The train was hurtling through blackness while I pushed through sliding doors from coach to coach. They were all empty. Even the engine car.

Once, in such a half-wake sleep, I struggled to throw myself out of bed. Mama came and tucked me back into the sheets. She asked what happened and I told her the dream and then, to keep her with me, spoke of the ghostly visitors. Not having the words to describe the other world I asked if the house was haunted. Mama sat on the edge of the bed with her face turned away from me, twisting a strand of her hair into a tight coil. She appeared unsure of what to say. Then giving herself a shivery shake – the family mannerism – she said, "There's nothing to fear, Sibyl. Sometimes when death catches one by surprise, the soul hangs around like a loyal dog." Before I could think of a response, her quick light step retreated down the hall.

They say dwellings take on the personality of their owners. But this house is so absolute that generations of my relatives born and bred under its influence have gradually assumed its character.

One day, while shelving and reshelving books in the library, I removed a used envelope marking a page in a history book about northern Ontario, published in 1943. The author was writing about our house. He described it as the oldest in the county: "...an unconventional dwelling built over time out of durable stones gathered from the surrounding fields. Because of the lack of right-angled walls and the irregular outline of the perimeter, it gives, if viewed from the south, a haphazard impression. The roof is flat as though a third story had been intended, but instead wooden parapets resembling a white picket fence have been added around the edge, while from the centre rises a small carved cupola. In its entirety, the edifice resembles a small eccentric fortress that was deserted before being finished."

The black-and-white photograph on the following page startled me...like seeing a picture of your parents before you knew them and realizing they are not who you think. Taken from a distance, the house looks proud, formidable, yet it wears a sorrowful expression. It must be late fall because the twisted arms of the oak, taller than the house even then, are naked and the flower beds have been dug up. In the foreground of the photo, the half-acre pond – scooped out by a retreating glacier thousands of years ago and filled each spring by underground streams – has dried to a swamp from which rise the decaying trunks and limbs of trees. The smooth surface of the water acts as a black mirror reflecting an upside-down crooked image of the house.

In the upper right corner of the photo, silhouetted against a sheer white sky, looms the tall wooden cross before it was struck by lightning. I can just make out the tangled web of leafless rose vines hanging from the crosspiece and clinging to the upright timber. The seeds, planted in Great-Gammer's burial mound at the base of the cross, had grown so quickly that within two years there were hundreds of crimson buds that opened to the size of saucers. The villagers jokingly told their children that, just like in the fairy tale of Jack and the beanstalk, the vines would keep growing until they reached the sky.

Because of the angle from which the black-and-white photograph was taken, the ridge of the escarpment rising beyond the cross is not seen. I remember though, as a child, I could look from my bedroom window and believe that the morning mist had transformed the ridge into giant limestone gates opening into another country. Not that I have ever been to another country.

Neither has any relative living in this house over the centuries. A fortress does not only hold people out.

The house, passed down from father to son, began as a one-room shack with a sod roof. Each Witherspoon generation built an addition, so the structure became a maze of rooms, halls and stairways. After more than a hundred and fifty years the locals still refer to it as the "house on the hill," as though the owners were unknown.

Gathering scraps of information from Mama and Gammer, I learned that our ancestors had not only been one of the original settlers here in the Madawaska Valley, but almost two centuries earlier, had also been among the early colonists in New England. Not much was known about them other than they were land-owners from the southwest of Cornwall in England and were fleeing because of religious persecution. In the beginning, many of their sons were educated in Boston as Presbyterian ministers but, according to Gammer, they must have been bad at preaching, or else how did they come to be backcountry tenant farmers? Family folklore has it that they were poor as church mice because they knew nothing about homesteading. Then, one of the daughters married into a hard-working Scottish clan – who were impressed that she could read and write and play the violin – and over the generations their large tract of land in the wilderness of northern New York State grew into an estate with fertile fields and houses and barns and slaves. When the War of Independence began, they sided with the British in the belief that they would provide them with the freedom to prosper.

I remember sitting beside Mama at this same kitchen table while she cautiously unwrapped the shawl that protected the ancient family Bible. In a hushed voice, she said how shameful that this book, which had to be one of the oldest in the county, was not displayed in a museum, but Gammer would not allow it out of the house. I remember how she opened it – as though it was alive and turning the brittle pages might kill it.

On page one thousand four hundred and six, where the family record begins, we leaned in close, breathing the dry smell of its disintegration while trying to decipher the names and birth dates that had vanished into watermarks on the mottled transparent paper. By page one thousand four hundred and eight, the ink had become legible, and Mama pointed out George James Robinson, the first ancestor of our branch of the family tree. She told me how, while acting as a scout for the British garrison, he stepped into a bear trap concealed under vines and fallen leaves. Unable to release the jaws, he knew his only chance of survival was to take the hatchet from his belt loop and chop off his own foot. This was the place in the story where Mama always gave herself a little shake and Gammer, who was listening from the rocking chair, would add, "The will to live runs strong in our blood."

After the war, the Robinsons and their seven children were driven off their property by neighbours who accused them of hiding fugitives from the British Army. Gammer claimed they were jealous of their aristocratic heritage and the rich soil that their cleared hardwood forest yielded. "Just another way of stealing," she always said. "Someone moving in before the fire in the stove has died down."

Once a year, on a winter Sunday, usually when it was so cold we had to stay close to the wood stove, three of us would sit, knee to knee, with the ancestral flatware that had never been laid on the table in our laps. As we polished, Gammer would hold up a spoon or a fork and say, "Solid silver." If the bread baked that morning had risen well and her arthritis was not too bad, she would add, "Don't forget, these are good as money in the bank."

This is the way she began the telling of how my Loyalist fore-fathers, exiled from the property they had been clearing and plowing and planting for generations, loaded up four packhorses and two oxcarts full of possessions and journeyed north to Upper Canada. They had no money and sold many of the eighteen place settings, piece by piece, in exchange for food and lodging. Often, there was no habitation and even the children had to walk long distances through wilderness, camping on the side of the trail. Whenever I left food on my plate Gammer would snap, "Eat! Your ancestors were so hungry they were forced to cook up the family dog. The children got the paws." Her voice, each time she repeated it, conjured the image of me as a starving filthy child gnawing on a bloody paw and my stomach heaved as I fought down the food.

It took them six months to make it to Montreal by the first snow. They wintered with thousands of other Loyalist refugees who had gathered by the Lachine Rapids. The next spring, many of them were loaded into open barges and pulled up the St. Lawrence River by horses and oxen. It was upon debarking at the Bay of Quinte that my unfortunate forefather found out that the hundred acres of riverfront property granted to him by the British Army was lowland, mostly cedar swamp.

Gammer's family history stopped abruptly at this point, as if to conclude that the world has always been against us. I know the year was 1784 because the document granting them the Crown land is folded in the back of the Bible. Whenever I asked Gammer how our family had ended up even farther north in Madawaska Valley, she shrugged, saying, "It's as good as the next place," and wiped her hands on the bib of her apron to signify the end of the conversation.

Although unable to speak of it to Gammer, I learned from my Grade 10 history textbook that the loyalty of my ancestors was not to the British Crown but to the American Dream…the dream of wealth procured by mastering the land. It was not a king they had wanted but bigger government land grants, and this is what had driven them farther and farther north. Unfortunately, their dream of once again owning a sweep of hardwood forest that could be cleared to yield good cash crops of corn, oats and tobacco distorted into a nightmare: a bitter struggle of wrestling a land that grew more and more barren as the lumber companies clear-cut the forests of tall virgin pines and the topsoil washed away into the rivers. That's why for generation after generation the weight never lifted from my relatives' shoulders, fat never cradled their lantern jaws and everything and everyone remained their enemies.

That's why over the long loop of the centuries the house became a fortress. It was Gammer's great-grandfather who cleared the land (far up from the rich valley basin, because to be higher was to be better) and built the original log-and-sod cabin. These walls, now coated in plaster, form the kitchen and parlour. After that, generations of men performed the back-breaking work of clearing hundreds of stones from the surrounding fields, arranging one on top of the other, bonding them with mortar. It was a monument that served each as a last will and testament.

As a child, unable to sleep, I sometimes lifted the corner of the blind and peeked at an outcropping of rock on the escarpment called Bald Skull. Over time, wind and rain had sculpted hollows, ridges and gullies into the limestone that I turned into features – long crooked noses that were ghost white in the moonlight, and stern baleful eyes. These were the faces of my forefathers. Silent. Immortal. Complete in themselves.

What made me think I could escape?

When my great-grandfather, bent and fleshless as his ancestors, laid his last stone and was himself laid in his square pine box, Gammer was a thirty-four-year-old spinster who had never been away from the valley for more than a day. Whenever I asked about Great-Grandfather, her face darkened and her eyes flashed as though lightning were behind them. If pressed, she would mutter that he had been a good man in his own way. Mama said the storm in Gammer's head was because she loved and hated him at the same time.

Both Mama and Gammer preferred to answer questions about my grandfather. They told me he was a DP – a displaced person – from the Second World War. He had escaped from one of those border countries between Russia and Europe that are always changing their shape and language. He had been hired as a carpenter and machinist on an immigrant boat, but after being seasick for fourteen days he had jumped ship in Montreal. With no family, no money and an English vocabulary limited to "thank you," "goodbye," and "no smoking" (the sign above his bunk), he figured it would be easier to find work in a northern community. He was hitchhiking to Sudbury, hoping to get a job in the mines, when a trucker dropped him off at the gas station in New Salem. According to Gammer, he looked up at the house on the hill and knew he had found a new home.

Unaware of Gammer's mistrust of people, especially strangers, he climbed over the locked gate and banged on the kitchen door. Holding his hat in his hand he showed his tools and pointed to the collapsing back porch. He stayed a week, sleeping in the barn. Since he wasn't much of a talker and Gammer could do with the help, he became a permanent boarder.

In Grandfather's knapsack – along with a bag of tools, a change of clothes and a pipe – was a small book with strange writing and delicate pencil drawings of mushrooms. It had been created by his mother. One day during the chanterelle season in the first months of the war, she had been scouring the woods behind her home when, mistaken by a neighbour for an enemy spy, she was shot and killed. It was after Gammer found the book on the hall table in which Grandfather had inscribed, "To Sibyl I am growing more fond," that together they began to forage for mushrooms. Over the seasons, Grandfather taught her all he knew...but as his interest dwindled, hers grew into an obsession.

She found them in every nook and cranny – sprouting from stumps and dead logs, hanging like icicles and protruding like shelves from tree trunks, hiding under leaf mould in scrubby woods, flowering from cow dung in pastures, glowing in the crevice caves of the escarpment. Each mushroom, whether a wrinkled grey morel or a ten-pound orange puffball, was a miracle of nature popping out of the earth as fully formed as a baby out of the dark of a womb.

Grandfather's passion was carving wood, and he chose to woo Gammer by transforming the flat tin roof – her father had intended, in fact, to add a third story – into a terrace similar to those he had seen when his ship docked in Mediterranean port towns. A place for Gammer to take the air, he said, with the best view in the valley. The first year, he built a waist-high wooden parapet around the perimeter of the roof. The next two years, he designed and constructed a wooden cupola – a smaller, less ornate version of the one on the church overlooking his childhood home.

Perhaps creating something concrete out of his memory helped him to feel less displaced. Gammer said when he dozed by the fire in the evenings, he whispered foreign words under his breath. Thinking she heard him murmur "Rosenkreux," she mentioned it was her mother's maiden name. That's how they discovered they might be second cousins, since Grandfather's mother's sister had married a Rosenkreux – a fairly common surname in his country. To commemorate their kinship and to complete his creation, he spent the third winter carving a rose the size of a human head, which he painted a gold colour and placed on top of the cupola. An emblem, he said, of their shared destiny.

I don't know if Gammer considered his offering too ostentatious, but not once did she climb the narrow steep stairs leading from the second floor hall up to the roof. However, the many bats living in the crevice caves of the escarpment loved the cupola. This convinced Grandfather that farmers could keep a colony of bats, like a hive of bees, to protect their crops against countless pests and that town people could use them to rid their backyards of black flies and mosquitoes. He dreamed of breeding a type of bat, tame as a canary, which could be trained like a passenger pigeon. Because bats squeeze through cracks, he said, they could bring emergency drugs to victims trapped in mines or buildings. In times of war, they could carry small bombs and release them in enemy barracks.

When I was a child, Gammer showed me the photograph of Grandfather that she kept – along with the land deeds and the papers certifying births, deaths and marriages – in the lap desk on the parlour sideboard. The picture, taken on the day he proposed marriage, shows a small gnome-like man with a wide crooked mouth and curly hair that, according to Gammer, was redder than a robin's breast. Even from a distance, his exuberant handlebar moustache – waxed to a point at each end so it looks like it's smiling – shows off the broad high sweep of his Slavic cheekbones and his deep-set eyes. He looks as though he would rather be anywhere else but standing on these front steps with the house looming up behind him. The angle of the camera gives the house a deranged look, as if all my hunchbacked lantern-jawed male ancestors, who had bent their bones to build this place, were furious that this outsider, this displaced person, would one day own it.

At dusk, a few days after having his picture taken by a travelling photographer, Grandfather climbed to the railing of the parapet in order to better observe the hundreds of bats flying out of the cupola. When it gave way he tumbled past Gammer, just as she was putting a bread pudding on the kitchen windowsill to cool, and crumpled soundless as a handkerchief in the rhubarb patch by the back door. She never had a chance to tell him she was with child.

Since I was an only child and had no playmates, I didn't ask about my own father until I started school and learned that everyone else had one. According to Mama, he was a U.S. draft dodger. I thought that meant dodging currents of air, but he was an American avoiding the Vietnam War, although that is not what he told Mama. He claimed he had been searching for a peace nowhere to be found in his homeland. After leading an anti-war demonstration in Boston that had erupted into a riot, he had been jailed for a month. Every night the same star peered between the bars of his cell's high window and he said he knew by its fierce shimmering that it was God's eye.

Finally, unable to escape the eye's scrutiny, he had cried, "What do you want?" and as the words fled his lips a cold thrusting light, like a bayonet, had driven him to his knees. He had been called.

Upon his release from prison he began walking towards the first star that appeared in the evening sky. And he just kept on walking.

Years passed and he was still following its light, walking at night and in the day earning money for food by making chalk portraits of people he met on the street. When a person refused to pay for the sketch, claiming it did not resemble him or her,

Papa would reply that it was a portrait of his or her soul where the vertical light of God and the horizontal dark of the Devil had intersected.

One early evening, while walking through Madawaska Valley, he saw a sign for New Salem and it came to him – like a lightning bolt out of the blue, he told Mama – that the peace he was missing had been inside him all along. Salem. Salaam. Shalom. *Peace* in every language is the same. Looking up, he saw the rising moon balanced like an angel on top of the great charred cross behind our house. "Yes," he cried out, throwing himself on his knees and kissing the ground, "Yes, yes, yes."

Mama said when she answered his knocking on the kitchen door her heart jumped like the trout she had caught in the pond that morning. She couldn't recall what he said. Only the warmth of his voice wrapping her in light. He wore a caftan and sandals, the same as the preaching Jesus in the picture that she had cut from a magazine as a child. He had the same shoulder-length brown hair, the same melancholy dark eyes that appeared bottomless. The young men of New Salem, on the other hand, wore faded overalls and trimmed their hair into a brush on top that was called a crew cut. Their eyes, I know, were dangerous.

He stayed from spring until late fall. In return for room and board he repaired the house that had not known a man's touch in twenty years. I used to imagine him after a day's work wearing a red wool cardigan (Gammer would have none of "that ridiculous garb") and smelling of Old Spice aftershave lotion. Just like the men in the mail-order catalogue, he stood with one foot on the bottom rail of the fence smoking a pipe while the steaks cooked on the outdoor barbecue.

I had to use my imagination because Mama spoke of him infrequently and always with a burst of words rushing like water through a broken dam. Without being told, I knew I was forbidden to mention his name, particularly if Gammer were present. If I had not caught her off guard one day by asking why there was a picture of Christ in the bottom drawer of the dresser, she would never have told me how they had met. And she never told me his surname either. "Your father," she said in a slightly projected and solemn voice as though about to recite the Lord's Prayer.

Gammer always referred to him as "that Peacenik," spitting out the words as though her mouth were a nest of snakes. Although she made him sleep in the alcove off the kitchen like a hired hand, he did persuade her to bring running water into the house. She wouldn't admit it, but I think it was his interest in mushrooms that won her over. Through the decades she had experimented with hundreds of varieties and had learned which should be boiled or fried or dried or pickled. Her obsession made her fearless. She tasted them all whether they smelled like rotting fish or sun-ripened apricots. Even the poisonous ones, she discovered, could be potent cures, especially if combined with certain mosses or lichens to create a balm or a salve.

Gammer was gathering horsetail ferns on the far side of the pond the day Papa first appeared at the back door in his caftan and Mama – enthralled, she said, by his beatific light – invited him to stay for dinner. Passing by the racks of mushrooms drying in the summer kitchen, he pointed at a red-capped one with white dots. "*Amanita muscaria*," he said, "the divine mushroom of immortality. Rare in these parts." Mama found this amusing since she and Gammer called it "fly killer," leaving bowls of it crumbled with sugar around the house. She described the effect on the insect and how, in the midst of mad whirling flight, it would fall dead to the floor.

Over a dinner of pan-fried trout, Papa related the history of *amanita muscaria* (Mama's pronunciation made it sound like the name of celestial bells), so highly valued in eighteenth-century Siberia that those who became divinely possessed by ingesting it would urinate into a bowl and sell the urine to another. This person would drink the urine and then repeat the process of urinating and selling. The mushroom was so potent, according to Papa, that the urine could be sold to five people. Although he could not convince Gammer or Mama that, by partaking of its power, their souls would soar from the tentacles of reality to join with the cosmos, he did, over time, talk Gammer into taking him mushrooming.

It was she who pointed out the clusters of orange-headed mushrooms growing in a crevice cave on the escarpment and told him that, although it was too bitter to eat, it could be rubbed on the orifices of a first-time birthing sheep, causing it to relax, roll on its side with legs kicking the air, and bleat in an odd way – a kind of phlegmy laugh like an old lady who had drunk too much gin – until the labour was over. Then the sheep would get up and gambol about as though nothing had happened.

Papa, convinced it was similar to the sacred mushroom used by the laughing monks of Tibet, watched while the caps grew from the size of marbles to small jack-o'-lanterns. Then, as the red October moon, swollen to its fullest, floated free from the horizon, he secretly harvested them. Late one night when everyone was asleep, he boiled a potent concoction for himself. Hearing him stumble about, Mama crept past Gammer's closed door and down the steep stairs. When she didn't find him in the kitchen, she ran out and eventually caught up to him standing under an apple tree. Something had changed. His dark melancholy eyes were cold and too bright – glittering like a pond in the moonlight – and he had disappeared below the surface of himself. She wrapped her arms around his shivering body. Pressing against each other they swayed slowly and then began to dance as Papa crooned, "Fly me to the moon and let me dance among the stars…"

I like to imagine how romantic they looked waltzing between the rows of trees in the orchard while the last fruit swooshed to the ground and the moonlight stroked their flesh, calling for the egg, which was me, to be released into life.

The next day, bringing a morning cup of tea into the room off the kitchen where Papa slept, she found in the hollow of the pillow – still warm from his head – a note saying that he had willingly given up his freedom for peace, but there was no peace in New Salem – except for those resting in the graveyard – so he must forfeit his great love for her to keep following the evening star…the shimmering of God's eye…

All this I learned one winter night when I woke to find Mama in my room. At first I thought she was one of my ghostly visitors. The blind on my window had been rolled up and she stood huddled in a grey blanket staring out into the night. Over her shoulder I could see the moon covered by a frilly white cloud like the peignoir set that I had cut out of the mail-order catalogue as a Christmas gift for my paper-doll Mama. The north wind howled down the stovepipe and she, pulling the blanket more tightly around her shoulders, began to speak in a voice so distant it could have been coming from the moon. It made me afraid. Cut off from her, from everything familiar, I stared with all my might across the suddenly vast unknown space that was my room to where she stood in silhouette against the window. As I was staring, it seemed her words were gossamer threads flung endlessly out of her dark shape, filament by filament building a bridge between us. And from us to the clouded moon.

I am sure my eyes didn't close, but the next I remember the lowered blind was washed with morning light. Although I was forbidden to utter the word *Papa*, I couldn't help blurting, "Why does God only have one eye?" as soon as I saw Mama. She spilled the milk she was pouring into my mug and, with the pitcher frozen in mid-air, asked sharply who had told this to me?

Gammer entered the room and I half-answered that the words had been spoken by someone in a dream. "Dream figures often speak nonsense," she replied, with such conviction that I began wondering which one of us had been awake and which had been sleeping.

For months afterwards, watching her closely, I grew more and more aware of the unhappiness gathering around her. By squinting I could make it appear – a translucent film of cloud like the one covering the moon on the night she'd come into my room. Gradually, as her unhappiness hardened, the cloud turned into a white plaster cast. I didn't know it was her attempt at mending a broken heart. I thought she wanted to hide from me. To be visible but not here.

And Papa? He was invisible but here. Like God whose name could never be spoken but who we carried around inside.

Like Mama, too, after the summer when the river took her.

I don't recall how long Gammer and I had been alone before the envelope addressed to Sibyl Witherspoon arrived in our mailbox. I knew it must have something to do with Papa because Gammer muttered, "That no-good panhandling Peacenik," as she turned it over and over trying to decide what to do. Then, lifting the lid off the wood stove, she threw the letter into the fire while announcing in a loud voice that the Devil comes in many disguises. I said nothing, but I wanted to throw myself into the stove after it.

Just now when the phone rang – three long and one short – I jumped out of my skin because I could see myself sitting at the kitchen table with a pen in my hand. Just as fast I came back, gripped the edge of the table and closed my eyes. The knocking of my heart was louder than the ringing phone. It might be Gammer. No. She doesn't know I am here.

Who, then, was phoning? I can't recall if I left Mrs. Janowski, my landlady, the phone number. What could she want? Probably inquiring as to when I'm coming back. I got here yesterday afternoon but it could have been an hour ago. It could have been a minute ago that – to escape the fear of returning to the nightmare – I sat down with a pot of tea to wait for morning. Although there has been no marking of time by the grandfather clock, I know the sun has been long up by the length of the shadow of the oak branches on the pulled kitchen blind. As I write these words, I listen for Gammer's footsteps at the back door, home from helping the Muellers with the lambing.

The house is brooding over her absence. I can feel it.

Standing up to stretch, I wonder why I'm so stiff and then, remembering how I slid and rolled down the escarpment last night, I lift the window blind and press my face against the corner of the glass, hoping her slow-moving bulk will be cutting across the empty field that borders our property and the Muellers'. Nothing moves, except for the glimmer of the pond that I can see out of the corner of my eye. The pale wavering light becomes flickering images, like a malfunctioning television screen…a snowy film of naked bodies with no sound. Why am I shaking? Screaming inside my head? Screaming about what happened but I don't know what it is. I'm not safe awake or asleep – at any moment images rise like the dampness from the root cellar beneath my stocking feet.

I go to the phone on the wall next to the pantry door and dial the number of the Muellers. One long, one short, one long ring. They're probably in the barn tending the newborn lamb. I'll have to walk over, maybe meeting Gammer on the way who will scold me for leaving the house without eating breakfast.

Careful not to step on the line between the black-and-white squares of the linoleum, I cross the kitchen and cut two slices of bread. While I toast it on the wire rack over the dying fire, I remember how Gammer returned an electric toaster I bought for her with my first earnings because she said toast tasted better made on a wood stove. Staring into the red glow of the embers, I see an exit sign at the end of a long hall with doors on each side. I am being propelled forward between two people. I hear laughing. I am struggling to speak. Nothing comes out…but the screaming in my head…

Taking a deep breath, I focus my mind on a pentacle scratched into the black tin of the stovepipe close to where the dampers are located. I must have been very young because I cannot recall making this squished circle with the five points of the star so uneven they resemble fingers. I keep staring at it, thinking of Mama's long restless fingers. It comes back how she beckoned to me on that last morning as I sat cross-legged on the bed watching her brush out her hair.

After eating the toast and licking the buttery crumbs from my fingers, I try again to reach the Muellers, but there is still no answer. I haven't seen them since leaving New Salem and, dreading their judgmental questions as to why I never come home, I decide to wait a bit longer for Gammer's return. But perhaps I'm procrastinating. I have a tendency to sit back and wait for things to happen. Gammer says I'm a navel-gazer, which means physically lazy. In relief, I make a cup of tea and open my journal…

That last unforgettable morning. Perhaps Mama sensed the effervescence in my veins, it being my birthday. Although we lived on the wrong side of things in New Salem – of church on Sunday mornings, of piano lessons after school, of parties on birthdays – there still would be a gift ordered from the Sears catalogue. I yearned for a bicycle but it would have been too expensive, so I circled a night light shaped like a penguin, which might stop me from falling into the dark through the trapdoor in my bed.

Whatever her reason, Mama changed our daily ritual that morning. She stopped brushing her hair and turned from the mirror to face me. As her long graceful fingers beckoned me to come, she smiled, but her sorrowful expression (was it a premonition of leaving me?) did not change. I crossed the room and leaned against her knees, breathing in the sweet lilac smell from the purple bottle on her dresser. As though wanting to do something, she began to brush my hair.

"Today you are ten years old," Mama spoke with fearful determination. "Old enough for me to share a story about one of your ancestors that has been passed by word of mouth through the generations…"

Pausing with the hairbrush in mid-air, she turned as though looking for guidance. I, too, turned, watching the sheer curtain that covered the window moving in and out as though breathing. Mama began to brush my hair in slow strokes. I leaned against her as hard as possible without moving my feet. She sighed.

"It happened so long ago."

"How long?"

"Before the first name was recorded in the back of the family Bible."

"Who was she?"

"A young girl about your age who committed an act more deadly than any of the Seven Sins."

I wanted to ask what the Seven Sins were, but a cold invisible finger pressed against my lips. I thought of the trapdoor nailed shut. Of my relatives held in the ground by the weight of their tombstones.

Suddenly the rising sun filled the loose white curtain with light. It glowed. I could feel a presence. Mama, giving the family trait of a wee shake, continued speaking, but slowly, with small silences.

"Hundreds of years ago, when people believed God and the Devil battled for their souls, they also believed witches and magicians were helpers of the Devil and that the work of the church was to root them out. Our distant ancestor, also an only child, was the first to point her finger and cry out 'Witch! Witch!' This simple word began a craze of accusations that caused twenty innocent people to be hanged. It's written in the history books as the last witchcraft trial in America."

"Is her name Sibyl?"

"No, Elizabeth, but they call her Betty."

"What happens to her?"

Mama pulled me onto her lap. I sat dangling one leg on each side of her thighs as though riding a pony. Not wanting to see myself in the mirror, I closed my eyes. The ends of her unbound hair tickled the back of my arms as her voice flowed over me...

"Months pass. Betty watches more and more young girls become possessed. They accuse the people around them of being witches and magicians. A daughter, whose mother had been pointed out as a Devil's helper, stood outside Betty's home and damned all within. On and on she went, praying that their seed – and the seed of every generation to follow – be tainted with misfortune and that their souls find no peace in this life or the next. Nothing could stop her curses until her family came and took her away.

"After this, Betty – helpless to stop what she herself has put into motion – suffers a feeling that her tongue is burning like the flame of a candle whenever she speaks. Her Papa, the minister at the parish church, says the fire will cease if she stops believing it. She can't. She's afraid. She refuses to speak. Her dark eyes appear empty as though her skull is a burnt-out house. She becomes cold to the touch. The warmth of the sun or the touch of a human hand on her body causes her to scream in pain.

"Her parents send her to live with an uncle in Boston. Still she refuses to speak. Even though barely more than a child, she runs away at every opportunity. It is said she could be found down on the docks performing a strange kind of dance. With head bowed, arms crossed over her chest, left foot grounded as the right one moves, she turns in circles. Spinning faster, her skirt and petticoats open like a rose, and then – extending her arms and lifting her face to the sky – she rotates so rapidly her body appears to dissolve into a whirlwind. Wine-flushed sailors cheer and throw coins as she slowly falls to the ground, smiling, ecstatic.

"A few years later, a laundry basket is left at the front door of her uncle's home with the note, 'Fathered by the wind that fans the fire.' On the flesh over the heart of the newborn infant there is a crimson birthmark the shape of a flame."

At this point in the story, Mama has placed her hands on my shoulders as if to somehow protect me from her words. I did not move or open my eyes...

"Betty is never seen again. It is rumoured that she stowed away on a ship sailing to the Old World. Her daughter grows into a golden-haired girl adored by the aunt and uncle. Years later, a sailor from abroad tells the story of seeing the woman who whirled like a dervish on the Boston docks perform the same strange dance outside St. Paul's Cathedral in London. Each day he said the crowd grew, as did the coins raining down. Soon people were calling out "Blessed Betty" and attempting to touch her twirling skirts which emitted flashes of blue light and a high humming sound. When it came to the attention of the bishop, he proclaimed that black magic would not be practiced outside the doors of his church and pronounced her a heretic – the most wicked of all sinners. She never stood trial because, according to the sailor who read about it in the *London Daily Mirror*, when a constable came to take her to jail he found a smouldering corpse lying on a cot. But what is strange, the straw mattress didn't burn and her clothes weren't scorched. A sweet smoky smell permeated the tiny rented room but nothing else showed signs of fire."

Mama drew in a long breath. I was about to ask the meaning of *corpse* (the way she pronounced it made the flesh on my arms creepy and cold) when she continued, "Back in those times people believed that humans could catch fire from the inside and burn to a cinder – *spontaneous combustion* it was called – just as they believed in werewolves and witches and all sorts of things that defy explanation. But regardless of what is true, or not true, through the centuries there has been a smouldering in our family tree."

Mama hesitated and then said, as though thinking out loud, "It would seem that the body never lies, or else why has a flame-shaped birthmark appeared through the centuries?"

It was not the question that made me open my eyes, but the way her voice had gone slack, dull as a dead stick, while her fingers tightened their hold on my shoulders and she mumbled something about a terrible deed, a curse never to be shaken off...

I found myself looking directly into the mirror of the dressing table. Behind the reflection of our faces, framed by her unbound hair, the glow of the sheer curtain covering the window had the intensity of an apparition struggling to reach our side.

Time passed. Mama let go my shoulders and began to pull the long gold-red hair from the wire bristles of her brush, winding each strand around the fourth finger of her left hand.

When she spoke – more to herself than to me – it concerned the migration of souls after death (I pictured a flock of swans flying overhead), and how it was common to many religions all the way back to ancient Egypt. I couldn't follow what she was saying, except for the story of how the native people who once lived in this area believed that when the body of a dead baby was buried by the wayside, the soul would find a new mother in a passer-by – particularly if she were a member of the same family or tribe.

After telling me this story, Mama hugged me fiercely. We stayed unmoving, silent, my cheek pillowed against her breastbone. Her terrycloth robe, softened by many washings, comforted me. Her bright hair smelled of the sun-ripened apples that I gathered each autumn. How I loved her then. Wanting these moments to go on forever, I asked, "Why would a soul want to live in another body?"

"Perhaps it's lonely."

"Then why doesn't it go to heaven rather than hanging around?"

"Perhaps it's not ready to leave."

"Why?"

"Ohhh, I don't know. My soul could never leave."

"Why?"

"Because," she sighed, "of our Witherspoon blood."

"Where would your soul live if it weren't in your body?"

"Some place close by," she nuzzled my neck, "so I could watch over you."

"But where do you think?"

"How about the oil lamp on the fireplace mantle?"

"Why there?"

"Think how snug and safe I'd be…just like when you were living in my womb."

Just like I was, right then, inside the magical circle of her arms. How snug and safe I felt, and how special because it was my tenth birthday and Mama had shared a family secret with me. She swayed us gently from side to side. We could have been in a canoe on the river. With my head against her chest, I could hear the rushing of her blood and it seemed I was holding an empty shell against my ear, listening to the ocean murmuring…

Then her voice broke in, low and soothing, "Sibyl, you mustn't be afraid of going to bed at night, of falling through the dark. What you are doing, people call 'falling asleep.' Everyone does it."

Mama hesitated. "Perhaps, my dearest, it's like falling in love."

Leaning her head gently against mine, she sighed, "I had a similar feeling after your Papa went away. It seemed as though the bottom had fallen out of the world and there was only an endless emptiness…inside and outside. I'm telling you this, my precious, so you can understand that these strange unpleasant sensations can happen to anyone. It means, at that moment, we are thinking ourselves to be alone…apart. But we aren't."

Mama kissed the top of my head. "Do you remember I told you about your great-grandmother's family who arrived every summer in a brightly painted caravan pulled by a white horse?"

I loved the story about how they settled on the banks of the Mad and the adults gathered lichen, mosses and ferns from crevice caves of the escarpment. Because they did not flower and grew in hidden dark places, these exotic relations of mine believed they were plants from the underworld holding the secrets of life. Mama said this could be true, because when the dried-out lichen – forgotten in the back of the cupboard in our summer kitchen for generations – was sprinkled with water, it started to grow again. I imagined the mother and father in colourful clothes with kerchiefs wrapped around their heads boiling and pounding and sifting and combining and muttering strange words as they transformed what Mama called *cryptogams* (a word sounding like telegrams from the dead) into a magical elixir. I also imagined the younger children playing naked in the shallow water of the river while the older ones collected flat stones, painting them with symbols of the sun and moon and stars. Afterwards, they sold them door-to-door in the village as wishing stones to put under pillows.

"What I didn't tell you," Mama broke into my reverie, "is that on both sides of the caravan were written in large letters AS ABOVE, SO BELOW. This was a phrase from the Emerald Tablet which, according to legend, contained all the wisdom of ancient Egypt. In it is stated" – at this point Mama held out her hand with the palm down – "That which is above is the same as that which is below." Then placing her other hand beneath it with the palm up, "And that which is below is the same as that which is above." Hugging me even closer, she brought both palms together, "And thus all things have their birth from this One Thing."

The last two words she said slowly and solemnly while turning her hands into prayer position. I did, too, and together we repeated the words "One Thing."

Mama smiled at me in the mirror and went on to explain how, from a mail-order collection called *The Books of Knowledge*, she had learned that the Emerald Tablet was a sacred document inscribed by their most revered prophet of mystical power (with a name she couldn't pronounce) who lived around the time of Moses. She told me my ancestors, with their belief in magic and their knowledge of plants, must have embraced the Emerald Tablet as holding the key to all mysteries. For them, the universe was the same as God, God was the same as man, man was the same as the cell, the atom was the same as...

Not following her words, I picked up her brush from the dressing table and began running it through my hair. Mama stopped her story. Inhaling sharply, she said, "My poor precious one, how can I expect you to understand something so obscure and convoluted, something I've been mulling around in my head for years?"

She kissed me again on top of the head. "Let's just say if we are all part of the same thing – and I believe we are – then there is nothing to fear. We can never really be alone. And even if you feel yourself falling as you go to sleep, repeat the phrase 'As above, so below,' and imagine the veins of your body stretching to the roots of the oak tree outside your window, your hair to the feathers of the crows roosting on Great-Gammer's charred cross, your soul to the light of the stars webbing the sky...everything...One Thing..."

Mama and I looked at each other in the mirror while repeating together, "As above, so below." Then she hugged me close, her voice caressing my body. "So you see, dearest one, it's all how we look at what happens to us. What we do with it. That's what the stories that come down from generation to generation teach us."

When I asked to know more about Betty and the flame-shaped birthmark, Mama's face clouded. "Perhaps when you're older I'll let you..."

Knowing she referred to Betty's diary that I had never seen because it was too old and fragile, I interrupted, "But I'm ten now and can read almost every word – even in the Bible."

Mama stared at me quizzically in the mirror and then, with a little laugh, tossed her head back, "No doubt your Gammer will disapprove but I don't care, we're going to look at the diary together."

I scrambled off her lap and, as I waited eagerly for Mama to pin up her hair, she warned, "Don't be disappointed, my pet. This writing has faded so much over three hundred years that, no matter how I struggle to read it, all I can make out is an odd word."

She left the bedroom and I heard her quick light steps going down the stairs. Upon returning, she kneeled before the hope chest and fit a large iron key into the lock. The hinges creaked as she opened the humpbacked top and then, taking out a small brown book, she came to sit beside me on the bed. I was surprised how insignificant the diary appeared with its shabby leather cover and broken clasp. Before we had a chance to look inside, Gammer began stamping her boots in the back stoop to knock off the mud. Mama, promising that we would open it later, slipped the diary into the drawer of her bedside table and, scooping me up in her arms, whispered, "Trust, Sibyl, like the river trusts the sea."

That is how Mama and I spent our last morning together. How prophetic her last words. Or have I made them up? Certainly I had never heard her talk so much. If fact is the solid black outline of what happens – as Mama said – then my colouring in the memory of it changes with each telling inside my head. What does not change is the storm and the flash flood of the Madawaska River and Mama's disappearance and the long hot summer of waiting for her return. That was when Betty came into my life…not as a friend but as a haunting.

Perhaps because of Mama's promise that we could read Betty's diary together, I took it from her bedside and hid it in my secret cave under the high round table in the parlour. Here in the lacey shadows of the floor-length crocheted cloth, safe from Gammer's prying eyes, I struggled to make out the faded writing of my ancestor. I stared at each page, thin as tissue paper, waiting for her words to reveal themselves. What at first resembled the tracks of an insect across spilled flour gradually took the shape of letters. Although my distant kin wrote in a strange way, little by little I was able to figure out the words, and the more I understood, the less alone and afraid I became – especially when I discovered that she was ten, exactly my age at the time.

It felt as though Betty had slipped through the invisible membrane that separated me from the rest of the world. Sometimes, while struggling to decipher a word in her diary, I felt a prickly crawling between my shoulder blades, and I believed she was writing the word on my skin. Sometimes at night, waking from sleep, I heard a distant voice in my head and I recognized her chanting, "Don't leave me alone, don't leave me alone."

It was because of Betty that I taught myself to spin. First, I turned with both feet until, dizzy, I fell to the ground. In time, with one foot firmly planted, I learned to whirl faster and faster until, one day, lifting my face and spreading my arms, the ground rose up to meet me and the sky came down and the two joined and, suddenly, I left my body and I was flying, flying, flying, and then the world rushed away and Betty and I were One.

It was because of my spinning that Gammer found out about the diary. The heat wave was over and, while Gammer dug in the garden for the few root vegetables that had survived the drought, I was trying on shoes ordered from the Eaton's catalogue. Instead of the usual black loafers, Gammer had picked brown suede shoes with laces. Pleased by the style, I decided to find out how it would feel to spin in them. I was in the parlour because it had the largest space, but before my whirling could reach its zenith I heard the clattering wood rings of the curtain rod. As Gammer's head poked through the faded velvet curtains covering the entrance, I fell, knocking over the round table.

"Sibyl," she gasped. "What are you doing?" Ignoring her question, I scrambled up and attempted to pull the table upright. As Gammer helped me, she caught sight of Betty's diary through the tangled lace cloth.

"How did you get this?" she pounced upon the diary and waved it in my face. When I told her I took it from Mama's bedside table, she shook her head in disbelief, saying through clenched teeth, "Your mama would never leave this cursed book where you could find it."

"Yes, she did!" I yelled, grabbing at Gammer's hands to get the diary. She swatted me across the top of my head and, turning on her heels, spat out, "Devilish thing, it's going into the fire!"

And it did. Nevertheless, Betty remained, not like the ghostly figures I saw in my earliest years going silently about their business in a parallel universe, but like the flickering light behind my closed eyes after I'd been staring at a candle flame.

Closing the journal, I stuck my head out the back door to check the weather. I was surprised to find the sun directly overhead. I had been writing for hours about my childhood, the pen moving automatically back and forth across the page like the pendulum of our now-silent grandfather clock. And to think I believed that I had finally escaped the umbilical cord that slipped like a noose around my neck during my birth, almost choking out my life, and which Gammer claimed to be the unbreakable lifeline tying me to the generations of the Witherspoon women who had lived in this house. She always said that the more I struggled the more it would choke me. Regardless of her warnings, my only unwavering desire has been to accomplish what Mama had not…to live the life she had not…to go the distances I had seen in Mama's eyes.

I walked to the Muellers, still safely focused on the past – on the newborn lamb that Gammer brought home the spring after Mama died. Born with a harelip, it could not suckle properly, so old Mueller had given it to Gammer in return for her help with the birthing. I adored this animal, cuddly as a child's toy. Every morning I woke to her bleating for the warmed milk I fed her from a baby bottle. At the end of my school day I rushed back and, releasing the lamb from her pen, we would gambol in the nearby meadow, plucking clover that she ate and I wove into garlands. Although the lamb followed me around like a dog, Gammer would not allow her to be named, warning that it was not a pet. I reminded Gammer that the Bible called lambs the children of God but she just shook her head telling me, no matter the scriptures, that sheep have been raised as food for thousands of years. I said nothing but knew, just as God had sent Jesus to save the people, Mama had sent this heavenly creature to be my saviour.

The lamb was my constant companion all that spring and summer and then, one day in late fall while walking up the road from school, Old Mueller drove past me, his truck jammed with bleating sheep. When I arrived home my lamb was not in her pen. Gammer had warned me over and over that, not only did we have no barn to keep the lamb in the winter, but more importantly, by the next spring it would be too old for its meat to fetch a good price.

I have completely blocked what I did or said to Gammer, but writing these words I am shocked by the stench of hate flowing from this long-buried wound.

I thought I might meet Gammer on the path, as I hadn't seen the Muellers since leaving home three years ago. They were our closest neighbours and therefore the most dangerous according to Gammer. Keep your distance, she warned. It was old Mr. Mueller who bought our land, piece by piece, when Gammer couldn't pay the taxes. Now the farm is run by his son who Gammer calls Young Mueller (even to his face), although he must be close to forty. He has always been soft and slow in mind, as well as body, while his wife Bridget – who he calls The Bride although they have been married for close to fifteen years – is quick-witted and vengeful: "He is her watchdog," they said in the village, "kept on a short leash."

As I cut across their back pasture I noticed the sheep pens behind the barn were full – a larger than usual flock this year – no wonder Gammer had stayed overnight. I was about to enter the barn when Young Mueller appeared, staring at me as though I were a stranger. Pushing his cap back on his head, he flashed what was meant to be a smile, and I noted to my amusement how wide his mouth was, showing teeth unnaturally long and pointed like those of a dog.

"Sibyl!" he exclaimed. "It's been ages. You've changed. Look more like your…" I cut him off by asking for Gammer. He looked surprised and said Gammer hadn't helped with the lambing at all this year. "It's a pity," he said, "with her know-how, even breach birthed twin lambs could be saved."

Without my asking, he told me that she had been helping out at the store that had once been the Methodist Church in New Salem. He carried on about the shame of people being forced to drive all the way to Bancroft to attend Sunday service. Although the church had been locked up for years, still, Aggie Porter had shown no respect for a sacred place of worship (The Bride had been baptized there) by turning it into a business and how pretentious of her to name it The Country Church Craft Boutique.

Young Mueller wiped the corner of his mouth with the back of his hand and went on about Gammer's fancy bottles of remedies selling for outrageous prices – the latest was a face serum from morels, the first mushrooms of spring that she claimed made wrinkles vanish. "Twenty bucks for a tiny jar," he exclaimed, "yet your granny can't concoct enough of the stuff to fill orders from those city folk – one following the other dumb as sheep in a herd. Aggie Porter's going to be the richest woman in Madawaska Valley. But then, as The Bride says, what can we expect from a second wife, an outsider, twenty years younger than the Old Doc, who cashed in on his savings and bought the church before he was even cold in the grave."

Pulling his cap back down on his forehead, Young Mueller gave a quick smile, baring his teeth. "Your granny's a strange one. We're her closest neighbour but not once have we been invited inside for a cup of tea or a drop of whiskey while she and Aggie have become thick as thieves. Never knew her to leave the house on the hill. Lived like a hermit but then this past year I see her walking up the road from the village. Pretty steep for an old lady. No wonder she has to sit down and rest. The Bride got so upset she went to the shop and gave Aggie a piece of her mind. Since then we see your granny driving by in Doc Porter's ancient black Chevrolet – that is, when it hasn't broken down. No reason Aggie can't buy a new car. Everyone knows she's got socks of money stashed under her floorboards."

Standing there – shifting my weight from foot to foot as I tried to maintain eye contact – I was surprised by this outpouring from a man who had never strung more than five words together. At the same time, I was embarrassed by Gammer's behaviour being the butt of villager's jokes.

Both Young Mueller and I ignored the sharp rapping on the upstairs window, but it gave me the opportunity to say that I must hurry back as I was expecting an important phone call. I was closing the gate when I heard The Bride call, "Hey, Sibyl, it's been years. Never seen you with hair so loose and wild. Looks real glamorous."

I knew by the way she said "real glamorous" that she meant "ridiculous," and I could not stop myself from breaking into a run. As I loped across the field, ugly and awkward as a camel, I heard them laughing.

Why have I returned to New Salem? One encounter and the self so carefully created over three years has shattered like a mirror. Gammer is right – The Bride carries a snake in her bosom. Gammer insists it's because of what happened ten years ago when The Bride had her purse stolen and so had no money for the bus fare from Kingston. Of course she should not have hitchhiked home. Gammer says she's lucky to be alive. Now she can't hold a baby to term but won't go to a doctor. I remember once she hemorrhaged so badly that, if it hadn't been for Gammer's remedies, she would have bled to death.

Thinking about this, I grew so cold my teeth rattled together and my mind erupted – suddenly, violently as a seizure – with hands on my flesh…my breasts…weight pressing me down… pressing my thighs apart…

Even now, sitting at the kitchen table, I continue to shiver uncontrollably. I clench my jaw as tight as I am clenching this pen, watching the words flow across the page. No wonder so much of my return to New Salem has been spent writing in this journal about my childhood. Living in the past, I have control –

not like the present when images can erupt more real than any dream. And what is real? What I am writing in this journal? What remains unwritten in my head?

To keep myself focused, I make a list of what I must do. First, phone Country Church Crafts. The answering machine picks up announcing that the store is closed for inventory. It makes sense that Gammer will be assisting Aggie. Next I carry my suitcase upstairs and unpack. It doesn't take long as I brought only one change of clothes. Then I fill the woodbox and neaten the kitchen. Since that's everything on my list, I am about to relax in the rocking chair by the stove when a voice says "Idle hands make an idle mind" so loudly I can't tell whether it's inside or outside my head. Half-sitting, I freeze, convinced Gammer's admonishing me. Worry and lack of sleep, I tell myself, but still the skin tightens on my scalp thinking that her thoughts have invaded my brain.

In an effort to keep busy, I go to the pantry to see what I can make for dinner. I am surprised to find how well-stocked it is. Besides the many jars of home-canned food, there's an array of store-bought tins with bright labels. In the past Gammer scorned commercially made products, but I counted five different kinds of Campbell's soup as well as tins of ham, sardines, tuna and (unbelievably!) baby clams. Young Mueller's right. Gammer's tonics and cures must be selling well. Come to think of it, in one of Gammer's first letters to me she mentioned that she was being paid for helping out.

I'm sure she will come home tonight, even if Aunt Aggie's car has broken down. In all her years Gammer has never stayed away for more than one night. Maybe I should head down the road towards New Salem but, if she comes by car, Aunt Aggie might take the long route and if she's on foot she might take the path along the stream to look for morels. Better to stay here so I can prepare a good dinner. Aunt Aggie may come in. Perhaps for dessert I should open a tin of those fancy canned peaches and add some cinnamon and homemade chokecherry cordial.

I keep phoning Country Church Crafts but get only the answering machine. Unfortunately, Aunt Aggie – who lives behind the store in rooms that once held the children's Sunday school and the minister's private study – doesn't have a personal phone line. In my frustration at being unable to leave a message, I throw the receiver against the wall.

It's almost night. Where can Gammer be? The house doesn't want me to leave. I can tell by the way the glass eyes of the deer head are following me as I pace around the kitchen, careful never to step on a black square of linoleum or the trapdoor to the cellar. With the grandfather clock no longer marking the time, I don't know what the hour is as I climb to the narrow window at the turn in the stairs, or how long I stand in the dark watching for Aunt Aggie's car headlights to come up from the village.

Along the gravel road, shivery pools of light from the high full moon are leaking shadows into the ditches and the edges of fields. I watch for some sign of life – an owl gliding low over the treetops, a fox tip-toeing daintily through the bulrushes around the pond – but with the deepening night, the familiar landscape grows strange and foreboding. Behind me the house pulls into itself as if anticipating danger. I have never felt so alone. A wave of nausea sweeps over me. Closing my eyes, I lean my forehead against the cool glass of the window.

When I am calmer, I force my body to walk back to the kitchen table and my left hand to pick up the pen. Then, taking a deep breath, I force my mind to return to that night…to bring back every detail.

It was five o'clock on April 24th – Thursday evening of Easter long weekend – and for the coming three days I had no plans. I stood on the steps of Robarts Library listening to winter retreating down gutters and drainpipes. The unseasonable warmth had transformed the grey isolated streets of the city into a spring carnival. Although I had been living in Toronto for close to five months, there was nobody I knew among the people strolling along with open coats and bare heads.

Louella Carvalho suggested we go to Murphy's for a beer as she had a two-hour wait for her ride home to Sault St. Marie. Lou and I were both from northern Ontario and had started at Robarts as fetch-and-carry-go-fers around the same time. Although we often took our breaks together, she had never asked me to join her outside our working hours. I was flattered and a little nervous. Walking the block to the pub I thought how odd we must look – me, plowing along with head down like a raw-boned dray horse and she, mincing gingerly due to her bunions and spike-heeled shoes. At one point she put her arm through mine, saying, "Whoa there, girlfriend, not so fast."

It was Lou who first saw the Panman playing his flute and dancing for the people lined up at the bus stop. He winked at us. I pretended not to notice, but Lou blew him a kiss. "Don't you love his vibe?" she said. "The way he can zap you with his eyes. I swear there's nothing you can hide from him. Yesterday I was wearing my new red spring coat with a red-and-orange striped scarf and he told me I made myself bold and beautiful as a tropical bird only to camouflage my shyness."

"You, shy?" I laughed.

"Don't tell," she poked me lightly in the ribs with her elbow, "I wouldn't want to ruin my reputation."

The pub was packed. Three guys invited us to squeeze into a corner table with them. They were third-year students who had just finished their final exams and were celebrating by ordering rounds of beer for the five of us. For me, not being a beer drinker,

they ordered something called a pina colada. John and Jack –
cousins with similar nasal voices and bold brown eyes – wore
white T-shirts that showed off their broad shoulders and fore-
arms whose muscles swelled each time they lifted a beer to their
lips. The other one, appropriately called Sandy or Sandman, had
vague features with hair, skin and eyes the same dull beige
colour. All three kept their eyes fixed on Lou, who flirted and
laughed a lot – her full breasts swaying under the tight sweater.
She appeared to find the guys amusing, but the music blaring
through the speakers prevented me from hearing much of what
was said. I recall her saying we worked at Robarts, and one of the
cousins replied that with our good looks we should be airline
hostesses. Lou said that would be a lot more fun than pushing
carts of books around the stuffy old library, and then she reached
over and unclipped the barrette holding my upswept braid. Lou
knew that my hair, which had never been cut, was my glory, and
as I shook it loose she said, "Sexy as Lady Godiva," and the guys
whistled and applauded. Lou and I began moving our upper bodies in time to the music. Jack, sitting beside me, pressed his
thigh against mine. I pressed back.

Suddenly Lou jumped up, saying, "Oh my god I'm going to
miss my ride," and picking up her bag, rushed out. Left alone I
felt awkward and said, "I must leave too," but when I stood up I
grew dizzy and headed to the washrooms. Jack followed and
grabbed me, running his hands all over my body. I was too surprised to stop him. Returning to get my coat, I discovered another pina colada waiting for me.

After that it's as though a piece of my life had been sucked
into the black hole my body falls into each night while going to
sleep.

I came back to myself with everything moving in and out of
focus as though I was emerging from an anaesthetic. Reaching

up I touched my face. I felt a nose, eyes and mouth but they were in the wrong place. I stamped my feet because my legs were wood. As my mind cleared I realized that I was standing in a bus shelter on College Street close to the library, the Panman hovering a few feet away. I tried to speak but my words were so slurred I didn't understand them.

He shook his head and began to dance in a circle, chanting, "Rub-a-dub-dub, three men in a pub; and who do you think they be? A butcher, a baker, a candlestick maker all jumped out a rotten tomato. 'Twas enough to make a god stare."

It didn't make sense, but his voice was as rich and full as a preacher reciting a prayer. I found myself sobbing. At least I think I was, but there were no tears and it sounded more as though I was strangling. I covered my face with my hands.

"Oh no, oh no, I am so sorry," he crooned, as if soothing a sick child. "I was trying to make you smile." His eyes were closed but he had the kindest saddest expression on his face as he massaged his temples with his fingertips. Did he sense the pounding pain in my head? Then he began mumbling about temples to the goddess, the throb of the drums calling us to divine worship.

As I stumbled down the street I heard him calling, "Please don't be frightened," but I didn't look back until I got to the corner. College Street was empty. The Panman had vanished, yet somehow he was still there – a dark shape with a white aura, the negative of a photograph – set against the lurid city sky. Was he the reason the buildings leaned inward to form a tunnel, or the billboards in the bus shelters yelled obscenities, or the sidewalk rose and fell in gentle waves? To avoid the blinding spotlight of the street lamps following me, I crept along in the shadows…my feet knowing the way.

The last I recall was lying fully dressed across the bed in my rented basement room and listening to the phone ring in the upstairs hall. It was light outside and my alarm clock read three fifteen in the afternoon. I ached all over. Wobbly, I got up and made my way – slowly because of the pain in my pelvic area – to the bathroom at the end of the corridor. In the mirror above the sink I saw my swollen and discoloured cheek, but I couldn't remember falling. Then, undressing to shower, I found my underwear inside out. I allowed the hot water to beat down on me until it turned cold, but I felt no better, no closer to knowing what happened. The more I tried to think about it, the more my head and my body were somehow separating.

❧ DAY THREE ❧

Once I had made concrete on the page all I recalled of that fatal Thursday of the Easter weekend, my nausea and headache dwindled. I wanted to rest, but every time I closed my eyes I would begin falling – not into the bottomless night of my child-hood – but into the sharp cutting fragments of images from the nightmare that I can't remember, but is real…scattered like a broken mirror in my brain.

Why did I write these words? Must be the two nights with-out sleep. Of course a nightmare can't be real…or I would have to accept knowing…knowing every moment for as long as I live. Still, I can't help wondering what the Panman had seen that night. In the following weeks I stayed on the lookout for him around the library and made sure to duck out of sight before he saw me. I was ashamed of course, but more, I was afraid of what he would say to me in front of Lou or my other co-workers. The bruise on my cheek faded, but always over the black hole in my memory the Panman's face glimmers like the moon at mid-day.

To stay awake for the remainder of the night, I fetched an arm-ful of split logs from the woodbox and laid them on the dying coals in the stove, and then I filled the black iron kettle with water to boil for tea. Recalling how, on a winter Sunday after-noon, we used to polish the ancestral silverware, I took out forks and spoons and bone-handled knives that were wrapped in soft blue flannel from the armoire in the dining room. Making a pungent paste of warm water, baking soda and dried wormwood leaves, I pulled the rocking chair close to the fire and began by cleaning the five large serving spoons.

Trying to keep focused, I reminded myself of the story that Gammer often repeated as she polished – about how our Loyalist forefathers were exiled from their prosperous land after the American war for independence. "Solid silver," she would begin, holding up a piece she had lovingly rubbed until it glowed, "Good as money in the bank." She went on to describe how George James Robinson, the first ancestor of our branch of the family tree, packed whatever fitted into two oxcarts and walked through the wilderness of northern New York state, selling off – piece by piece – the flatware to feed and lodge his family. She never failed to say that it cost six of the eighteen place settings plus two silver foot-high candlesticks to pay passage on the barge that hauled them up the St. Lawrence River to the waterfront property granted him by the British army. At this point Gammer, wiping her hands on the bib of her apron, ended the story with, "Of course the land turned out to be two hundred acres of bog fit only for beavers and mosquitoes."

That the world has always been against the Witherspoons gave us a hidden pride in our bent backs and broken hearts. It vindicated our smouldering anger at being cast out…like Ishmael…and like Ishmael we formed our own nation. Although Mama and Gammer never spoke of it in this way, why else, on so many occasions, did they open our ancient Bible to where the births in our family had been recorded as far back as the seventeenth century? Mama would delicately run her finger down the pages of names – so faded in the beginning that they seemed to have been written with invisible ink – until she reached our branch of the family tree.

It was the beginning of the nineteenth century, and two generations of Robinsons had been attempting to eke a living out of their Quinte Bay homestead. Regardless of their desirable waterfront property turning out largely to be a cedar swamp and with no slaves to help, the first settlers cleared the little arable land that was available and planted crops of tobacco, convinced they would be highly profitable. Unfortunately the yield, more often than not, went mouldy. Then they drained part of the swamp and planted crops of corn to sell for animal feed, but only the blackflies multiplied – along with my ancestors' bitterness at losing their rich land in America, especially while their neighbours were prospering.

Although the growing number of Robinsons laboured endlessly, constant hunger forced the men off their land to work in the logging camps, and then in the building of the Rideau Canal. Designed as an alternate route in case there should be another war with the Americans, the canal took six years of hard labour with only axes, picks, shovels and wheelbarrows to clear the forests, drain the swamps and excavate through the steep outcrops of limestone and Precambrian rock. The camps were so rough two sons died of dysentery and two more of malaria. Pointing to their names in the family record, Mama said that dying was the only thing the Quinte Bay clan did well.

With only women – too old or too young to marry – remaining, the homestead was put up for sale, but no one wanted it. And after more than forty years of toil, the place was abandoned and the ground, which never should have been broken, gradually returned to the beaver and the alder bush and the redwinged blackbird.

The youngest daughter, Mary Anne Robinson, took what would fit into her hope chest and fled north to Perth which, with the building of the Rideau Canal and the free land grants to

European settlers, had become a boom town. In 1845, after working six years as a seamstress, she married Alfred Cole Witherspoon whose wedding gift – a silver needle case engraved with the initials M.A.W. – has been used by the six generations of women unfurling on the Witherspoon branch of the family tree. Alfred, a British immigrant discharged from the Napoleonic Wars, had received a free land grant to settle in Upper Canada, but he lost the hundred acres in a card game and spent years gambling in the hope of winning another parcel of land. In the end, this tall handsome charismatic (according to Mama) forefather finagled another land grant from the government, which was eager to push northward in its colonization.

The Witherspoons were among the first white settlers to travel along the rough trail, later described in books as a road of broken dreams. After the lumber companies ravaged the pine forests and the gold rush frizzled out, there was only the rocky soil, too infertile for farming. By the end of the nineteenth century, many homesteaders in the Madawaska region, broken by years of near starvation, had fled to the west. But not my forefathers. Too proud and too stubborn (stupid according to Mama) to admit that nature had defeated them, generation after generation stone-picked the surrounding fields and built this house on the hill as a testimony to themselves. Everything and everyone outside the family turned into a potential enemy. By the time Gammer was born, the only refuge from the perilous world was inside the closed gates to the property. No one left except by dying.

After rolling the last dessert fork in blue flannel and returning it to the box, I rise up from the rocker and find the grey of dawn seeping under the kitchen blind. It's too early to phone Aggie and find out why Gammer has stayed another night. Aunt Aggie, asleep in the rooms at the back of the store, wouldn't hear the ringing, and early-bird Gammer would never pick up the phone. Once the sun is up, if still no one answers, I'll take the shortcut down the hill and be there in twenty minutes. In the meantime, to overcome the powerful urge to sleep and to stretch my stiff legs, I begin prowling along the narrow corridors connecting the old stone house to the limestone and weatherboard additions that flank both sides.

Each time, as a child, when climbing a staircase that joined the front or back of the floors, I felt compelled to stop on the landing and run my hands over the wall, trying to find the half door that hid the winding metal steps to the flat roof. According to Mama (who told me not to say anything about it to Gammer), when Grandfather fell to his death, Gammer took off the knob and sealed the crack between the door and the wall. Once the wall was painted no one could tell that a door had existed. Even Mama did not know its exact location.

I had forgotten all about the half door but, now that the guardian in the front hall has stopped counting the moments, time is sliding backwards. I am being pulled into the past by what I thought I had forgotten – the moist odour of wood smoke and Lyle soap in the pantry, the faint but biting reek of bat droppings in the second-storey rafters, the creaking complaint of the fourth step on the back stairs, the whispering of the threadbare silk curtains when I open the door to the dining room.

Nowhere is there any colour. Even the large green ferns on the parlour wallpaper have faded to shades of grey. No matter which of the fourteen rooms I enter, the gloom and bitterness, collecting since the house was built, swirl like fog around me. Somehow I can't make myself open the curtains that have been closed for three years in the front of the house. People might suspect. That Gammer is not here. That I am.

The more I wander through the house, the more it becomes a labyrinth I can never escape. The cracks in the plaster are hieroglyphics. I feel I must decipher them to find my way. The wet patch where rain leaked above the front hall mirror has changed its shape from a fish to an eye – unblinking – not one for weeping. The mirror, when I mistakenly glanced into it, seemed to be pulling me into the glass. It took all my willpower to turn away.

And just now, passing by it again, I found myself touching my body as if to make sure it was there.

In the same way, passing Mama's closed bedroom door, I found myself bending to peer through the keyhole. I can never bear to enter, but for Gammer the room is a shrine to be kept exactly as Mama left it on her last day. Through the keyhole I saw the window with the hope chest beneath it. Made from Cedar of Lebanon, it is the size of a child's coffin. My Loyalist ancestors brought it here from New England. The chest – darkened by many polishings – has a slight indentation on the front as though something were scraped away. As a child I once ran my fingertips over the hollowed place in the wood and recognized the faint etchings of letters that I thought spelled the word EVIL. After that, I had nightmares about a bride in a white gown locked in the chest by an evil stepmother. When I showed Mama the secret word she took my other hand and moved it in the opposite direction across the indentation so that the letters spelled LIVE.

Although, as far as I remember, Mama only spoke once of our ancestor's diary and only once unlocked the humpbacked top, she often told me (in a whisper so Gammer couldn't hear) that the package sent to me by Papa after my birth was waiting there. Each time I asked to see it she would say, "When you are ready, the hope chest and its contents will be yours."

After Mama was taken by the river, I spun daydreams around myself, sweet and pink as cotton candy, about Papa coming for me and our wonderful life of travel and adventure. I lived inside this cocoon of hope throughout my childhood. But as my body blossomed, so did my anger at Papa for deserting us. I needed to find out what was in the package, even if I must enter the forbidden room. When I asked Gammer for the key to the hope chest she snapped, "There's nothing inside so why would you want to open it?" Remembering how she threw the unopened letter into the fire saying, "That damn panhandling Peacenik," I lied, telling her I hoped one day to be married.

She gave me an odd, slightly surprised glance and then, wiping her palms vigorously down her apron as though she couldn't get them clean, said, "Hope is the worst of all evils. It'll tempt you with something better in the future. Don't you waste a moment in hoping, Sibyl, it's the dirty end of the stick, turning each day into a mouthful of dust."

I heard her repeat these words just now as I was staring through the keyhole. The hope chest itself appeared smaller, more fragile than I remembered, and the ornate brass lock had tarnished. The only other object in my line of vision was the patchwork quilt covering the bed. Mama made it by cutting up the clothes Papa left behind and stitching the pieces together in an intricate design of pentacles as beautiful as a stained-glass window. It took her years. Snip by meticulous snip, stitch by tiny even stitch, she assembled not so much a comforter of warmth but a canvas of her despair and grief. The brilliant reds and oranges of the large five-pointed star in the centre was, for me, a destroying angel of flames, while spinning out from it were other angels that grew darker, duller, more cold as their size diminished until they reached the dark blue border of death.

The mornings I watched Mama brushing out her hair, I always folded the quilt across the bottom of the bed. I was afraid to sit on it. Afraid of the power that flowed out of it.

Now, after all these years, what made me bend to peer through the keyhole was not to see what's inside, but to try and suck in that special odour…the smell of her hair and the sweat of her neck mingled with the lilac of her cologne. The cologne that she would dab behind each ear after pinning up her hair. The cologne in the purple glass bottle that, in my grief, I stole and poured into the pond.

In my wandering through the house I stopped at the end of the long upstairs corridor to poke my head into Gammer's bedroom, still hoping against hope that she would be taking her daily nap. But the quilt over her bed, patched from the blues of Grandfather's overalls, continued to lie smooth as the pond on a hot summer day. And on the night table her false teeth lay curled like a shellfish in a glass of water. I find it odd that Gammer would leave the house without them. Perhaps, with the money earned from her remedies, she has replaced the ill-fitting upper plate that she complained about for years.

I should go into her room and check the closet to see if her good black dress with the tiny blue flowers is in the closet. Is it because she so rarely allowed Mama or me into her bedroom that now I can't make myself step through the door? The air, more dense and clammy than in the rest of the house, has created an invisible wall through which my body refuses to pass.

Instead I stare at the sample, cross-stitched by Great-Gammer, hanging above the bed. Although intricately decorated by faded violets and trailing clematis, the words *Those who know do not speak and those who speak do not know* remind me of how I have tried to escape the brooding silence of this house and the day-to-day struggle of Gammer's life. Most of all, I have tried to escape the unrelenting rage that turns her to ice on the outside while on the inside she burns like a witch at the stake. Writing these words, I feel my own body dwindling – smaller, colder, more numb – into a ghost.

I am familiar with being a ghost. It had already happened on the day that part of me died. I actually felt my soul separate from my body – only it couldn't escape because it was tethered, just like an unborn baby is connected to its mother by an umbilical cord. I know what I say is true because of that afternoon when I learned what happened to the one who was my first friend…

Rosie O'Sullivan – writing the letters of your name pulls me into the perfect summer of my fourteenth year. It actually started the previous fall. You were living with your aunt and uncle, the Pitkins, and their six children on that ramshackle farm I passed on my way to and from school. When you first came to New Salem we both used to walk home alone, drifting along in the same direction like sheep crossing a field to a barn. A barn was where it all occurred – an abandoned barn on the vacant lot that signalled the end of the village. The day we began to be friends, you waited for me in the corner of that vacant lot where some old kitchen appliances had been dumped. You were hiding behind a rusting refrigerator and, as I walked by, you threw chestnuts at me, asking if it were true about Gammer being a witch. No one before had asked to my face and I blurted out, "Yes, she knows how to bring people back from the dead." You – green eyes fierce and calm as a cat – replied that you would like to learn.

After your parents died in a car accident, you were bounced from relative to relative because of your uncontrollable temper tantrums. You were such a scrawny scrappy kid, two years older than me but a head shorter. You hated bathing and never combed your hair, just cut off the tangles so that ragged remainders stuck up all over your head like orange feathers. Gammer said you looked like a chicken pulled backwards through a wire fence.

You were the only one at school not afraid to come to my house. The only one not afraid of anything. Your acceptance of me has been the only miracle in my life. Since the first grade, embarrassment had become routine. Children don't forget. Roving clutches of girls hunted me down in the cinder playground of the schoolyard and one of them chanted, "Silly Sibyl stinks of shit," and another replied, "That's because she's illigit." Then they took turns pushing me and yelling "bastard," but never hard enough or loud enough to alert the teacher on yard duty. When I defended myself by pushing back they spat at me, and when I yelled, "I'm not a bastard," they chanted, "Liar liar pants on fire, hanging from the telephone wire." There was no way to escape their taunting.

You, on the other hand, were shunned. Standing in the corner by the chainlink fence, you pulled a blade of grass, placed it between your thumbs, and with palms together in prayer pose, raised your hands and blew into them. The screeching from this ancient reed pipe split open the air as though the Devil himself were gaining entrance to the world. Every kid was awed by the sound but afraid to approach. That was because of the razor-blade edge to your voice that could tear strips from the schoolyard's biggest bully. And you never stopped talking. Motor Mouth they called you. Everyone was your enemy. Except me.

I adored everything about you – the perfect little teeth revealed by your lopsided grin, the bitten fingernails flaunting an ever-changing gaudy polish, the knobby elbows and knees that seemed to move before you did. But above all I loved your small pointed face with its round curious eyes. Whenever you glanced sideways I was reminded of a fox.

By June we had been inseparable for the entire year, and rather than being the two individual outcasts of the schoolyard we had, by some special providence, become one...invisibly joined at the soul, I like to believe. You believed it was because we were both orphaned at the age of ten and that we both had the word *rose* in our names (your given name was Rosemarie and Grandfather's last name was Rosenkreux).

I think the other kids sensed our combined strength because they grew a little afraid, even though they still called us freaks or weirdoes. It was you, Rosie, who claimed our supernatural powers after yelling, "Break a leg!" when Willie, biking by, splashed us with mud and then before he reached home, he slipped and sprained his ankle. It was you, also, who stole *The Complete Book of Magic and Witchcraft* from the library truck because it pictured a five-pointed star inside a circle on the cover and you knew of Mama's and my obsession to draw a perfect one. We discovered together that it was a holy sign, officially named a pentacle, and had been used since ancient times as a powerful amulet to protect people against evil. We who believed in black magic named it a Witch's Cross or a Goblin's Foot. Others, like nuns and priests, referred to it as the Star of Bethlehem.

It was my idea that we should make our own amulets as a secret sign of our being special. The five-pointed stars were easy to construct from picture-frame wire and we hung them on strings around our necks. I wore mine with one point of the star upwards (the way I had always drawn them), which the book regarded as a symbol of the earth goddess. I could actually feel her protection around me – this female figure with head, hands and feet touching the circle of the cosmos – like electricity in the air before a thunderstorm. You wore yours with two points upwards signifying the horned god, the Prince of Darkness. So potent, you announced, that it burned against the bare skin of your chest.

On that fateful June afternoon, we were walking home from school when Billy Parson suddenly appeared waving a green-and-brown striped garter snake. He was with his younger brother and Ned Nickels, the fat grocer's son who we called No Neck.

"Drop it down one of their shirts," No Neck shouted. Fear sprouted wings from our feet and we got away, racing across the vacant lot. Crouching behind the rusted fridge we watched the three boys pass and then decided to hide in the abandoned barn in case they were waiting up ahead to jump out at us. As we pulled open the door there was the rush and flap of pigeons rising like disturbed cherubs out of a hole in the roof. I threw myself down on a pile of mouldy straw in the corner. You kept watch through the slats in the boards.

When you whispered, "They're coming," I thought it was a joke, but then you raced up the ladder leading to a loft where the pigeons had been nesting. I barely had time to burrow under the straw before the screech of the rusty hinges announced the boys. From my hiding place I heard Billy making some kind of bet with his brother Freddie that snakes are the same as worms and if one is cut in half, the tail becomes like the head so there will be two of them.

Crouching on the floor, Billy held the snake behind its head and No Neck held its tail. It was quiet with the late afternoon sun slanting through the hole in the barn roof, spotlighting the boys as they huddled. I recall peering through the hay at the dusty motes slowly dancing and whirling in the beam of light. Far off, I heard the murmuring of bluebottle flies. For those few moments time ceased to exist.

Then Billy brought out his pocketknife. It was said his father used a leather belt to strap him and I could see the welts on his legs. With a sudden downward movement he sliced the snake in half and then both boys let go and jumped back. How vivid is my memory of those crazed parts whipping across the floor towards my hiding place…separate but somehow together…both halves twisting around and around in a kind of duet…each part unable to escape its bloodless silent pain. I could see the jaw opening and closing, the tongue flickering in and out. I heard its deaf-mute snake sound that seemed to be coming from me…twisting and turning inside my own lungs and I closed my eyes and held my breath. But still a sound came out – a kind of "Euf, euf." Then a hand grabbed my ankle and I was dragged out of the straw.

"It's Silly Sibyl."

"Motor Mouth must be here."

"Let's get her and stuff the snake in her mouth."

"Ya, that'll shut her up."

No Neck twisted my arm behind my back. While struggling to get free I heard him demand to know where Motor Mouth was hiding. The sweet stench of doughnuts on his breath churned my stomach. When I didn't answer he twisted my arm with such force I fell to my knees, crying out with the pain.

Freddie, who was standing guard by the barn door, snuffled, "I want to go home."

"Shut up, big baby," Billy said, "or I'll make you take out your teeny weeny and stuff it into Silly's mouth."

"No, no," he blubbered, "she'll bite it off. She's evil. Her ugly granny turns into a witch at night. You told me she can walk through walls and pull me out of bed."

Billy always picked on his dumb snip of a six-year-old brother, who he took everywhere since their mother's constant coughing confined her to bed. All the Parsons had bland features and pale, almost corpselike colouring. The villagers had nick-named them the Parsnips.

Billy dragged Freddie over to where No Neck had me pinioned and pulled down his pants. Then he grabbed me by the hair and yanked my head back, saying if I didn't lick Freddie he would ram the head end of the snake – twitching in its death spasm on the dusty floor – into my mouth.

I stared up at the sky through the hole in the roof. The brilliant blue radiated down, accumulating around me, soaking up my terror. I felt my insides soften. It was all right. She, the goddess of my amulet, would protect me. I closed my eyes. I stuck out my tongue. I expected it to feel cold and slimy like a frog or a snail, but it was warm with the velvety texture of a mushroom.

Then Billy let go of my hair and said, "Come on, No Neck, let's take off her blouse. If she's a witch there'll be three tits and if she's a werewolf there'll be fur." Their rough hands yanked at my buttons while I punched and kicked. Then Billy sat on me and No Neck pinned my arms to the floor above my head. Billy seemed disappointed that I was not an aberration of nature. Although he said my tits were flat as oatcakes, he ordered Freddie, who was back standing guard by the door, to suck my nipple.

"It'll poison me." His voice quavered.

"Big baby," scoffed Billy, "Don't you want some titty milk?"

Freddie started to sniffle, wiping the back of his hand across his face.

"If you don't suck each titty until the count of twenty, I'll tell Ma how you wet the bed."

"No I don't."

"Yes you do. I should know. I have to sleep on the same mattress."

Then Billy forced him down and pushed his face against my bare chest. His eyes, squeezed shut, were beaded with tears. The touch of his thin silky hair could have been moth wings.

Looking back I recall how easily his small pink mouth found and fastened on my nipple. Like a blind newborn puppy. It brought a warm pleasant sensation that, spilling downward, grew more intense. Then suddenly the air was split open by the familiar call of your screeching whistle. And there you were, standing in the loft high above us, your palms in a prayer pose over mouth and nose, your body outlined in the golden glow of the late afternoon sun pouring through the hole in the roof as though – like Mary, Mother of God – you were about to be raised straight up to heaven.

The image shattered as you yelled, "There's someone coming." At the sound of a truck the boys jumped up and ran away. I lay curled in a ball on the floor with my hands over my face. "Quick," you said, "Here's your blouse." We slid out the door and, without a glance at the pickup truck slowing to a stop, turned towards home. For once you didn't say a word. Neither did I. Not even when I realized my amulet was missing. Everything we passed on the road looked too sharp as though it were made of broken glass. I kept my eyes half-closed. And my mind.

At the gate to your uncle's farm you said without looking at me, "See you tomorrow." But you didn't. I couldn't go to school. My throat was on fire. I had a fever too. It raged for weeks, in spite of Gammer's poultices and sponge baths. Old Doc Porter had not been to the house since Grandfather fell to his death so many years before, but whenever his name was mentioned Gammer would grumble, "Highway robbery to charge ten dollars for a death certificate." Now she was forced again to call upon him. All I remember is his being so shrivelled and slow-moving that, when he sat down beside me, the bedsprings never complained – not even a little sigh. I knew that even though his eyes had fallen into their sockets, he could see the snake when he looked down my throat. It had slipped in when I was sleeping and it clung there by its fangs, sucking my blood. The voice in me cried bite, bite. I did – again and again – then I spat out the pieces…and they wound around each other and became one again, creeping away through a knothole in the cupboard door.

Once my fever broke I plugged the knothole with paper. Even though I understood that Doc Porter was right and the snake had been a feverish hallucination, my heart lurched slightly whenever I opened the cupboard.

Weakened by the glandular fever, I was relieved of my chores. You, on the other hand, were a servant to your Aunt May – not only taking care of the bratty kids and making the meals but repairing her chipped nail polish and backcombing her bleached hair until it resembled a hay stook. However, we had a signal. Whenever the phone rang once, I knew to go to our secret place – the small muddy beach hidden by head-high reeds and bulrushes. Mama and I had discovered it the time we were pick-ing wild blueberries on a duck hunters' path that meandered along the banks of the Mad.

On hot afternoons you and I skinny-dipped and afterwards sunbathed on mats woven out of reeds. I counted the freckles sprinkled over your body. Some days there were fifty-seven. Other days a hundred and three. If I squinted, the tiny hairs on your arms and legs became a golden aura.

Yes, that summer when I turned fourteen and you turned six-teen, we found a magical enclosure, a gateless garden where no evil could enter, no words could come out wrong. We talked for hours – babbling, Gammer called it – our tongues loose as the river flowing past us.

I told you about Papa – the few facts divulged by Mama that over time I had woven into a bedtime story – of how they met, and instantly fell in love, until God forced them to part so Papa, like the Magi in the Bible, could follow the evening star, and how

Mama found the footprints of his departing sandals in the muddy lane and stuck a nail into the deepest one, hoping it would bring him back...and then seven months later when she was walking under the blossoming apple trees, gathering boughs broken by the winter storms, she glimpsed what seemed a brown bear rummaging around a dead stump. She screamed and then, as it was rearing up, recognized Papa holding a handful of mushrooms.

Before Mama knew what she was doing her arms were wrapped around him and they were leaning into each other, straining and trembling at the edge of their skin. He moaned, "Come away with me, let the dead bury the dead," in her ear while she, her face pressed hard into his thin rough coat, said nothing...did nothing. Then, ripping his body away and falling to his knees, Papa put his hands on her tummy whispering that he loves me and will always watch over me in the same way that the evening star watches over the world. And then, getting to his feet, he reached into his baggy pocket for a metal ring meant to hold keys and slipped it on her fourth finger. After kissing her hand, he glanced over his shoulder and said, "Before the eye of God appearing over the far hills I take thee for my wedded wife." They looked into each other's eyes for a long moment and Papa whispered, "There is always room on the road for three." Mama shook her head ever so slightly, and slowly, without a word, he turned away. She stood like stone watching him leave.

Even when he turned and waved before climbing the fence into the neighbour's field, she did not wave back. Instead she remained motionless until he was out of sight and then tentatively lifted her hand to touch her burning cheek. That's when she found the imprint of his coat button. And she wanted to run after him, to leave with him so they could always be together. But at that moment I moved in her tummy and she knew a child needed a home, not a life on the road. Over the years she waited for him to come back to see me...

At this point I began to cry and you, Rosie, put your arms around me and said, "As soon as we're legal we're going to hit the road and find him." I confessed that over the years I had expanded and polished the story so many times in my head that I no longer knew how much of it was true, except after Mama was gone I vividly recalled how I discovered one of his sketchbooks, filled with chalk drawings of people he called "soul portraits," and how Gammer grabbed it and, forbidding me to ever speak his name, burned it – page by page – in the kitchen stove. At the time I was too young to understand I was illegitimate.

That's when you confessed to me that your parents had not been killed in a car accident but, after your mother left, your father had committed suicide by driving off a bridge. You didn't miss your blonde and placid baby sister who had been adopted immediately, but sometimes in your sleep she sobs "Wosie, Wosie," her last words as the social worker took her away.

You also told me that Aunt May and Uncle Horace were not relatives, but people paid by the government to take you in. You hated everything about them, especially how your so-called aunt wore her nylon stockings rolled to the ankles and no underpants. Since her thighs were so fat that there was no space between them, when "on the rag," as you called it, she smelled high as a catfish that sometimes washed up on the shore of our secret place. It was stronger, you said, than the smell of your so-called uncle who only took off his greasy cap when he went to bed. He had so few teeth that when he chewed tobacco you used to count the number of times his chin reached up to touch his nose.

Now, reading these words, I wonder if we were aware of the current underneath our voices – that silent current of love –

shaping everything we said. It's strange how I recall your every word but not much of what I said…except for little secrets that slipped like silk into our conversation. Maybe they seemed little because I felt no shame with you. But, if that's true, why didn't I reveal that one of my ancestors was responsible for starting the last witch hunt in America?

Instead I told you that, according to family legend, I had a distant cousin who believed that by whirling like a toy top she got close to God. Then I told you about teaching myself to spin. How, standing with feet apart, arms folded across my chest, head bowed, I took three deep breaths and, with the left foot planted on the ground, I turned with the right, faster and faster, gradually extending both arms and lifting my face…until at the climax, just before falling to the ground, I left my body and became a whirlwind of singing colours.

"Cooool," you said. "Show me how."

After that, one of us would spin until dizzy and breathless, and then the other would catch the reeling body and lay it on the mat of woven reeds.

"Like being one with the universe," I said. "Like having an orgasm," you said…a word unknown to me, but sounding as though it were music for an orchestra or church organ.

I loved to watch you spinning to dry off after a skinny-dip in the river, hair bleached by the sun to the colour of hard butter, skin glistening. You twirled with such speed that your body lost its form…becoming a golden funnel…a guardian angel of light. Finally you fell spread-eagled into my arms as though in a mystical trance. I couldn't help but stare at the translucent half-moons of your breasts, the delicate pink flower of flesh between your parted legs. Then one afternoon you took my hand in yours and showed me how to stroke those soft warm petals. I was fascinated but at the same time appalled by the force that was released – not in the way a blossom bursts into flower, but in the way Mama spoke of a body spontaneously bursting into flames.

Always we stayed too long and shadows crept up from the ground while we walked single file, quiet as deer along the path, eyes ever watchful for the first star above the ridge of the far hills. Ever since I told you about Papa leaving to follow what he called God's eye, we vied to be the one to point out the solitary light – bright, fierce, cold – in the deep purple of the summer sky. Then, joining hands, we repeated out loud, "God's eye," and made a wish.

Always during those moments I knew that somewhere near or far Papa was looking up because he felt the star's power. And I knew that he, too, was making a wish…for what is a wish if not a prayer.

In September I returned to the two-room brick schoolhouse while you were bussed thirty miles to the large cinderblock high school – the only one in the county. Most afternoons I walked slowly along the road watching for the yellow school bus to pass. The first week you waited at the end of your lane to tell me about the cafeteria, the library, the gym, the locker you shared with a girl who owned a genuine leather book bag. By the second week, the girl who sat next to you in the math class – who shopped for clothes and never ordered from a catalogue – had loaned you a denim jacket.

By the end of the month all you could talk about was Mr. Baxter, the physical educational teacher, who looked like a movie star. You pinned a photograph of Robert Redford over your bed saying your teacher had the same baby-blue eyes and wave of shiny blonde hair that fell over his forehead.

It was my idea to ask Gammer's advice on how to make a love potion to give to Mr. Baxter. I pretended it was to be part of a school science project on the many curative powers of plants and mushrooms, but Gammer said love was a curse, not a cure. I should have known she would refuse to help because whenever the word *love*, and by association *sex*, was mentioned, she clenched her hands as though she was about to engage in a fist fight.

Both of us remembered about *The Complete Book of Magic and Witchcraft* stolen from the travelling library truck. You, Rosie, found the love potion under a section on Hoodoo and Voodoo in the South Sea Islands, but you let me help to make it. The book said to place a small piece of clothing on which one has sweated into a conch shell (you ran until the band around your forehead was soaked and we substituted a clay bowl) and then to let fall on it seven drops of blood from a finger pricked with a javelin (we substituted a penknife). Next, the book said to set the piece of clothing on fire and, while it is burning, to sprinkle in a strand of hair the size of a baby finger and nail parings from all of one's fingers and toes. Most importantly, the ash, mixed into sweet food, must be eaten by the victim before the next full moon.

Since your school was having a bake sale to raise money for gym equipment, you decided that we would make brownies with chocolate icing. The day of the event you walked up to Mr. Baxter with an extra-large square and, when he saw that it was decorated with his name, he smiled (you told me his teeth were straight and white as a toothpaste ad) and said, "How can I refuse?" But he didn't eat it right away and you worried for a week, until after gym class you asked if he had enjoyed the brownie. He gave your shoulder a little shake saying, "It tasted somewhat gritty. Are you sure, Miss Rosie O'Sullivan, that you didn't mix in a forbidden substance?" Then, as your heart was pounding, he started to laugh, saying, "Don't look at me like that! I'm joking."

Did Mr. Baxter know about the love potion? We talked of nothing else all that fall. You overheard the older girls in the lunch room whispering about something they called weed, forbidden by law, but it was smoked in a cigarette so we thought that couldn't be what he meant.

Meanwhile, you began bathing and washing your chopped-off hair so it curled naturally and shone like copper. The green shadow you wore in the hollow of your eyes made them appear even larger and bolder and they gleamed like emeralds when you spoke of Mr. Baxter. You joined the girls' volleyball team that he coached and suddenly, as if by magic, your knobby arms and legs grew lissome and long. When Mr. Baxter passed you on the road, hitchhiking because of a missed school bus, he stopped. Then he began to drive you home every afternoon. I would hide in the ditch by the gate to your farm and wait for his car, but you arrived later and later and I had to be home by sunset, which was coming earlier and earlier.

After weeks of not seeing or speaking to you (Gammer would not allow me to use the phone), I had a nightmare that you were caught in the current of the Mad, drifting farther and farther away while I stood helplessly on the shore. I woke sobbing. I had to see you. Not yet knowing what I would do, I dressed and slipped out into the night. There was no moon or stars. No light or human sound. My flashlight made the familiar landscape press in too close and not in a protective way. Better the dark, my feet leading me down the same familiar road I walked every day to school.

By the time I reached where you lived I had a plan. Not wanting to wake the dogs locked in the barn, I moved stealthily around to the side of the sleeping house and threw a pebble at your bedroom window. Only on my third attempt, with a handful of gravel that rattled the glass, did your face appear around the side of the blind. You were angry when you crept outside and pulled me, shivering, into the shed full of chopped wood. With the door shut it was black as the inside of a cow.

"I'm in enough trouble now," you whispered, "without sneaking out in the night."

Although I couldn't see you, it was enough that I was able to inhale the sweet musk of your skin mingled with the pithy odour of the fresh-cut wood. You didn't even acknowledge that I was there. You spoke of how your foster parents were threatening to take you out of school. You were too late coming home. Aunt May claimed she couldn't do your chores and prepare supper and look after the kids all at the same time. The more you talked, the more agitated you became. I could sense you pulling at your hair. You spoke of running away, except you couldn't leave him. You spoke of getting a night job and living on your own, close to him. Over and over you repeated, "I won't give him up. They can't make me. No one can make me."

When I broke into your monologue and asked if you and Mr. Baxter would marry some day you shoved me and spat out, "Don't ever mention his name. He warned me that it's over if I tell even one person. So stop pestering me."

Then, pushing past me to get out of the shed, you hissed, "And stop spying on us. I've seen you hanging around like a mangy dog."

Somehow I had the presence of mind to catch the door before it could slam.

When I peeked out you were disappearing into the house. I wanted to throw myself sobbing on the ground. I wanted to take the axe leaning against the wall and drive it into your heart. Instead I did nothing.

I have no memory of walking back except, when the clouds covering the moon thinned, I saw what appeared to be a giant crooked forefinger pointing up from the ground behind the house. Afterwards, regardless of the time of day or from which angle, whenever I looked up at Great-Gammer's cross hit by lightning, that's what I saw. And it personified evil. If God had been everywhere in the summer – in what we saw, we heard, we spoke – he died that night. From then on, the world looked the same but it wasn't. I lived in the shade of the Prince of Darkness. A shadow that lay over everything.

While I was acutely aware of the ripplings and shiftings in my body, as well as the monthly drops of blood – Gammer called it the curse – the kids at school knew only that you were not there to protect me. Word of the incident in the barn had spread like an oil slick on a puddle. Boys ran by me at recess whispering, "Silly Sibyl suck my snake." Billy Parson ignored me, although sometimes I caught him looking sideways at me. When Miss Corbet asked for examples of onomatopoeia, Meli wrote, "Stupid Sibyl is a slut," on a piece of paper and passed it around the room. Three days later she broke out in boils and I lied, telling everyone I caused it by sticking pins into a voodoo doll I had made from her stolen mitten.

After that they left me pretty much alone except for Meli, who had scars on her face because of infected boils. Every day she found a new way to torment me. Once, when she was sent outside to clean the blackboard brushes, instead of banging them together to get rid of the chalk dust, she banged them against the red bricks of the school, leaving the graffiti Sibyl Fuckhead in big white letters. At recess, while everyone was looking and laughing, I saw a flash behind my eyes and electricity shot through my body. I grabbed Meli by her long black hair, throwing her down easily as a rag doll. As I beat her head on the ground, blood began to seep from her nose. Then pour. I couldn't stop even when her screams brought Miss Corbet.

Miss Corbet, my nemesis. She had picked on me for years. I don't recall her face except I have the sense of something pale and slippery. Like a peeled egg. She suspended me from school for a week. I pretended to be sick and afterwards I signed Gammer's name on the pink report slip. Since Gammer never answered the phone, she never found out.

When I returned there had been a shift. Not that the kids respected me, but they made room in the way a flock of migrating birds will accommodate a stony peak of a hill.

I must have grown much taller over the summer because when we lined up in order of size to go out for recess I was at the end. Behind me there was only Billy Parson. One day he whispered into my hair, "I'll give you a dime if you come to the barn after school." How surprised I was to hear myself blurt, "Give me a quarter and I'll come." It was afterwards, as I walked home turning the money over and over in my hand while skeins of geese passed overhead, that I figured out if I could raise fifty dollars – the price of two one-way bus tickets to the city – then Rosie and I could escape New Salem.

As weeks passed, the sock of quarters that I hid between my mattress and box spring grew heavier. I don't remember what I thought or felt. Day and night I dreamed of you, Rosie…of you and me living in an apartment with a balcony and a shower in the bathroom, of you and me working as waitresses in a fancy restaurant with a candle on every table, of you and me saving enough money to go on the road and find my father. I convinced myself that together we would do what Mama – because she had to look after me – never could.

Because I was already certain that my world was ruled by Powers of Darkness, I took what I did for granted as something that must be done in the same way Gammer must make solitary expeditions at dawn to gather mushrooms. And – just as that first time with little Freddie – it was like licking the cap and stem of a mushroom…the same smooth roundness, the same musky woodland scent. I remember how, with eyes closed, I would play a version of blind man's bluff where, depending on shape and size, my tongue would attempt to name each one after a type of mushroom such as chanterelle or fairy's house or puffball or horn of plenty.

Winter was late that year. By the time banks of snow had blown against the barn door and the boys were bundled in too many clothes to unbutton, I had four dollars and fifty cents in the sock under my mattress.

As one of the oldest and biggest children in the school, I had been accepted as the only girl in a loosely linked gang controlled by Billy Parson who called me Sibyl Spitfire. This gave me amnesty in the schoolyard – if nothing else. I allowed a select few to see the scar from the pentacle I had attempted to carve into my palm, claiming it was a birthmark that proved my powers as a witch. When I showed Billy he reached out and gingerly stroked the scar. Afterwards my palm tingled each time I thought of his touch.

It was Billy who instigated the snowball fight, but I threw the one with the stone inside that sent Meli running to the teacher with a swollen eye. And it was I who told little Julie to lick the icicle. Even when it froze to her tongue she was too afraid to tattle.

In early spring the snow had melted enough for Billy and me to push open the barn door. Finding it too cold to unbutton but not wanting to leave, we buried ourselves in the old straw in the corner and played I Spy. Then, since there was little to spy in the barn and both of us were too shy to suggest Truth or Dare, we made up a game called Catch the Mouse, in which my hand was the mouse and his hand was the cat. And then we stopped playing and, with his hand over mine, we just lay there. I remember his gritty cinnamon smell that reminded me of baked apples and how it made me feel safe...so safe I told him my plan. When Billy said he could never leave New Salem because of his sick mother, there was a catch in his voice – like the quick pain of a zipper catching the flesh as it closes – and we spoke no more.

When we left the barn, it was almost dark and Billy offered to walk me to our gate. As we were turning on to the high road a car sped by, swerving to miss us. I recognized Rosie, her head on the broad shoulder of the driver who had a hat pulled low on his head. I waved but she didn't wave back, although she must have seen me.

That same day, *whore* was carved into the wood top of my desk and Gammer found out.

Opening the back door to the kitchen the first thing I saw, a few inches from my face, was the scarab brooch quivering on Gammer's bosom. She towered there, silently staring down at me. I concentrated on the tiny bristling hairs on her chin. Then her big square hands grabbed my shoulders and she shook me. Shook me so violently I thought my head was separating from my body, little pieces flying off in all directions. Suddenly she stopped but her fingers still dug into my shoulders. I could taste the warm salty blood where my teeth had bitten my tongue.

"Sibyl, how could you? Miss Corbet told me everything. That no-good tramp Rosie, she's to blame. She talked you into doing those disgusting things. I'm going to wash your mouth out with Lyle soap and you're forbidden to speak to that hussy again."

The air around me turned to ice, "Don't you dare blame Rosie," I said. "It's in my blood."

Gammer stared at me stone-faced.

"You were born six months after your parents married."

"Who told you that?"

"Their marriage certificate in the lap desk."

Gammer's eyes widened, radiating rage.

"I also know about Mama."

She turned her back and started to walk away.

"She was a bastard and so am I."

I had no time to escape her fist smashing into my face with a force that hurled me across the kitchen. Hitting against the sink, I fell on my knees. Still, I said what I had done and how many times I had done it and with whom. I said she had driven Papa away and stopped Mama from leaving. I said she was the cause of Mama's sorrow and I had become a whore to escape her and the house. While the hate spilled out, I watched Gammer take the big wooden spoon from the hook beside the stove. Her blows landed on my back, shoulders and arms covering my head. I heard my words soften, diminishing into the whimpers of a cornered animal.

I didn't return to school. One week of simmering silence followed another. Gammer made bloodroot poultices for my bruises and for my nose, so swollen it must have been broken. Even though spring blew through the loose joints of the walls carrying the scent of budding leaves and the cold rising water of the pond, my body never left the perpetual dusk of the house.

Until I disconnected it, the phone rang our code incessantly with girls politely asking for "Sibyl the Slut" and boys yelling obscenities. The word *nympho* was scrawled with chalk on the front door. Kids hid in the cedar bushes beside the house chanting "Witherspoon Witherspoon fucking by the light of the moon, fucking so often they're now in their coffins and Silly Sibyl will be there real soon." Gammer kept the curtains closed and hung the shutters on the screened veranda and the summer kitchen.

117

Even when Gammer was asleep, her good ear against the pillow, I did not turn on a light. I lay with the blankets over my head waiting for the thud of rocks being hurled against the sides of the house. Someone tried to set fire to our shed, but it was built of stone and stood almost empty of chopped wood now that winter was over.

Looking back, all I see is myself cleaning endless baskets of pale delicate-shaped morels – a seldom-seen spring mushroom that was a constant reminder of my sin.

But then everything changed. How vividly I recall the afternoon that Gammer again pinned her scarab brooch on the dress with the lace collar. It must have been early summer because the oak tree was in full leaf. I was staring at its frilly shadow dancing on the pulled kitchen blind when she pointed her finger at me and motioned that I was to go up to my room. I lay on the bed listening to the distant whistle of a passing train. It brought back the image of railway tracks running straight and shiny through the valley and of travelling along them, escaping New Salem forever. But this time I vowed to myself that you would be with me, Rosie, and Billy would join us later in the Big City. I was so preoccupied with talking to you inside my head that only gradually did I become aware of the muffled sounds recognizable as conversation, drifting up from the parlour. And only when Miss Corbet and Gammer came out into the vestibule could I separate their talk into words.

I tiptoed to the banister at the top of the stairs to watch Miss Corbet pick up her brown hat with the feather in its brim and her brown knit gloves from the hall table. She was speaking of my missed months of school and how I must write the final examinations or fail my year. When she finished, Gammer replied that I would not return to school because – the same as Mama – I would be receiving my education by correspondence.

Her voice swelling with pride, she told Miss Corbet that Mama had graduated from secondary school with the highest marks in the province and she had done it by correspondence. "She even refused a scholarship to teacher's college," Gammer announced above the chiming of the grandfather clock. Of course she hadn't gone, I figured out the arithmetic. Mama was eighteen and pregnant with me.

Gammer, opening the front door, said in a tone hushed with hate, "I trust, Miss Corbet, there will be no future need for us to meet." Although the feather in her hat trembled violently, Miss Corbet made no reply.

And so Gammer and I continued as before – side by side, but silently – through the wet cool days of that summer. While Gammer scoured the countryside every dawn, the big wicker basket over her arm soon filling with mushrooms, it was my job to sort and clean, and then dry on large trays in the sun of the summer kitchen, what she had gathered.

It seemed as though Gammer's ancestors, who had arrived in a caravan each summer, beckoned from the back of her brain, because to her daily foraging she began adding strange-looking plants – mosses resembling curly brown pubic hair, or green wooly caps and grey lichen that were like shrivelled bits of brain. She kept them in the damp darkness under the sink, concocting new and more potent remedies and cures. Until it was too dark to see, she ground and chopped and mixed and mashed and boiled and sieved, muttering words I couldn't understand.

From the shelf in my bedroom, I took out the well-thumbed biology book that Mama used while working in the gardens of the restored Old Mill Inn. I found out that the mosses and lichens, and also the glutinous lumps of algae Gammer wouldn't let me touch, were called *cryptogams* from the word *kryptos* meaning hidden and the word *gainos* meaning marriage. I thought of Mama and Papa and their hidden marriage and how I was the cause of her unhappiness because she could not go with him and how – even after she was taken by the river – rather than going to heaven, her soul stayed close by so I would never be alone.

Through the chilly days of late fall, Agnes Porter arrived on Sunday afternoons to buy Gammer's medicinals that she later put into fancy bottles, selling them for ten times the price. She was old Doc Porter's second childless widow. He had died suddenly the previous winter, and with the money from his will she had bought the disused little brick church on the main road and converted it into a shop selling local produce and crafts. City folk en route to their cottages, who never slowed their cars driving through New Salem, were now beginning to stop.

Mrs. Porter insisted I call her Aunt Aggie. She reminded me of a tough old chicken past her egg-laying days that Gammer would fricassee one autumn Sunday because it wasn't worth its price in winter food. She was small and skinny with a stiff-legged walk, and when she spoke her head bobbed as though she were pecking at seeds.

I had not been out – except to the mailbox at the end of our lane – since Miss Corbet's visit in the spring. The curtains and blinds remained drawn on every window and Gammer, who considered turning on the lights a waste of electricity, was always in bed before dark. I was afraid to stay up alone so I'd lie awake, dreaming with midday clarity, of the two of us, Rosie and me, living together in the city. The showers of stones rattling against the house and the graffiti scrawled on the doors and windows had lessened, but on Halloween night village kids pushed over our grave markers and attempted to set fire to the charred cross, the lingering smell of smoke confirming that the Prince of Darkness was watching over us.

On Sunday afternoons Aunt Aggie picked up the ever-increasing supply of salves and syrups and teas and tinctures, paying more cash than the house had seen in years. Gammer and I were forced to speak to her and – although she didn't realize it – through her to each other. Gammer began wearing her good navy-blue dress and inviting Aunt Aggie to stay for tea and cake, which she served in the parlour. Because the tall windows looked out on the now shuttered veranda, Gammer had no choice but to turn on the hanging lamp, drawing my eyes to the gleam of the silver tea service on the round table beneath it.

While the two old women sat on the Queen Anne sofa drinking tea and arguing about what would sell and for how much, I studied, sitting in my little cubbyhole five steep steps up from the parlour. It was originally a sleeping loft, the first addition to the one-room log cabin, but for generations it had been used as a storage room. In September, after I'd registered to repeat Grade 8 by correspondence (Miss Corbet had failed me), I cleared a space and made myself a desk by laying a leaf of the dining room table across two stacks of boxes. For a chair, I put a pillow on top of an old tin trunk.

Gammer – if we had been speaking to each other – would have told me I was crazy to hole myself up in this tiny space when there were so many unused rooms in the house. She never understood how, here, snug as a squirrel in the hollow of a tree trunk, with no one to torment me and no teacher to berate me, letters stopped shifting inside words, and the words moved along a line orderly as railway cars along a track. Behind the closed door, I could read and study and brood over my weekly assignments while the cedar bush outside the ten-by-eighteen-inch window cast an underwater glow on my books.

On this particular Sunday, while passing through the parlour with my completed work to be left in the mailbox for Fast Mac, the postman, to pick up, I noticed Aunt Aggie's bold beady eyes following me. "That child's pale as a ghost," she clucked.

"More fresh air would put some colour in her cheeks, but I can't get her away from her desk," Gammer's voice was loud and bright. "She just received her first report card and she got A in every subject. Her mama herself graduated from high school with the highest marks in the province."

That's the first I knew that Gammer had read the report card I had deliberately placed on the kitchen table. Mr. Wordsworthy had given me A+ in American History, adding a note that spoke of my talent for writing. When I'd asked for more information on the seventeenth-century Salem witch trials, he'd sent a box of library books and mimeographed sheets, saying I could keep them until the end of term.

Of course, what I secretly wanted was to discover more about the family secret that Mama had revealed on the morning of my tenth birthday, with me sitting on her lap, her unbound hair tickling my arms. Had it really happened the way Mama told me? And why did Gammer grow so angry when she discovered I was attempting to read the diary?

I desired, and feared, to learn more about this ancestor called Betty who had haunted my thoughts in childhood and whose words I had been obsessed with deciphering until the terrible day that Gammer burned her diary. From Mr. Wordsworthy's information, I did find out that her last name was Parris. Although the names of those recorded in the back of the family Bible were faded past recognition, I was convinced – with the help of a magnifying glass – that there was a letter *P* and double

R in many of the surnames of my descendants born in the mid-
to late-seventeenth century. I also discovered that her father was
an ordained minister – the same as our Presbyterian ancestors –
who was preaching in Salem in 1692. Mama was right when
she told me Betty was the first young girl to be possessed by
evil spirits, but I was to learn that she accused her black nanny
of being a witch as well, and that her cousin, Abigail, who lived
in the same house, also became possessed. None of the history
I was reading explained why Betty became what they called
"deranged" or what happened to her afterwards. It felt as though
I'd been handed a feather and told to imagine the bird it came
from.

I have little memory of those winter months, except for Aunt
Aggie's weekly visits. The rattle of the north wind shaking the
windows always seemed louder after she left, as did the silence
between Gammer and me. I only ventured outside on Monday
mornings to leave my weekly assignments in the mailbox and
again on Wednesdays when the next set of notes was delivered
from the correspondence school in the city. I was working hard
to get good grades in the hope of getting a better job than wait-
ressing when Rosie and I (and maybe Billy) would be living
together in the Big City.

In my hole off the parlour, like a hibernating animal feeding
on its own fat, I fed on my assignments, the information I was
absorbing being as real as my daydreams. From one of the history texts I copied out a quote by the clergyman, Reverend
Cotton Mather, who lived during the witch trials. *If the invisible
world is not real then we shall come to have no Christ but a light
within and no Heaven but a frame of mind.* I would sit and stare
at the words, believing that they held the key to the mystery of
Betty who had been my comfort after Mama died. If there was
a membrane separating this world and the spiritual world – like

the membrane that separated the left and right brain – I was sure Betty had found a thin place to slip through.

The day I received the information from Mr. Wordsworthy about the Board of Education annual writing competition, New Salem had been snowed in for three days. It had taken an hour to shovel my way to our mailbox, and when I returned my fingertips were frostbitten. The reason I recall the weather is that my numb fingers tore the entry form removing it from the envelope and – since we had no Scotch tape and the closing date for the competition was in two weeks – I was forced to return the completed application in three pieces. The winner received a hundred dollars plus publication in *Ontario Teacher Magazine* and, best of all, a summer job at one of a select number of public libraries in the province. Closest to me was the town of Perth, an hour south by car, where our ancestors had lived before migrating to Madawaska Valley.

I imagined winning the competition. My brain raced thinking of how, finally, I would escape this house, and if Gammer refused to let me go, I would run away. I also daydreamed of how jealous the kids at school would be and how Billy would brag that I was his girlfriend. Most of all, Rosie, I thought of you, picturing how you would wait for me after school. With your lopsided grin and green cat eyes, you would say fiercely, "You did it! You kapowed these hayseeds," as we walked along the road arm-in-arm discussing how you, being eighteen, could get a job in Perth…that is, unless you'd already run away with Mr. Baxter.

I wanted to write about my ancestor who started the witch hunts, but the more I struggled for the words, the more they disappeared. A week passed. I stared at my open notebook, my brain a beetle in amber. Then one evening, long after Gammer had gone to bed, after I'd banked the fire for the night and stood brushing out my hair before the warmth of the stove, I was suddenly taken back to the summer of our Paradise and you, Rosie, spinning to dry off after a skinny-dip in the river, your wet skin and hair glistening in the sun. Then it came to me. That's what I must do. I too began to turn, faster and faster, until suddenly I fled my body – or so it seemed – because I was watching from somewhere else…from another time, for what I saw – like a wisp of dream – was the sight of myself spinning in circles around the kitchen, arms outstretched, face lifted, unbraided hair rippling around me like water over stones in a brook, and all the while repeating in a singsong voice heard before in my sleep, *donn't leeve me alone, donn't leeve me alone, drown'd in your blood, trap'd in your bone, trap'd in your bone, drown'd in your blood, donn't leeve me alone, donn't leeve me alone…*

I saw myself fall into a chair at the kitchen table, my pen – a live thing – crossing the blue-lined pages of my notebook, transcribing the words of that other, whose shadow loomed from the back of my head…

My Birthdaie

September 9th, 1691. I am ten yeares. Mama hast giv'n me a diary with a tiny gold key. She saies I be old enuff to keep an account of Gods dealings with me. Papa saies since what happens daie to daie comes out of the providence of God, the leest event can have portenshus significance. I thinke I shall tell my life in littel stories & other children will have instrucshun even tho I cann't benefit from it at the finalle reckoning.

I should beginne by telling you I am an only childe. I live with Papa & Mama in a village named Salem on the edge of what Papa saies be the most hideous, boundless, unknown wildernesse in the worlde. My cousin Abigail – everyone calls her Abbie – lives with us 'cause her parents died of th' influenza. We hast two slaves of coloure, Tituba & John Indian, who come from Southern Seas.

My name be Elizabeth after Mama, but everyone calls me Betty. I be born when a comet appear'd between Andromedes & Pegasus winge. 'Twas so bright it could be seen in daielight moving towards the sun. Tituba saies 'tis an omen that God has speshul plannes for me.

Papa be Reverent Samuel Parris. When he speaks I hold my breath. When he frownes his eyebrows meet, curving into batt wings. The batts that flie 'round the picture of Hell in my Catechism Book, Milke for Babes Draw'n out of the Breast of both Testaments.

Mama hast no milke, but Tituba hast a stillborne so she be hir'd to suckel me. That made my insides blacke. When I be three she rubb'd mustard on her nippels to ween me. I remember 'twas swallowing fire. Still, I wanted it. Throwing myselfe into her lapp like a moth into burning birch loggs.

Right now it be late afternoon. The help be out in the stable helping to blood a sick horse & Mama rode with Papa to the Putnam Farm. 'Tis forbidden for Abbie & I to leeve the Parsonage. Iroquois warriers be glimps'd in Devils Den – a woods just beyond the bounds of the village. I hast never been there but John Indian saies it be so dark & dolesom that no flowers growe. No birds sing. Once while he be riding by a firie flying serpent attack'd him. Mama saies 'tis more likely that he fell into a flesh-tearing thickett after drinking too much hott canarie at Ingersolls Ordinary.

'Tis my birthdaie so Abbie & I hast no chores. We be playing hide-the-thimbel in the parlour and when my turn comes I place the thimbel under the pewter lampe on the mantel. Abbie will nev'r look there 'cause we be told not to touch it. This most beeutiful object hast alwaies been pass'd to the old'st girlchild in Mama's family and noing it will be mine makes my legges want to jump about with joy.

Once I telled Mama the lampe be preshus as the sword of th'Angel leeding the chosen people out of the desert. She cover'd my mouth with her hand. Beware of vanitee, she wisper'd, it comes from th'Evil One who – just like an Angel – cann enter a personne as light.

Papa

I never touch him. He never touches me 'cept to press his palms against my forehead when I saie goodnight and he saies Ne tradus Bestus quando nos dormus. Deliver us not to the Beast when we sleep. When I look up into his eyes – the coloure of molt'n lead Abbie saies – I think of the firie furnace on Judgement Daie. Hair burning like bedd strawe. Skin oozing fatt like a goose on a turnspitt.

Papa be only here in th'evening. But 'tis alwaies evening at the Parsonage 'cause of shaddowes that spring alive from walls & floore. Tonight the wind rattels the leaded casements & he hunches before the hearth in his grey hooded cloak. Only his forehead sticks out like a white cliffe. And one hand.

I hear the scratch of his titmouse quill as he notes in his sermon book any decay of Godlinesse he hast found during the daie. Mr. Blackburn who just open'd a tavern on Ipswich Road owes us firewood for two winters. So do the Putnam Family over by Whippel Hill.

During the bigg snow storm last Spring we hast few loggs & no candels. Papa, Mama, Abbie, myselfe, the blackes slep't on a littel strawe in front of the kitchen hearth. Like a parcel of doggs Mama saied. Tituba fetching hens from the barne & putting them under the quilts at our feet. Thus prison'd they staied quiet & gave off a dunghill heet.

'Cept once when Papa roll'd over on Tituba's pett browne hen & was stabb'd in the hollowe of his ankel. In a rage he grapped the hen by the necke and flung it against the wall. I hid my face but Abbie saies the body slid down & jerk't towards her. Its head & necke dangling.

All at once Papa snapps the book shutt. He hawkes. Spitts into the Fire. Knaves & Cheaters he hisses. May the Foul Fiends climb into their bedds & splitt their wives up the middel. A gust of wind blows smoke down the chimney. As the room dimms it settels slowlie across his shoulders and down his back in the shape of a Crosse.

Lost Sheep

While looking in a tangel'd thickett, Abbie – her green eyes fierce & calm as a cat – throwes burrs at my haire. Haire, she saies, the coloure of bleeched bone. I think of the half-buried skull of a wolfe we found last Spring near the Beaver Dam. Inside it a birds nest with seven eggs speckell'd the blue of a hot summer skie.

Maybe words be like eggs waiting in the nest of my brain. Waiting to be hatched into the world. I take the tiny gold key that hangs on a string 'round my neck & kiss it. Stopp that blasphemie saies Abbie. You be enveus, I saie, cuz you be old'r than me but you hast no diary. She saies nothing altho her eyes turn cold as jade.

On the waie home my eyes turn inward so I donn't see the dead snake droop't over a stump. Abbie picks it up. Tells me it looks the same as the belt John Indian stole from a savage. Only his, he claims, be made of human skinne.

Then Abbie shoves it in my face saieing she will stuff it downe my blowse if I donn't giv her the key from 'round my neck. My hearte slammes from side to side. I trie to run but she tripps me. The pain in my skulle be bright as sunlight dancing on water.

The next I knowe a hot ruff tongue be licking teers from my face. The lost sheep hast found me. Then I see Tituba coming with Abbie. I nev'r told what happen'd tho there be a bump the size of a robins egg on my forehead. Tituba put on a poultice of mutton fat and red clover so I shall suffer no mental defect. At supp'r Abbie gave me her portion of deep plumm pie & thick creem.

Mama

Her heads alwaies bowed. Eyes lidded as tho she be afraide to look up t' Heaven. In th' evenings she spins in the corner. The great wheel humming like bees making honey in a hive. Her hands – the same size as mine – hast nuckels swoll'n & cross'd with tinie cracks.

She be fourty-four. Five of her children died before they could saie Mama. She told me their Soules flie in & out of her like sparrows looking for seed. Dead to God from the beginning, they'd rather be hungrie on earth than in the easiest roome in Hell.

Mama's lower lippe alwaies be trembeling. Prayers no one can heare. They be webbes of light I can see shimmering in th'air when I half-close my eyes.

Most daies Mama makes errands of mercie. This afternoon I stood at the edge of the path & watch't her growe small'r & small'r. Skimming over gold pools of leeves in her grey hooded cloake she seems a ghoste who hast put on a body.

Mama be taking a remedy to Goodwife Roebuck, a Church Member who laies out the Dead in the assemblies of God.

She lives alone in a sodd hut by Hawthorne Swampe. No one likes her 'cause she be fatte, toothless & smells of fry'd bacon. Before stuffing cotton into the mouthe & rectum of the dead she puts an iron ringe on eech finger to stop the Dark Ones from leeping into her.

When she laied out old Mr. Williams a ringe dropped off. Jump'd like a Cricket she saied. At the same moment stones the size of goose eggs broke every winddowe in the house. Passer-byes saied they fell out of a cleer skie.

Since then Good Roebuck be curs'd with boils. Tituba made an ointment by mixing together the dung of a goat & menses blood. If smear'd on the boils at sundowne they'll be gone by morning. Mama shakes her head. She saies it be Divine Wrathe, not elfshot.

She takes it anyway, but warns us not to tell Papa.

Full Moon

The Hutchinson boy who stole a sovereign from his father hast been stripp'd, tarr'd, feather'd and placed on a hogshead on the Common. Everyone hast gone to laff 'cept Mama & me. I be too weeke 'cause of the purge I took for bad dreems. As alwaies Mama spins in the corner where the shaddowes lie umbrok'n & thicke. I'm suppose to studdye, but my minde drifts loose as smoak.

The bigg'st picture in my primer be the burning Martyr, Sir John Rogers, bound to the stake with hoops of iron. They saie his nether parts smoulder'd for hours 'cause of a Court Order that the fire be kindeld with no more green faggots than two horses could carry.

In the picture the bladder of gunpowder hast burst between his leggs & the merciful flammes wrapp him in a downie cape. Sparks cluster in his haire. He beets his breaste with one arme. His other arme hast fall'n off, but his hande be stuck to the iron around his cheste. Blood dropping out of it like beeds from a brok'n bracelett.

The Martyrs eyes be shutt. His large white face be patient as an old sheep, Sweet Jesus have mercie upon me be his last words. Altho his swoll'n tongue hanges out so he cann't speak they saie his lippes went on praying 'til they shrunk to his gummes.

I shiver. Pull my stool closer to the hearth. Resting my elbowes on my knees I hold my numm fingers out to the fire. In the copper warming pann the refleckshun of my face glows & flickers. Theres a harsh hollowe crying inside my eares. Listen, Mama saies, Geese! Winter'll be earlie this yeare.

I look over my shoulder to where the moon – a scalp'd head with no eyes – hangs in the winddowe. Why am I so colde? Colde as the shaddowes. Cold as the moon.

Mama! You bind us all. A spider reciting our sinnes.

Mercie & Mary

I hate them. Hiding behind the barn 'til Papa & Mama leeve then giggeling & pushing eech other thru the back doore. Mercie & Mary. Skirts smear'd with muck & dung. Haire tied in greasy kerchiefs. Reddn'd hands clutching the ribbon & buttons that Tituba locks in her ebonie boxe. Time befor last she read their palmes. Now 'tis tea leeves to know their future husbands calling. I tell Tituba Fortunetelling be an Evil Art. She paie no attenshun.

Mary, the Servant of Master Proctor, hast a long nose and one eye small'r than the other that rowls round by itselfe. Like a strip'd marble. When it drifts up to her skull she sees the night skie – or so she saies – with starres bursting like rockets. Mama saies 'tis no wonder she alwaies be taking a vomitt to cure a headache.

Mercie works at the home of her Uncle Dr. Griggs. When she talks her thin voyce clawes my insides like Abbie running her fingernail across a writing slate. Over & over she tells the story of why she be sent here from northern Maine. 'Twas after her young'r sister disappear'd. She'd been carrying a baskett of food to where her Papa & brothers be harvesting a patche of corn.

The next daie they found Iroquois footprints by a brooke & follow'd them to the baskett. Inside it her sisters finger laie on a bedde of moss. When Mary comes to this parte she shoves her round flat face, like a saucer of milk, right into yourn. Her sour breath makes a belly turn.

Mercie & Mary. I hate them. They sit in th' inglenook drinking tea with sugar lumps between their teeth. Weesels sucking eggs whispers Abbie. She jogs Mercies arme. Spills her tea. Git at your chores, Tituba saies, & chases us out with a broome.

Earlie Morning Omen

I dreem of Mamas head frying in a bigg iron skillet. Smoak swirls from her eares. Teers drip from her chin sizzling like pork fatt. Help me, she cries as the flammes leap high'r. I run from room to room but eech be dark'r, cold'r, more emptie. In the kitchen the fires dying. Mamas heade shrinks – littel, wrinkel'd, brown – a walnut rowling about in the sooty pann.

At first I thinke the sound comes out of me. I cann't tell if it be a screem or a laff. But then I open my eyes and find its outside the howse. A gull & raven fighting among the oak branches. A storm must hav driv'n the gull inland. I open the winddowe to shoo them awaie. The raven dares me with a sheeny black eye but the gull rises – absolute as the Holy Ghoste – over the brown orchard…the emptie pasture…the leafless woods…on & on…disappearing into the sunn as it comes to light our daie.

Wanting something that hast no name I leen out the windowe. The raven laffs at me & flapps like a black ragg cawt in the tree. I watch a winge feather drifting downe. 'Tis then I feel th' emptieness – a live thinge inside – & knowe my Soule hast escaped againe.

Tituba saies my eye be too bigge. 'Til it returns I be afraide lest the Dark Ones squeeze in.

October Appel Picking

Mama hast rid'n off, saddle bag stuff'd with horehound & wild plums, to comfort Goodwife Murray whose husband and three children be tak'n to the Pest House with the Pox. Papa hast gone to consult with the Elders about a petition by dissenting members.

I be told to gather windfallen appels from the seven trees round the back pasture. My basket full, I sitt with my backe against the ruff silver bark. Lifting up my skirt & petticoats I look at my legges. Too longe & thinn. The sunlight thru the leaves mottels them into a snake.

I pick out the bigg'st redd'st appel. Holding it in my hande I imagine it be a cage for a Soule. As I bite into it I see above me a long-legg'd spider swaying on a long thread. It be the same as Mama – wishing to bind what it touches. I wish only to obey. To thinke littel.

This morning Abbie giggel'd againe during family prayers. To teach her a lesson Papa tied a rope round her waiste & lower'd her downe the well. He dunk'd her three times, eech to the count of tenn. Her wails still be echoing thru me.

I reach up, take the spider & carefullee pull off eech legge. In a lowd voyce I saie the children of the wick'd shall be butcher'd peece by peece. I look up to the skie but it remaines emptie & verrie blue.

As I walk home I try to balance the baskett on my head the way Tituba does. On an outcrop of rock at the farr side of the pasture I notice for the first time how a lone pine hast been blast'd by lightning. I remember that other lone tree on a hill. The swaying rope. On the end an emptie noose like an O in th' aire. Mama cover'd my eyes so I couldn't see but afterwards Abbie told me how the hanging body jerk'd. Armes & legges stiff as a puppets. Tongue rolling out like old Shep in the heat.

I feel my handes moving up to circle my necke. Squeezing mor & mor hard. Coughing & splutt'ring my heart leapes with feer. Why do I like what fright'ns me?

Dearest Dread in thee I put my trust. I am only a rotting appel core under Thy Tree.

Balde Hill

While Tituba & I pick crimson pokeberries to dye haire ribbons for the Thanksgiving Feast, we see a ratt run out of the brambel bush. Coming closer we heare flies singing. I hold my nose 'cause the smell grippes my gutt. 'Tis a deade lambe. Wandered awaie from the flock saies Tituba.

Climbing to the topp of the hill we lift our skirts & sitt on a rock wide & flatt as an alter. Would Abraham have slitt the throat of his son? Tituba shakes her head. Saies too much sacrifice makes ash of the hearte.

In the distance clouds be gath'ring. I look for a face. Below us the pathless marsh meaddowe seems to suck up all the light. Here & there a clump of balding cedars leen on eech other. They remind me of old ladies gossiping at a Social. On the other side of the marsh lies the track of land that Papa wants. But the Nurse family owne it & they be our Enemie 'cause they won't paie the Ministry Tax.

Between the marsh & the road to Topsfield Tituba pointes out the place where a nak'd woman viel'd in miste beckons to men riding by after dusk. Papa saies it be the spectre of a witch. At this very moment the shaddowe of a hawk glides over us. Feering its a bad omen I burrow between the soft bundels of Titubas breasts like a worm into a flower. She runs her fingers thru my haire. Everythinge be hush'd & gold'n. I count her heart beets. Keep my breath in time with hers. Between the living & the dead the space be so narrowe.

Before Bedde

I open the winddowe to emptie the chamber pott. The smell nipps at my nostrils as it hisses downe like a gold'n serpent into Mamas herb garden. No winde. No moon. No comfort from the lavender scent'd aire. A mist slippes out of the long grasse by the barne. The dammp sticks to my skinne like a curse. A feeling comes over me that somethinges going to happen no matter what be done to stoppe it.

I aske Abbie if she feels it. She shrugges. She be catching moths. Scorching their winges in the candel flamme & then tossing them into the aire to see if they can flie.

Why doesn't she feel what I feel? The dark thats in us. Thats spreading. Unbound like night & the wildernesse surrounding us.

Lecture Day

I must staie to stack Psalm Books & collect the hickory sticks set round the Meeting-House to keep the boys in mind. Afterwards Papa hauls me up behind him on the broad back of Prince. There be a barn raising at Captain Putnams farm.

We take a short waye. Down the long open slope speckl'd with daisies & red clover. Across the road leading to Wolfe Pitts Meaddowe, a boggy waste fur'd eech Spring with sweet purple moss that lures deer then wolves. Papa saies they be the Devil's doggs. Mama remembers wolfe heads nail'd to the Meeting-House door. She saies they stared like unshav'n old beggars.

At the north forke of Crane Brooke we leeve the sunlight. 'Tis along these shade-woven banks that Tituba gathers blotchie toadstools that look like the shrunk'n heads of Fairies & smell like they sprung from the dead when she brews them into a drink against Witchcraft.

A sharp turn. At the edge of a small clearing I glimps something white. I think its a spect'r but coming clos'r I see the frothing of petticoats & the panick't face of Sarah Miles. She be on all fours with haire every which waie. As she struggels to get up a breast floppes out of her bodice like a brok'n gull winge. Behind her an animal be rearing. Then I recognize Mr. Burnhamthorpe neeling with his breeches downe. His loins be shaggy as a doggs with the same dangelling pink growth that I once saw on old Shep. With his fingers clawing the ground he seems about to flee.

Papa raises his fist making a sign of the Crosse. Evil demons, he screems. Spooking Prince who charges into the trees. My hood falls. Twigs like finger bones slash at my face. I close my eyes. I squeeze Papa. Squeeze hard'r the hott flanks of Prince. The pound of his hooves & our sobbing breath be one wild rhythm. Faster. The rubbing between my thighs. Flammes be whips licking me all over. I'm hott. I burn with no paine. I am Daniel in the firie furnace. Sweet Jesus, Prince of Light, flie me to Thy bossom. Let me be consumed.

From farr awaie the barking of Captain Putnams yellowe hounds. The comforting odour of wood smoak & manure. Papa calls whoa, whoa, as tho an arrow be in his throate. My Eyes won't open. Mama lifts me downe, fluttering and cooing. Whats wrong, childe? she asks, you be flush'd redd as a savage. I goe to crie Help but it be like trying to shout in my sleep. Behind my eyes a comet be streaking across the blacknesse.

Supper

All daye the burnning between my thighs be spreading like a forrest on fire. I am trap'd inside my heade pounding against walls while my lippes behave as tho nothinge be happening. I help Abbie heeve the table board on to the trestles & set out the dishes. We sit, bowe our heads & folde our hands. Papa gives thanks. I keep my eyes open. Watch from somewhere deep inside.

Blood begins to drip from the loaf of bread. Slowlie it trickels between the bowle & trencher, under the handel of the spoon & downe into my lapp. O Dearest Dread, let this not be happening. I begg You to burn awaie my sinnes like flesh from bone.

We eat in silence. Black-eyed beans & cold partridge. Whenever I look up, John Indian be staring at me the waye a wolfe stares. As it saies in the Bible – Out of the eater comes forth meat.

Later It Dark'ns

Titubas breasts rippel under her calico gowne as she leens over to put the candels on the table. Papa pushes back his chaire, wipes his hands on the back of old Shep asleep at his feet & beginnes to talk. With the light & shaddowe dancing together over the surface of things 'tis as if the seen & the unseen be one.

Too many be wandering from the sound of the Silver Trumpet, Papa saies. Thats why a streem of lightning hit the church tower in the city & throate distemper be carrying off so many children. He will make an example of Mr. Burnhamthorpe & Sarah Miles. They must confesse publickally next Sabbathe. Afterwards she must stand on the pillary with her back bared & be whipped 14 stripes. Mr. Burnhamthorpe must paie half the cost of a plank footbridge over Crane Brook.

Sarah Miles be a runaway servant. They saie she had a bastard by her Virginian master. Deliver'd it herselfe on a creek banke. Then flung it in. The children of the house found it under the hump'd roots of a cottonwood. Swaddled in a muddie linen ragg, it look'd like a logg. Now she be endentured to Mr. Burnhamthorpe whose wife died last Winter in travail with their 17th child.

While Abbie washes the dishes & I drie, she whispers that she would rather live in a hollowe logg than with Mr. Burnhamthorpe who hast yellowe-grey tufts of haire sticking out his huge ears. Whenever he passes at a social, she saies, his eyes snip off her bodice & petticoat.

Can she see me burnning? Cann she see the guilt I cann't name?

Going on the back stoop to throwe out the dishwater I hear a rustling like a silk banner in the wind. I look up. The skie above the north pasture be cover'd with a blood-redd vapour. Urg'd by my comet the thinge that be going t' happen hast begunn. I hear Papas heavie steppe behind me. Smell his meaty breath as he saies Aurora Borealis so farr south, what does it mean?

November Wind

The blasts of cold aire coming down the chimney makes the hanging onions & peppers & fennel into dancing witch puppets. The fire in the kitchen hearth has been burning for weeks. After our chores Abbie & I must sitt on our stools – Abbie calls them Soule racks – and practis needel work. Papa claims 'tis an amusement to improve the mind. I be embroidering a sampel that saies Christ be the true vine. I long to write in my diary but must wait 'til Papa & Mama be out. They may ask to read my accounts of Gods deelings. Then they would know I hast been cutt from His roots.

Wind slashes at the roof. Whines through the keyhole like a knife as it be sharpen'd on a grindstone. In the distance the sea roars. I think of hungry lions. I see myself enter the great stone amphitheatre. In the ash'n light of burning crosses the bones of Christians glowe like scatter'd jewels. I hold up my armes to the Emperor Nero. A gold cape fluttering like winges from my shoulders. I am the wheat of Christ, I crie out, to be ground bye the teeth of wild beests so I may be found pure bread. The crowde cheers Bless'd Betty, Bless'd Betty. The iron gate lifts. The lions charge. One by one they lie downe & lick my nak'd feet.

As I planne my direct ascent t' Heaven in the strong armes of the Archangel Michael, Abbie be raking the dead embers out of the hearth. She wispers that she be scratching the belly of a living Beest – a creature with giant winges that Tituba saied would carry us to an Eden of coco nut trees & hammocks & sugar canes. We will die of boredom, she saies, if we sitt on our stools any long'r.

Then looking wildlie round with eyes that donn't seem to see what she be looking at, Abbie picks a hott pok'r out of the fire & burns the word LIVE into the front of Mamas preshious Cedar of Lebanon hope chest. Next she picks up the tongs & takes logges out of the hearth & throwes them about the roome. I watch her petticoats rising & falling.

Just then Papa comes inn & even tho she yells 'tis the Devil be making me, he locks her in the closett under the stairs. She be tied necke to ankels cuz last time she kick'd the door 'til her toes broke. When Tituba cut off her shoose she never cried out, altho her swoll'n toes be pinke as little pork sausages.

No Sun

'Tis my turn t' emptie the sloppe pail. The path to th' outhouse be muddie so I goe thru the garden. Still no snowe. No coloure anywhere 'cept for the last red bloom of a poppee. Dying vines grapp at my ankles. Cornstalks rattel like skeletons. The scare-crowe shivers in the sudden breeze.

All at once everythinge stoppes. The world holds its breath while the clowdes part & a finger of fire flashes downe to touch me. My blood bursts into a whirlpool of blazing raine. A trumpet sounds. Cymbals. Drummes. A tambourine. I dance round & round with armes outspread. My heads full of light. The dead grasse under my feet be crackling flammes. My clowthes be chaines dropping awaie.

Dearest Dread, show me the Angel whose breath like th' aire driv'n from bellows will open a burning path for me to follow. Yes, Yes, Fire be all. Whether I shine in Paradise or burne in Hell.

They Saie

An excess of yellow bile be the cause of the hott loins & delu-sions. When Dr. Griggs came with his bleeding cups I heard faintly thru the roofe a few wild shreeks as tho somewhere above a childe that lied be going to his Father in Hell Fire. Later, watching the blood drippe into the vial I felt a chill run up my spine. They saie it means someone be walking acrosse the ground where my grave will be dug.

Seventh Day of the Storm

The snowe be above the winddowes. Papa, Mama, Abbie & I gather for morning prayers. In the dimme underwater light we seem to be wading slowlie & smoothlie with the current.

No one speakes. Silence plugges our eares. Our solitude sets us apart. We be the chosen ones seal'd in their inner sanctuary. All within safe from all without. How reel be Papas musket over the mantel, the wood'n water buckeet, the eggs in the bowle, the white china plate with its fancie gold trimme.

Here, in this fosforus gloom, for the first time I see the Soule. It be outside the bodie. A littel rainbowe hook'd over our left shoulder. Even the catt washing its face on the winddowe sill glowes in its owne prism of light. A light so solitary, so simple, so clear, that I know at once that the Soule lives in God.

The sise & coloure of eech Soule be the same. However, when I twist my heade, mines pale as a bruise whereas Abbies be the singing shades of a sailors parrot. My heart shrinks into a fiste that wants to hitt & hurtt. I hear myselfe interrupt Papas prayer by saieing in a lowd strange voyce – Our Soules be but pretty baubels for the Lord to admire. I remember no more.

Dark Day in December

Owles be hooting. Ratts behind walls tapp like fingers. Tenn feet of snowe hast fall'n in a fortnight. The dead can not be bury'd.

Not even Goodwife Simpson, one of Papas old'st most loyal church members, who crav'd Salvation so much she genuflected three hours a day. Her knees, she told Mama, were hard & numm as a camels. She be neeling to milk a cowe when she died in a fitt of feer. The barne catt she thot be rubbing against her thighs turn'd out to be a starving lynx too weak t' attack.

In the last blizzard the Town Magistrate who hast a gold front tooth and much land by the sea lost a hundred sheep. Their eyes be so glaz'd with ice they wander'd into the water & drown'd. 'Cuz of the drifting snowe afterwards it took Papa & John Indian two weeks to digg a tunnel out to the sheep penn. Since it be on the lee side of the barne th' animals became slowlie entom'd under sixteen feet of snowe. Four out of fifteen staid alive by eeting the wool off their dead companions who be so naked, John Indian saied, so rosie, they seem'd like cherubs sleeping on a clowde.

But for me the worst calamitie came last night. Neeling beside my bedde I hear a buzzing inside my head. When I try to pray the sound growes lowd & angry like I be caught in a spiders webbe & the words come out tangel'd. Looking up I see Tituba in the doorway rolling her eyes as tho they be oil'd. She saies they test for witches by making th' accus'd repeet the Lords Prayer. If it comes wronge its 'cause prayers be recited backwards at the Witches Sabbath.

I begg her not to tell Papa. She sighs & kisses my forhead. Her mouthe be soft as an over ripe plum. Papa calls Tituba to come at once! While I still be neeling she blowes out the candel & closes the doore. It be so dark I can feel it. Or is it His shaddowe growing over me? His hands on my hands. His body on my body. His mouth on my mouth.

Quicklie I crawl under the quilts. Am I witch? I whisper to Abbie. Curl'd with her back to me she stays quiet as a pond under ice. I am afraide. I want to be a snaile & go back into the howse of myselfe. Slidding furth'r & furth'r inward I hear a sound like the slithering of eels thru mudd. The darker it getts, it seems to saie, the deep'r you see.

Teers

Witches cann't crie. I crie all the time. Papa saies teers be Gods meat & looks thru me with eyes cold & cleen as bullets. I run awaie. Hide in the root cellar. Huddeling in the loose earth. Darknesse flowing into me like blacke milke. In the low bulbous voyce of someone speaking from a well or a barrelle I hear myself saie – No wonder you be afraide when you see what God hast in store. But if there be no God there be no sinne. If there be no sinne there be no Devil.

No Earth, No Skie

Nothing but whitenesse. Clean. Cold. Pure. Snowe hast form'd domes & towers where trees & corn cribs & outhouses should be. The cedar bush by the gate looks like fatte little Dr. Griggs in his loose-flung cloak & cock'd hatte. He comes to blood Abbie & me no more. He told Papa we suffer no natural ailment. It be an evil hande.

Th' afflckshun be spreading. Yesterdaye Mr. Putnam came to fetch Papa. His daught'r Ann frothes at the mouth & screems like a truss'd pigge with a stick in its necke. A woman no one can see prickes her. Pulls at her bowelles, she saies, like they be weeds.

Mary the Proctors servant be darning a stocking when some-thinge cold as a crabbes clawe grabbes her by her throate & ankels. Drawes her body backwards into a bowe. Drawes it so tight they feer'd the skinne of her belly would splitt. She staid that way for houres screeming Lord have mercie. Even her master who alwaies seems too bigge for the roome could not releese her.

Neighbours gather in the parlour. Murmuring. Staring at Abbie & me. Mr. Beale the Tithingman with a brok'n veinne like a fatte red spider on his nose whispers to Mama as she be making tea that a calf be brought forth with one head & two mouths & three eyes. A portent of worse to come he saies. His small bright eyes dart acrosse the roome to me while he picks a louse from his haire & squashes it in a dirtie handkerchief. Mama saies nothinge but in the hearth I hear the damp logges spluttering over & over – Fire be life, Life be fire.

After that everythinge goes blacke before my eyes like the time Abbie & I stared at the noon sun.

Fever

Dr. Griggs saies it be the mark of an impure fire in the bloode. Thats why my tongue be swoll'n & black as an ox.

It no longer belongs to me. Sometimes slithering out of my lippes to strike at whoever passes. Sometimes coiling inward as tho a string be tied from its tip to my vitals.

I tell no one. Not Papa or Mama. Not even Abbie or Tituba. No one knowes about the Revelashun. No one knowes that the Devil be God gone madd with love.

Fever

I can't thinke. Sleepe. Eet. I be soft in the heade. Soft as the wax at the flamme of the candel. Tituba sponges me with squawmint & rosewater. She saies I be so shrunk my veinnes stick out like a blue nett. I tell her it holds the Devil inside. To drawe him out she makes a plaster from black catt haire baked to a powder, my feces & the blood from the cutt throat of a pidgeon she found in the barne.

Fever

Night after night I shiver. Dreems freezing in my skull. Teeth rat-teling like a lock'd gate. Whenever I close my eyes I hear faint thunks under the ground as tho somewhere nearbye a horse be pawing the froz'n earth. Or be it someone digging my grave? I begg Tituba to save me. She holds out her armes. Enfolding me like a blacke cloak.

The Question

I sit on my stool. Papa stands. His armes folded. His shaddowe growing over me like a shrowde. Who torments you he asks. I turn my head awaie. He hast whipp'd Tituba for making a witch cake & sent her from the Parsonage.

I stare out the winddowe. Shaddowes thick'n by the fence. A firie skie. I think of Shadrack Meshack & Abednego. Be they as frighten'd as Abbie, Ann & me on that afternoon last fall? I remember the sound, like the snapping of small bones, when Tituba stir'd the fire. I remember the sharppe smell of the vervain she told us would ward off demons. I remember Ann neeling & staring into the glass ball. How it glow'd with a dead light. How she moaned please no, please no.

Pappa grabbes me. Who torments you he asks again. His frighten'd eyes shine like an ax. He wants to cut me to pieces. My toes, fingers, ears, flying off into chippes of wood.

I am Isaiah being chopp'd to death in a hollow logge. I grow small'r & small'r. Only Tituba can save me. Only Tituba can hold me to this world. Her armes soft as the sea, warm as velvet. Tituba! I cry out. Tituba! Papa leeves the room. Fetch the Constable, he shouts. Issue a warrant to arrest & trie Tituba as a witch. In my hearte a wound opens.

I goe to follow Papa. To tell him my tongue hast betrayed me. All at once I be stopped in my tracks as tho an axe struck my chest. My mouthe rips open. My tongue that viper, that fork'd flamme, releesing words bright as sparks in the emptie aire. I AM THE PROPHET OF THE DEVIL I roar & spring sudden as a lion to bite Papa's hand.

Alone

How far awaie everythinge seems. How smalle. How cleer. I lie on the cott in th' inglenook. My backe to the hearth. Watch my soule – a light emptie of light – wandering between the frost'd winddowe & the moth lying dead by th' unlit candel.

I listen for His voyce. There be only the easy breathing of the fire. Then I hear a faint tata-tat-tat, tata-tat-tat. At first I think it be the tapping of an oak bough on the winddowe, but 'tis the drum of the village crier calling everyone to the Hearing at the Meeting-House.

'Tis the second daie of Tituba making her statement. She claims that a tall black man with white haire made her sign a Blacke Booke. Nine other marks be in it. Red as Christs wounds. Two of them made by Goodwife Osburne & Goodwife Good. On clowdie nights they forc'd her to ride on a pole thru th' aire. She help'd them to torture Mercie & Mary & Elizabeth & Abbie. But not me she saied. She would never torture me. Not even if the Devil made her a strutting Queen with white lace sleeves.

I picture Papa at the Meeting-House standing before the gather'd in blacke cape and skull capp. He opens the sermon book as tho it be the jaws of a sick horse. Thank you O Lord, he prayes, for helping us in this cursed wasteland to struggel against the Devil and His earthlie helpers. On & on rolls his voyce like distant thunder.

For the first time I don't hold my breathe. Now I am not afraid. Now hate takes the shappe of a coil'd snake inside me. Tituba saies only the bites of cold-blooded creetures be poison- ous. Now I know what I must do. I cann't be a prophet if I cann't speek. I struggel to sit up. I feel nothinge. Knowe noth- inge. Not even if I am dead or alive. I light a candel. Open Tit- ubas sewing boxe. Take a needel & run it twice thru the flamme saieing loudlie THE TONGUE BE A FLAMME THAT CAN NEV'R BE TAMED.

I cutt a length of crimson thread that Tituba used to sew my haire ribbons for the Thanksgiving feest & pull it thru the eye of the needel. I knotte the end seven times to build a witches lad- der.

With my left thumb & forefinger I pinch my lips closed. Old Shep sniffs at a crack in the door & whines. High in the rafters batts squeek as they turn in their sleep. I start with the right corner of my mouthe. I go thru the upper lippe & out thru the lower. Ten stitches. One for every year of my life. Then it happens. The room caves in. A tide of blacknesse pulls me under.

Exodus

Nothinge be solidd. Nothing be save. The flammes hast devour'd all that be earthlie inside. My Soule be a piece of burn't parchment that hast blown away.

I'm a ghoste within myselfe. I live in the shade & trie to capture its edge to stop it from growing. 'Cause I see & touch only shaddowes, Papa sitting on the parlour settee be flatt as a blankett folded in the cedar chest. Mama, serving tea, be transparent & pale as a jellie fish thrown up by the tide.

I listen to what they be telling Doctor Griggs. How they found me sitting on my stool by the hearth. The needel & crimson thread still in my hande. She be transfix'd, Mama wispers, staring as tho the pitt of Hell hast open'd at her feet.

Papa closes his eyes and turnes his sunken face awaie. Mama wipes her teers on the hemme of her apronn. Nobodie speeks. Slowlie the silence closes round us. From the farr forrest comes the howl of a wolfe. Old Shep lying by the untended hearth picks up his head. Doctor Griggs absentlie scratches his groin. With a deep sigh Mama takes the pewter lamp from the mantel and lights it. All of us gaze at the flame.

Fire can not lie. I taste the ash but will not speak. I be an only childe. An only Hell – save from God and the Devil. Under my skinne there be nothinge. Nothinge but darknesse & the cold running of aire...

"Sibyl!" From a vast distance I heard my name. Then, a gripping of my shoulder and a gentle shaking that increased until my eyes were forced to open. I saw a weathered face cut from stone hovering above me. As I recognized Gammer and my own body slumped in a chair, that other life began to fade like a brightly coloured pebble lifted out of the river.

Gammer scolded me for staying up all night. I couldn't stop shivering and Gammer wrapped me in a blanket, saying I was sure to get sick as it had been the coldest night of the winter. I sat in the rocking chair by the stove while she laid and lit the kindling. As I reached my numb fingers towards the warmth, I heard *togeth'r in one body we giv birth to eech other like two dry sticks rubbed togeth'r giv fire.*

Wondering if the voice, that did not seem to be mine, came from inside or outside my skull, I watched Gammer shut the stove door and fill the kettle. Then, after a mug of steaming tea, I took the pages out of my notebook and – just as they had been written – bundled them up with the entry application from the Board of Education's writing competition. I told myself, as I wrote the covering letter to my sponsor, Mr. Wordsworthy, that I was its author even if the words had created themselves without waiting for me. I told myself I didn't care if I won, at least I had tried.

Hearing Aunt Aggie's knock on the door, Gammer invited her to come in but she refused, saying that Valentine's Day was almost over and she still had to deliver four more boxes of chocolates to the people whose crafts she had sold. Then she paused, and breathless with excitement, half-whispered, "I just left Mrs. Gilbert's place whose husband teaches at the county high school. She told me that yesterday afternoon Rosie, the girl fostered by the Pitkins who have the pig farm between here and the village...well, you won't believe it...she hanged herself...she's dead."

She's dead. The pain of those words...the letters are red-hot. And I hear myself screaming "LIAR, LIAR, LIAR" as Gammer pulled Aunt Aggie by the arm out to the veranda and then, as the door was closing, I caught the words "gym teacher" and "rope through a basketball hoop." Then everything went dark and distant. I thought this must be what happens when we are dying.

But part of me continued to live – the house sighing and creaking in the wind, the kettle whistling when the water boiled, the hall clock striking the hour. I went to bed. I got up. I did what I had always done. But I was keenly conscious of a chasm separating me from everyone and everything...even from myself.

As before, neither of us spoke. Gammer's muttering, which no more could be considered speech than the sound of distant thunder, was now constant, and the cloud over her head grew bigger and blacker. One afternoon, while Gammer sat mending in the rocker and I stood washing and drying dishes at the sink, her voice became distinct enough for me to hear, "Love's a Devil. Its eyes are mirrors that steal your soul."

She might have been referring to Mama, or even herself, but I was sure she was talking about my love for Rosie. Lying in bed at night I told myself that my soul, after receiving such a sudden shock, would naturally flee. Why shouldn't it? Even a child or a dog would run away from a fright.

With all my dreams gone, I returned to my childhood's twilit world populated by ghostly figures. Some days I glimpsed a shape, a shimmering mirage, waiting for me at the turn in the stairs or at the end of the hall. Other times, a slight displacement of air would make me look up. I would feel a tracing of words like cobwebs on the skin of my arm. It didn't frighten me. I hoped it to be a message from you, Rosie, but it disappeared so quickly I could never decipher what you were saying.

Not once did I cry. In the days that followed when I was at my desk staring blankly at an open book (I no longer cared about schoolwork), a drop of blood fell on the page. I thought it was coming from my nose that Gammer had broken when she hit me.

One supper time, while I was sitting across from Gammer at the kitchen table, another drop landed in my bowl of soup. I thought it was guilt when she started to cook my favorite foods – jam turnovers, coddled eggs, apple pancakes – and I choked down a few mouthfuls trying to appease her. I also thought it was guilt that melted her silence. "How did you sleep?" she asked each morning. "Fine," I replied. I was too numb to care.

One morning, just after dawn, I awoke to the tread of heavy boots in the house. Since Gammer wore carpet slippers I wondered who it could be. Creeping down the stairs, I discovered it was in fact Gammer wearing her good navy-blue dress and her only pair of leather winter boots, cleaned and polished. As she filled a shopping bag with carefully wrapped bottles, she reminded me that this was Good Friday and because Aunt Aggie's ancient car had broken down, she was going to walk the two miles to Country Church Crafts. For weeks she had been preparing what she called invigorating medicinals. Aunt Aggie was anticipating many local customers during the long weekend because of her advertisement in the Madawaska weekly newspaper. She was convinced that, after such a long cold winter, Gammer's spring tonics in colourful glass bottles would far outsell painted wood eggs, handmade candles, white silk lilies — even the live baby rabbits dipped in purple vegetable dye.

Both women, bitten hard by life, had become shrewd and calculating. They always haggled and each was convinced that the other was cheating. Although Gammer disliked making the trek to Country Church Crafts, the fear that she might miss making some money, or worse, that Aunt Aggie might somehow pull the wool over her eyes, was greater than the fear of unleashing the tongues of the villagers.

"Goodbye, Sibyl," she called as she opened the back door. I should have followed the family ritual by saying, "God speed you," and she would reply, "Safe home." Instead Gammer filled the empty air with, "I must go before the wind comes up and it clouds over. My bones tell me we're in for a bad storm."

Then she added in a voice sharp as her eyes, "Stop feeling sorry for yourself. Your relatives worked hard, they proved their worth, and you must too. Especially now..."

The door banging shut said the rest. Although I heard Gammer's words, I did not feel them. I was dead. I was unreachable. I pushed my icy feet into the slippers warming by the stove and picked up my notebook from the kitchen table. I stared at the black-and-white linoleum tiles, at the trapdoor to the cellar, at the aluminum stripping used to nail it shut. I put the notebook back on the table. None of it mattered. What did I care about the future without Rosie? If she couldn't live without Mr. Baxter, how could I live without her?

Opening the back door, I saw that the sky had turned threatening with long low clouds, black as furrows of earth, moving in from the west. When I reached the shed, the door, frozen shut, would not budge no matter how hard I pushed and kicked and pounded. I was turning back to the house when I glimpsed the rope that Gammer had used to lash a tarpaulin over an ancient, inoperative tractor. I wore no mitts, but I managed to untie and pull free the rope that had been there for years. A gust of wind lifted the stiff grey plastic sheet off the tractor, and it lurched and rattled around the yard like a skeleton escaped from the grave.

Back in the house, I blew on my hands and concentrated on the next step. In the addition built by Gammer's rich grandfather "Silverspoon," there was one unfinished room, a nursery for his stillborn child, that subsequent generations used as a storage place. It was unheated, so leaving on my coat and boots, I took the rope and made my way up to the second floor and through the connecting hallway to the last room. Inside were four or five cardboard boxes, a dresser, a headboard for a single bed, a standing lamp with a broken shade and three wooden chairs. The walls and ceiling had not been plastered and the rafters were exposed. Since no one came in here, the window had not been covered and through it I could see – dark against the white snow – the bare misshapen trees in the apple orchard.

I uncoiled the rope, wondering if it could be the same one that Mama had made into a swing for me by hanging it from a branch with an old tire on the end. It was about eight feet long. I stood on a chair and then climbed on the dresser and, on the second try, passed it over the rafter and then I made a slip knot – it was how Gammer taught me to attach the yarn to the needle when I was learning to crochet – and pulled it tight. I made another slip knot and passed it over my head. I heard the grandfather clock in the foyer strike ten. I wondered what time Rosie died. I jumped off the dresser.

I remember the choking, my arms and legs flailing, the colour crimson going to black, and then falling, crashing on the floor, gasping, my lungs desperately sucking in air…

Slowly I recognized the frayed end of rope dangling above me. The weight of my body had broken it in two.

I lay on my back for a long time. I heard the clock strike hour after hour. I heard the snow and sleet beating against the windowpane, the house shaking and rattling under the force of the wind. The phone rang once. I got up and, removing the rope from my neck, left the room and closed the door. In my hole off the parlour I sat at my desk and opened my notebook, filling page after page with five-pointed stars inside circles. My head ached. Swallowing was difficult and my skin was raw where the rope had burned it. I smoothed on a layer of Gammer's ointment that smelled of primrose and fennel, then wrapped a piece of blue flannel around my neck.

Gammer returned to find me asleep with my head on the desk and my pen still in my hand. I woke up and wondered if I had been dreaming, but then I touched the flannel around my neck. In a hoarse whisper I complained of a sore throat. Gammer, when assured that I had no fever, scolded me for not answering the phone and, even worse, allowing the fire in the kitchen stove to die. Never had I been so cold. Still scolding, she bustled about the kitchen, raking the ash and laying and lighting the wood. While Gammer changed from her town dress, I boiled the water for tea and unwrapped hot cross buns and hard-boiled eggs dyed yellow with purple crosses, compliments of Aunt Aggie. It was Easter.

Gammer told me all about the storm, which her aching bones had forecast. It had arrived early – hail and sleet coating everything with a thick skin of ice. Even though the weather cleared by late afternoon, the road up the hill from New Salem remained a frozen river. Aunt Aggie urged her to spend the night, but Gammer was desperate to get back, so she hammered nails into two cedar shakes and tied them to the bottom of her boots with leather cords, then left Country Church Crafts where she and Aunt Aggie had been marooned. It took three hours, but her makeshift spiked boots held together, spraying ice chips at every step.

I can recall the aroma of the strong sweet black tea as I raised my cup to drink. And those hot cross buns! I was ravenous. I could taste wheat rippling in the wind, milk churning into heavy golden butter, the ocean drying into salt. Each raisin contained the summer sun. Each morsel of dried apricot the entire orchard. Slowly the heaviness lifted inside me, loss began to roll away. Bite by bite the act of eating was a miracle...a miracle of being alive.

Gammer washed the dishes and I dried. She poured each of us a glass of blackberry cordial "to soothe the throat and chase away the chills" and as we sat, side by side, our legs stretched out towards the stove's warmth, she asked if anything had happened in her absence. I told her "nothing much." Gammer replied that she had seen my open notebook and hoped my overdue essay was finished. Confused and exhausted, I nodded.

Over the next few days the ice melted and, under Gammer's direction, I spent time outside hanging up laundry, separating split logs from kindling, and checking the property line for toppled fence posts. By the time Fast Mac drove up the hill in his green panel truck to deliver the next package from the correspondence school, the rope-burn on my neck had faded and my voice was no longer hoarse.

Spring arrived late and, as though to make up for nature's cruelty, it brought manifold gifts. It began with the unprecedented occurrence of Gammer coming through the back door with a bouquet of purple lilacs held high as a lantern in her big hand. "Never have there been such blooms," she said, placing them in a vase on the front hall table. And never had there been fresh-cut flowers in the house. The unfurling of the clusters of tiny curlicue blooms conjured Mama…as though she had pulled the stopper from her perfume bottle and, dabbing the cool sweet lilac scent behind her ears, was wandering from room to room. I followed her scent. I breathed her in. When she was alive we had never been this close, so close she warded off Rosie – whose name still brings pain – and held off the ancestor who had possessed me while I was writing *drown'd in blood…*

Four months passed before I found out my submission had won first place. I remember reading the letter and the thousands of tiny wings lifting my heart out of my body. I didn't recognize it, but the sudden rush was a feeling of freedom.

Mr. Wordsworthy included a note saying my essay had left him speechless. I felt special for the first time in my life.

Afterwards, while planting in the garden, everything, from the tiny seeds I was poking into the earth to the picket fence around the graveyard to the huge overhanging oak, seemed brighter and more fully what it was.

Mr. Wordsworthy contacted the librarian in Perth, who arranged my room at a boarding house in the centre of town. He also helped to persuade Gammer, first by a letter that I read to her, and then by a pre-arranged phone call where he fortuitously mentioned my salary would be higher than either Gammer or I expected. Since this windfall could be used to help pay off the back taxes on the house, Gammer permitted me to do what no other Sibyl had done – escape the house and its choking loyalties.

Of course, Gammer could read my thoughts, repeating over and over how the generations of Sibyls born in this house were joined to it by a cord that could never be broken. "You'll have to come home," she said, "or circle like a dog roped to a tree."

During the first milky light of departure day Gammer and I walked, each holding a handle of my packed trunk, to the end of the lane. As we stood waiting for Aunt Aggie, who was going to drop me off at Perth on her way to visit a cousin, I had only one thought in mind, a constant wheel of prayer: *Dear God, let me escape. Dear God, let me escape.* I hated this barren broken land and Gammer, too, who had taught me to endure it. I hated my ancestors, flesh squeezing out of flesh, and myself for being trapped in this corridor of family history.

It was the beginning of summer and the first blush of green over the skimpy fields had faded. As the sun appeared, so did the boulders and thistles and briar bushes. The pond in front of the house, grown stagnant too soon, was thick with algae and weeds and water plants. When Gammer, who had been shifting her weight uneasily, started to grind her false teeth until they clicked like crickets in a dry spell, I knew she was going to speak. I didn't want to hear. I spun the wheel of prayer faster. She wiped her hands down her apron and then she surprised me by turning and cupping my face. Startled, I tried to pull away but she held me firmly, her rough calloused palms smelling of the pound cake she had made for me. As her eyes, red-rimmed as though she hadn't slept, bore steadily into mine, she said, "Don't forget, Sibyl, what's bred in the bone..."

Before she could finish by saying "...comes out in the flesh," Aunt Aggie's car rumbled up the hill and I yanked Gammer's hands away from my face. As the car eased to a stop I hissed, "What's bred in my bone is the family curse and what comes out of my flesh is hate and hate is setting me free – free from this house – free from you."

As Gammer and I heaved the trunk into her car, Aunt Aggie kept talking in a tone meant to be sympathetic, telling me how Miss Corbet should be sued for slander for saying that I was backwards and prone to fits because, if it was true, I couldn't have won such an important competition.

Aunt Aggie's beady eyes darted between Gammer and me but we ignored her. Sliding into the front seat I said, "Goodbye," and Gammer said, "God speed you," but instead of replying, "Safe home," I leaned over and closed the door without looking up.

The car took off with a jerk, and as I looked back through the rising dust, I saw Gammer standing in the middle of the road, waving her apron above her head. A few moments later I looked back again and she was still waving. I watched her grow smaller and smaller until, when we rounded the bend in the road, she was the size of a fluttering moth.

And that's how Gammer remained in the three years I've been gone...tiny, far away, disappearing around a bend in my mind.

Driving through New Salem, I ducked my head and slipped as far down in the seat as I could without Aunt Aggie taking notice. After we had turned onto the main road running the length of the valley, I glanced back one last time at the house on the hill. I had never seen it from this distance. Against the green backdrop of the escarpment its motley stone walls and collapsing parapets took the shape of a cornered animal snarling down at the village. The upper windows, catching the light of the early morning sun, gleamed like eyes driven mad.

The first summer of my freedom was spent in a town that calls itself the prettiest in Ontario. And it is true. Under the dappled light of the canopy trees lining the streets, the five thousand inhabitants of Perth live in solid comfortable houses with detached garages, neat lawns and ornamental shrubbery. The room Mr. Wordsworthy had arranged for me to rent was in a large turn-of-the-century gabled house modernized by aluminum windows and doors, white plastic window boxes and a tarred carport. Each morning, walking to work, I gazed with delight at the window displays in stores with intriguing names like Debbie's Attic, The Happy Scrapper, Black Duck Studio, and Angela's Heavenly Designs.

The public library had been destroyed by fire the previous winter and was temporarily located in a stately red-brick mansion belonging to the National Historic Sites of Canada. I had been hired for a specific summer job, filing the catalogue cards for the huge number of donated books, and I liked my days working alone in a dusty makeshift room in the basement. During the first weeks, when I closed my eyes to rest them from the glare of the overhead neon tubing, I could intuit something – almost like a breath – slipping in and out of me. That's how I knew that I was still partly dead. Or else why would my soul, which ran away when Rosie died, refuse to stay inside my body?

Regardless, I looked forward to my days in "the bear pit" of the library. Too busy to think as I sorted and filed hundreds of book titles, the four-by-six-inch index cards became the interlocking paving stones leading me away from my life in New Salem. Eventually all that remained was a periodic feeling of otherness.

Often I would stay late or come in early, saying I had research to do for a summer school course, but actually I was pursuing more information about my ancestor – the one who had turned my world inside out…or, more correctly, had turned me outside myself. Although the library had a diverse collection of historical books and articles and personal papers because so many United Empire Loyalists had migrated to the Perth area, I found nothing that gave me a clearer picture of Betty Parris. But then history is made up of facts and facts are only the edges – the solid black outlines – that separate what is from what isn't.

I did learn that in early March of 1692, at the height of the witch hunt, Betty had been sent from Salem Village to the home of her uncle in Salem Town. Around the same time, Tituba, her nanny, had been committed to jail where she admitted that the Devil had entered her. Since a person who confessed and repented was not hanged, nine months later Tituba was sold for the cost of her jail fees – her master, Reverend Samuel Parris, having refused to pay them.

I also learned that after the witchcraft trials, after nineteen guiltless people had been hanged, the parishioners turned from the reverend's leadership, claiming he was a false shepherd who had mislead his sheep. Many families, torn apart by the persecution and gruesome public death of their loved ones, refused to enter the church in Salem. In 1696 Reverend Parris was dismissed. Even reading about it, three hundred years later, I felt a mixture of shame and blame and pity for these distant kin...especially little Betty who was as real to me as Gammer... Gammer who never hugged or kissed or even touched me, except for the morning of our parting when she cupped my cheeks.

This reminded me of the touch test that I learned about while researching the historical period in which Betty lived. A woman who was accused of being a witch would be forced to lay a hand on the possessed person. If the symptoms disappeared, it meant the Devil had been drawn back into the accused, thus proving she was a witch. Did Gammer believe she was born old because of the ancient evil in her bones, and did she believe that if she touched me then I, too, would become afflicted?

If I liked the order and precision of my days in the bear pit, then I loved the freedom of nights in my room under the gable. Since I was the only one living on the third floor, Mrs. Bothwell, who had cataracts and memory lapses, usually ignored me when I walked by the lounge where she and the two long-term, septuagenarian tenants were watching the six o'clock news while eating their TV dinners. I heated my frozen lasagna or cannelloni in the microwave and then took it on a tray up the back stairs to the attic.

Because of the steep slope of the ceiling I could only stand or walk in the middle of my room. But it didn't matter. The long narrow window with its Juliet balcony opened into the branches of a giant horse-chestnut tree which, with the slightest breeze, spun forth spangles of green light and rocked the nest of mourning doves that fluttered and cooed. The furniture consisted of a single bed covered with a pale-blue chenille spread and a dresser, a desk, and a straight-backed chair in matching maple. There was a tiny closet with an accordion-style folding door, a ceramic table lamp in the shape of a fish standing on its chipped tail and, above the bed, a framed picture cut from a calendar, of a thatched cottage with a woman in a long yellow dress and bonnet waving to a man riding past in a horse-drawn buggy. The quote beneath read, "As rain does not break through a well-thatched house, passion will not break through a well-reflecting mind."

Here, in this place where only people with no home had lived, my mind did not dwell on the sadness of my past. There were no dead weighing down each object. There was no feeling of hopelessness. Here, snug as the nestling doves, my soul did not come and go but remained content in my body. Each night, as I fell asleep, the bed did not open into a bottomless black hole.

Possibly this easing of the mind occurred because of the many evenings I concentrated my attention on making mobiles (how many times did I hear Gammer say that an idle brain is the Devil's playground?). The idea sparked while I was gazing at a dream catcher in the window of the Four Winds gift store. Dangling from a thread, the web-like structure in the shape of a circle reminded me of the five-pointed star inside a circle that, for years, I had been attempting to draw perfectly.

The same day, on my way back from the library, I stopped at the hardware store and bought scissors, construction cardboard and coloured felt pens. Thus began my preoccupation that lasted for the three months I lived in Perth. I began by cutting circles out of cardboard – some large as saucers, others small as quarters. And then, without lifting the pen, I drew a pentacle on each side of each circle. Although it took only a few moments to draw one, I often spent hours choosing from various shades of coloured pens and filling in the eleven pieces that formed the whole. The last part of the process was to attach these brightly hued shapes to different lengths of wire so that each mobile resembled a constantly changing kaleidoscope.

I don't recall my reason for showing a mobile to Miss Carnegie, the only full-time fully trained librarian in Perth, but it was she who suggested hanging three or four of them in the Children's Corner. After that, whenever I passed through the public section of this temporary library and caught sight of my creations, it seemed as though I were glimpsing a rainbow after a day of thin rain.

Miss Carnegie, a tall strapping woman in her late forties, always wore a dark-blue suit and cropped her thick brown hair as short as a man. Although she looked cold and imposing, there was a tiredness (or was it sadness?) to her face that seemed to pull down the corners of her eyes and the tip of her nose, which

was too close to her upper lip. When she smiled (which was sel-
dom), she revealed as much of her gums as she did her large,
even, extremely white teeth. When she walked, she rolled like a
boat in a storm because of a heavy metal brace on her left leg
that went from her ankle to the top of her thigh.

I found out about the brace because on the way to work one
rainy morning, I saw Miss Carnegie slip and fall on the wet
cement at the library entrance. I ran up to where she lay on her
back, floundering, with her dark-blue skirt flipped up to reveal
her underpants and shrivelled leg in its metal cage. She looked
up at me with rage in her wide-set hazel eyes. Without a word
between us, I grabbed her around the waist and she grabbed me
around the neck and together we wrestled her upright. It took a
tremendous effort and as I stood panting, she turned silently
away and heaved herself through the front door.

Although no reference was ever made to this incident, Miss
Carnegie warmed to my existence, and since I was her only full-
time employee I gradually learned about her life. She had become a victim of polio as a young teenager and remarked, without bitterness, that she had never experienced a date, or even a
dance, with a man. After obtaining a degree in library science
from Queen's University in Kingston she had returned to care for
her arthritic bedridden mother, and for the past twenty-five
years, any leisure time had been spent researching and writing a
column on local history for the weekly *Perth Courier*. Perhaps
that's why when she showed me the summer issue of *Ontario
Teacher Magazine*, the gold flecks in her hazel eyes shone.

Opening the journal to the table of contents, Miss Carnegie
pointed to "The Salem Diary" by Sibyl Witherspoon and said,
"You must be very proud." Seeing my name in print was odd…as
though she were showing me a photo of myself that I didn't recognize. I waited until I was alone in my snuggery under the slop-

ing roof. Then, propped up by pillows on the bed, with the doves cooing in the horse chestnut tree, I turned to page 104 and began: *My birthdaie September 9th, 1691. I am ten yeares...*

It was as though the words, made concrete on the page, also made Betty concrete...more concrete than when I was a child and she became my invisible companion. She was free, speaking to anyone where the printed word would take her. But of course nobody knew that she was my ancestor. I recall struggling to decipher her diary before Gammer burned it. How much of what I was now reading in *Ontario Teacher Magaine* were her words stuck in my memory? While writing, it had seemed as if she were whispering in my ear. What had happened to her? This Betty on the page was scary. No one I wanted for a friend. Somehow she had changed after I read about the Salem witch hunts. Had I imagined her? Had I recalled what I'd read in her diary when I was ten? I felt not pride in what I'd done, but confusion.

That night the nightmare began. I had been sentenced for hanging and I wanted to run away but I was rooted – literally rooted – into the ground of the family graveyard. The following nights I dreamed variations...I was digging in the graveyard or Gammer was digging...digging deep as a grave to try and find where my heart, or her heart, was buried...buried but still beating.

Sometime later Miss Carnegie asked why I was so dark under the eyes and I blurted out my nightmare and how, when my job was ended in a month, I was going to run away to Toronto and live on the streets because I couldn't go back to New Salem where everyone hated our family and threw stones at me in the schoolyard and called Gammer a witch and Mama had been taken by the river and my only friend had hanged herself from the basketball hoop in the high school gym and all this was why

I wanted to become a librarian like her because surrounded by books I felt contented for the first time in my life.

During this feverish outpouring, I could hear Gammer's voice saying, "She's high-strung, she suffers from nervous prostration," but there was no choking and gasping as though an umbilical cord were tightening around my neck. There was no tunnelling into darkness. Instead, I seemed to be watching myself from across the room – hands clenched in front of me, shoulders hunched like a boxer – talking at Miss Carnegie who was looking down, fidgeting with the pen in her hand. When the words stopped as abruptly as they had started, she said nothing, but there were tears in her eyes as she turned from me. Embarrassed, I began mumbling an apology, but she shook her head and walked away. Although I regretted my outburst, I sensed it had awakened Miss Carnegie's sympathy.

A week passed. Both of us behaved as though nothing had happened, but sometimes while I was bent over my desk, labelling donated books, I felt her staring at me from the doorway. Then, one Friday afternoon as I was putting on my jacket to leave, Miss Carnegie came to me with an open book and pointed to the inscription, "For Dale on her birthday, with love from Dad." Below, in the same odd half-printed, half-written lettering, was the verse, "Laugh and the world laughs with you, weep and you weep alone, for the poor old earth must borrow its mirth, it's got trouble enough of its own."

I couldn't think of what to say so I kept staring at the page until finally she cleared her throat, "My Dad would quote this to me when I got moody or felt sorry for myself. He was a land surveyor for the federal government so never read much, but it tickled his fancy that the author had my exact name."

We stood stiffly side by side with our shoulders almost touching and I could feel Miss Carnegie straining to speak. "Too bad he never knew that I became a librarian and the man famous for building thousands of libraries in the early part of this century had his exact name – Andrew Carnegie." With a tremor in her voice she murmured, "Like your mother, my father died when I was young – a week after my thirteenth birthday. This was his last gift."

Still I could not think of an appropriate response. Moments passed and then, closing the book and handing it to me, she said in a slightly projected voice as though giving a prepared speech, "This was the most influential book of my teenage years. It always has been kept on my bedside table and, in memory of my father, on each birthday I read it from cover to cover. Now, Sibyl, I am passing it on to you with the hope that the advice contained within will guide…"

We hugged, awkward as two bears on hind legs.

When the first maple leaves were tipped with red, Miss Carnegie told me she had heard that an old college acquaintance was looking for someone to help run her small second-hand bookstore in Kingston. She had contacted the woman, convincing her that I was the right person. Although the pay was little, I could live rent free in the tiny apartment behind the store and, if careful with my money and time, I would be able to work while taking courses towards my high school certificate.

As I hugged myself and rocked with joy, I learned that the woman, Jennifer Heaven, who worked in the cataloguing department of Queens University, was unmarried and lived with her younger sister, Penelope, in the family home in the historical district. According to Miss Carnegie, the Heaven girls had loved books since they were children. Jennifer, a voracious reader of two or three paperbacks a week, would pass each one along to Penelope who, although very shy and a little slow, loved to catalogue and order their growing collection. After their parents died in a car crash three years ago, Jennifer hoped to console and distract Penelope by converting the front rooms of their house into a used bookstore. Somewhere between a pastime and a passion, tending to the thousands of books in The Bookworm's Heaven had become their way of life. But now the insurance money had finally arrived, making it possible for Jennifer to fulfill her dream of enrolling in the library science doctorate program in Ottawa. For the next five years, she would be home only on weekends, and my job was to be a companion to Penelope in the bookstore.

Since I was underage, Gammer would never give permission for me to leave home permanently. The only way was for me to disappear like Mama in the flash flood of the Mad. The police would not look for me because Gammer would be too proud to tell anyone I had run away from home. When I told Miss Carnegie my idea, she shook her head and said to leave it to her.

The next Saturday afternoon, Miss Carnegie's blue Honda pulled up in front of the house. I called down and instantly knew by her toothy grin that the trip to Gammer's had been a success.

"How did you do it?" I asked.

"I simply told her what happens to runaway girls who live on the streets in big cities," she answered grimly.

Gammer had packed my winter clothes in two big boxes and sent them back with Miss Carnegie. I had to promise to write once a week and, since there was a regular bus service from Kingston that passed through Madawaska Valley, to come home regularly.

I recall my first weeks in a "real" city with buses, crossing lights, parking meters, billboards, boulevards, four-lane roads, office towers and indoor shopping malls, as a constant whirlwind of excitement as brightly coloured as my mobiles.

The Bookworm's Heaven with its big bay window was on the ground floor of a tall narrow house in the oldest section of Kingston between the university campus and the shopping district. Jennifer and Penelope Heaven lived above the store in a hodge-podge of rooms, and I lived below in what they called an apartment, but actually was a furnished room with a hotplate. The sisters, who could pass for twins, were tall and narrow like their family home. Their thick straight faded blonde hair looked as if it had been cut by placing a bowl over their heads, leaving their dark brown eyes to peer from underneath like curious mice. They had small voices that grew even smaller when they were forced to converse with anyone but each other. Wearing their baggy grey sweat suits and felt slippers, they would arrive silently as ghosts in the store (often when I least expected it) to look for a book or check the filing cabinet or fetch Our Lady, the white cat, sleeping in the sunny bay window. Fortunately, having always lived among shadowy presences, I found our living together almost reassuring.

Within a short time we settled into a peaceful coexistence. Five afternoons a week, Penelope (only Jennifer was allowed to call her Penny) and I would open The Bookworm's Heaven at noon. For the next five hours, humming under her breath, she would go methodically along the bookcases, dusting, straightening and checking the placement of the thousands of second-hand volumes. Once a week, she would make room on the shelves for newly acquired books, giving each a little pat and quick kiss as a welcome – or so it seemed – to its new home.

Since my job was to help customers I would sit on a stool behind the cash register, studying or reading while waiting for the four to eight people a day who pushed open the door.

Because Jennifer's reading taste for twenty-five years had leaned to mysteries and historical fiction, it was old people in the neighbourhood – unable to make it to the public library – who dropped in to buy or sell books. If Penelope recognized them she would stop humming but carry on with her work. However, if she didn't, then she would disappear into the tiny storage room at the back of the store. It was not only that she was so shy that she could not look directly at anyone, but if anyone touched her, even accidently as they brushed by, she would scream and jump away as though stabbed. As I became accustomed to her odd behaviour rather than being disturbed by it, I considered myself lucky to have a greater capacity for hiding my own strangeness. Thus Penelope and I, ignoring each other like an old married couple, worked comfortably side by side for the next three years.

On most weekends Jennifer returned from Ottawa, leaving me free to hunker down in my basement room. Like a wolf in its lair worrying a bone, I worried my brain over the courses I was taking, not only at night school but also by correspondence. Although I feared choking on what I had bitten off, I was determined to please Miss Carnegie by having my high school leaving certificate when I arrived in the big city of Toronto.

In the meantime, I enjoyed waking to the ribbons of light squeezing between the bars of the tiny high window and falling across my bed. In the evening I enjoyed talking to my potted geranium – trying to persuade it to bloom – as I boiled water in my electric kettle to make soup-in-a-cup or sliced cheese to put on bread. After all, who was to hear but Our Lady who often crouched at the top of the stairs…staring at me but not seeing, and I would think of Mama and how, in the same way, she looked right through me as if I were made of glass. Then I would call out, "Help me, Our Lady, to do what Mama did not. Help me, I pray, to live the life she did not, to live it for her." I would toss a bit of cheese and watch Our Lady pounce as if it were a mouse.

With my excitement at escaping New Salem and the House on the Hill, I forgot about the book that Miss Carnegie had given to me until I'd unpacked my last box of clothes during the Christmas break from school. The banner across the cover claimed that *How to Win Friends and Influence People* had been a best-seller for over thirty years. I recalled Miss Carnegie saying how, at my age, she had read it many times. It never occurred to me there was a method of making friends that one could learn in the same way, let's say, as one learned to ride a bike.

I read the book with care, especially the places where it opened most easily, where I sensed (almost a faint warmth) Miss Carnegie's eyes had lingered. The author's claim was simple. People are more interested in themselves than in anything else, and therefore to win them over you must, first, see their good points and, second, tell them what these are.

While I had always been aware of those around me, it was more a stray dog's sensitivity to a hand scooping up a stone or a boot lifting to kick. I didn't see people...only their reactions to me. Now, from my stool behind the cash register, I scrutinized everyone who walked into The Bookworm's Heaven and took mental notes on mannerisms, body movements, facial expressions and how – not what – they spoke. Still, I was never confident enough to put my observations into practice. And it was no better at my weekly night school class, which consisted mostly of immigrants who hung around with others speaking the same language, or women who were paying babysitters and so rushed in and out without talking to anyone.

But there was one girl I saw almost every day that I particularly wanted to approach – a student – one of thousands who gathered every fall in this college town like flocks of noisy migrating birds. She worked as a part-time cashier in the local convenience store where I bought my meager groceries, and I identified her as a college student immediately because of the tight neon-yellow miniskirt with matching leggings and the big hoop earrings. In awe of her ease with herself and people, I reread Miss Carnegie's book on winning friends. Then, rehearsing my lines as I waited in line at the cash, I said, "For weeks I've been wanting to tell you that I love your hair (which she wore layered and wild as if teased by the wind) and how much you remind me of the actress Farrah Fawcett."

I must have sounded genuine and natural because her face lit up – just the way the author said it would – and she looked at me with interest...not that she was seeing me...but that I was seeing her. She talked about how fabulous Farrah had been in *Charlie's Angels* as she rang up my groceries, and then, while waiting for me to count out my money, she fluffed her hair with her hand and turned her head this way and that as though I were holding up a mirror for her to look at herself.

The next time I entered the store she was standing outside and waved at me with a cigarette between her fingers. "Hey, kiddo," she called, "you live around here?"

Often during that long warm fall when I was picking up some item before the bookstore opened, Cathy was taking her morning break. Not allowed to smoke inside, she lounged against the side of the building and always called me over. I don't recall what was said...only how I unconsciously stayed in sync with her by paraphrasing her words and adopting her interests. I even found myself crossing my arms the way she did while talking.

Only now, as I'm writing these words, do I realize that by transforming myself into a kind of mirror, I learned to see the world as Cathy saw it. As a result, even when we were not together, the feeling of loneliness – of falling into emptiness – diminished.

With growing confidence I tried this technique with the Heaven sisters. Holding up a mirror to Jennifer, I discovered that this shy retiring woman took such pleasure in seeing herself that she would use any excuse to come to my room. It felt as though I had a secret power like a magician turning people into who they wanted to be...who they really were but didn't know it. The exception was Penelope, who refused to look in my magic mirror. And Gammer...

I wrote to her every week, but I did not visit until Thanksgiving. To fit in with the flocks of students who had migrated to this college town I had stopped braiding my hair and I now tied it high on my head in a long ponytail that hung to the middle of my back. I had bought a black fake-leather jacket at a garage sale and Cathy had given me a pair of her big hoop earrings – both of which I wore home. Gammer was basting the roast chicken when I walked into the kitchen and, although I had not seen her in four months, did not respond to my greeting. Instead she looked me up and down, then exhaling a kind of "pshaw" to indicate how ridiculous I appeared, turned back to the stove.

I refused to give in and, a few hours later, when Aunt Aggie came for afternoon tea, I added some fake flowers to the elastic holding my ponytail and smeared blue shadow on my lids because Cathy had claimed it made my eyes look less protruding. This, of course, infuriated Gammer, who maintained a cold angry silence for the remainder of the weekend. Swept into the hurt and helplessness of the past, I hid out in my cubbyhole study, listening to the creaking joints of the house, breathing in the dry rot of the beams mixed with the foul stench of mushrooms that Gammer was constantly brewing into teas and remedies. It felt as though all the love and loyalty that had existed in the house when Mama had lived with us was, once again, being transformed into a bitter poisonous concoction that seethed in my guts. After three days, it was as though I had never left New Salem.

On the morning of my departure, Gammer appeared as I was putting on my fake-leather jacket and, blocking the doorway, said in a voice that shook with the fury of her pride. "All this education is doing you no good. Look at you! You're going to end up in trouble just like your mother."

"Yes," I yelled, "just like my mother, but I will have escaped you and this house."

Before I could stop myself I pushed her so she staggered backwards, falling against the kitchen counter. My last words were, "I'm never coming back," as I slammed the door behind me.

"Hey, kiddo! What's with you?"

I stood mute and unmoving, watching Cathy rummage in her bag for matches to light a cigarette dangling from her lips. Three days with Gammer had smashed my magic mirror. Taking her first long drag, Cathy squinted at me, saying that I looked like death warmed over.

I collapsed on the bench beside her and, lost in the blue smoke of her cigarette and the fragments of my magic mirror, I heard myself say that my mother was dead, my mother who'd been a professional flamenco dancer bedded by my father who was in the U.S. military and I'd been an army brat living all over the world until two years ago on Thanksgiving weekend when my mother had died in a car crash while they were vacationing in Malta and my father in his grief had asked to be stationed on a remote post close to the South Pole and I'd not heard from him in months.

I started to cry. Shocked that my lies were causing me to weep, I hid my face in my hands. Cathy, wearing bright pink fingerless gloves, flipped her cigarette butt into the bushes and put her arm around me. "Chrrrist, kiddo," she said.

For the next three years, I continued to invent myself, helped by Cathy who pointed out long flowing skirts, embroidered vests, bangle bracelets – what she called gypsy chic – in fashion magazines and shop windows. I assumed an aptitude for reading palms, which I claimed was inherited from my ancestors, but actually was taken from a second-hand book I found in The Bookworm's Heaven. This made me interesting to Cathy's college friends. I was no longer a lonesome weirdo…just a loner…

The ringing telephone knocks the breath out of me. I recognize our code – three long, one short. I rush to where the phone hangs on the foyer wall. Just as the ringing begins for the third time, I grab the receiver. I hear "Hello…hello…hello." A familiar voice, thick, stringy, says, "I know someone's there by the breathing." Recoiling, I hear, "Tell Sibyl that Mrs. Janows – " and I slam down the receiver as a face looms up, collapsing flesh puttied by cosmetics, accusing eyes…

Slowly I back away as though the telephone were a small startled creature about to attack. Head spinning, I stare at the open mouth of the speaker. I return to my open journal and pick up my pen.

Think, Sibyl. Use your head. You know that face. It's your landlady. How long have you been gone from Toronto? Don't know. Head still spinning. Gammer? Gammer? No use calling out. Not

*here. But where? Now it's coming back. Yes. Young Mueller. He said
she would be helping Aunt Aggie at the craft store. You phoned last
night. Remember? You thought Aunt Aggie would drive her home.
Thought Gammer was phoning just now. But how would she know
you are here?*

*Nights of no sleep. Your hand moving back and forth across the
page. Guiding your pen – a live imp, a familiar, helping you forget
something you can't remember.*

My neck and head ache. I am hollow with thirst and hunger.
How long have I been sitting here in front of the cold stove?
Waiting for Gammer. Stiffly I retrace my steps across the worn
black-and-white linoleum to the front foyer. I stare in surprise at
the grandfather clock. Its frozen face. Motionless pendulum.
Then I remember. Time is dead.

I look up to the shade-drawn window at the turn in the stairs.
It's a golden rectangle of afternoon sunlight. I open the front
door. A rush of heat into the cool dimness of the house. I am
cold. Has summer come? How long have I been gone? Did I
never leave? Did memory, knowing no time, come alive and am
I dreaming me?

Later, when I had pulled both sides of my brain together and
realized I had been lost in the past since before dawn, I tried
calling Country Church Crafts, but received the same message
as last night – closed for inventory. With gnawing urgency and
foreboding I choked down large mouthfuls of the untouched
corned beef and cabbage. Then, as I was rushing out, I recalled
Bridget Mueller's jeering remark about my hair and – unable to
find an elastic, or even a piece of string, to tie it back – I shoved
my unruly locks under Gammer's straw gardening hat that she'd
hung on the hook by the kitchen door.

I took a shortcut down the stony hillside. The path, traversed
mostly by sheep, followed a small brook and then veered left

across an empty pasture pitted by hoofs and lumpy with clods of hardened earth. I had forgotten how early the black-fly season starts this far north and within minutes they were swarming around my head. I half ran, half trotted, disoriented by the flies and the sweat running into my eyes until, climbing over a fence, I entered a grove of scrub pine whose shadows offered a short respite from the unseasonal heat. On the other side of the trees the path levelled out, but in the bottomland there was a large boggy place where I had to jump from mound to mound of marsh marigold in full bloom. By the time I reached the edge of New Salem my canvas sneakers were soaking, my shirt ripped from the barbwire and my face itching with fly bites. I forgot it all as I stood staring at the Country Church Crafts store.

Aunt Aggie had purchased the village's only church a year before I fled Madawaska Valley and I had not witnessed its conversion. Every day on my way to school I had passed the one-storey brick building with its empty belfry (the bell stolen years ago) and rusting tin roof. Because of a dwindling population the church had lacked a congregation and, when I was a child, held services for the non-religious locals at Christmas and Easter. Then one day the double doors were padlocked and the windows boarded up. The sign saying St. James Methodist Church had been removed after being spray-painted with "Fuck Mary" and "Hungry? Eat a Virgin." Still, though forsaken and ridiculed, the church gave off an aura of cold unyielding strength that always reminded me of Gammer.

All that was gone. It had been transformed into a gingerbread house, the brick painted the colour of pink candy floss and the rusting tin roof replaced with cedar shakes that looked like chocolate wafers. The coloured glass along the top of the windows (which I'd never noticed because of grime) glowed bright as gumdrops in the late afternoon sun. The little wooden belfry had been repaired and painted mint green, as was the trim, and the window boxes were already blooming with red trailing geraniums. There were smiling garden gnomes with red peaked caps lined up on either side of the wide stone steps. Coming nearer I saw a sign saying Closed tacked on the outer double door.

I was about to walk around to Aunt Aggie's living quarters in the back when I heard "Yahoo, Sibyl!" Even before turning, I knew who it was. From our first day together in Grade One, Meli (honey bee in her native tongue and she'd stung like one) had picked on me. Meli was petite, agile and popular. Her smooth tanned face with its high cheekbones still had the scars from the boils that she believed were caused by my having made a voodoo doll from her stolen mitt. With one hand she flipped back her long black hair (the hair I'd grabbed to pull her down and beat her head against the ground on the day our roles had reversed) and said, "Sibyl, is that really you?"

I saw myself in her mirrored sunglasses – face swollen and red with black-fly bites, strings of hair hanging below Gammer's battered straw hat – and I realized that since returning I hadn't changed clothes or brushed my hair or even my teeth. Meli was saying something but all I heard was the schoolyard voices chanting, "Silly Sibyl stinks of shit. That's because she's illigit." I couldn't look away from the twin miniature versions of my face in Meli's face. It was as though somehow I were being hypnotized...sucked out of myself and into myself simultaneously...so somehow I was inside Meli and she was inside me...and her mouth was moving and my mouth was moving inside her dark glasses...and I knew that she knew that I am not who I am...and she knew that I knew that she is not who she is...

Suddenly the spell was broken. Out of nowhere a small yellow finch swooped down and began pulling and twiddling at the loose bits of straw in the brim of Gammer's hat. Meli burst out laughing and woke her baby who started to cry. While jiggling the carriage she asked why I had come back from living in the Big City, but then the baby began to howl so she picked him up, squirming and flailing, and he grabbed her sunglasses and put them in his mouth. When she put them in the pocket of the carriage he howled even louder and reached for a fistful of her hair, refusing to let go. All this distraction helped to deflect her attention from me. Helped me to pull my selves into me.

I told her about my trying to find Gammer who – I understood from the Muellers – was helping out at Country Church Crafts, but how every time I phoned, only the machine answered saying the store was closed for inventory. According to Meli, Aggie kept the same message all winter because she didn't want customers to realize the store was shut for so long. When I said that didn't make sense, Meli shrugged her shoulders saying, "Well, that's Aggie for you," and went on to tell me that the last time she'd seen Gammer she was getting into Aggie's car. Aggie, who was loading in boxes and suitcases, said she was taking a trip to deliver some craft orders to stores in Perth, Kingston and, for the first time, Toronto. Meli presumed she must have been going to drive Gammer up the hill, as she usually did, but maybe both were going. This had sense to me as it explained why Gammer had phoned my boarding house in the City. Meli said they had left the day before yesterday and were to be away until the end of the week. That would mean they would be back in two days.

While Meli was telling me Gammer's whereabouts, she was preoccupied with jiggling and juggling the baby who squealed with delight. Without her sunglasses I could see her strange, copper-coloured eyes glowing with pride as she talked on and on about how jealous the Muellers were of her having Wee Will after all those years of Bridget's miscarriages. "You'd never catch me going alone to Kingston the way the both of you did," she said. "Yet look at you now! Heard you're working in the Big City of Tor-on-toe where girls get raped every day but, of course, living there you know all about it."

As she spoke, darkness began to swallow me up...the darkness that is the nightmare...scattered like a broken mirror in my brain...cutting sharp fragments of images...a gold signet ring on a man's hand holding my wrist...a mouth moving in a face too close to see...a fluorescent ceiling light...

"No! No!" I shook my head emphatically.

Taking off Gammer's broken straw hat I fanned my face claiming the sudden heat was making me feel strange.

Meli, her eyes turning cold with malice – or was it pity for my dishevelment? – asked in a joshing manner, "Hey, you never told me why you're here? Something happen? No one from the Big City ever comes back without a reason."

She was kind of smiling but it was a mirthless smile, while behind her friendly words she was saying something I didn't want to hear, so I stopped listening – the words just empty shapes in my ear – to concentrate on the gurgling squirming baby with flaxen hair and washed-out blue eyes, bright as a hot overcast summer sky. That's when I realized Wee Will had to be one of the "Parsnips" and that his father had to be Billy...Billy... Billy...I called across the abyss of time while the scar of the five-pointed star tattooed on my palm began throbbing and I recalled our last afternoon in the barn...his hand closing over mine... closing over my heart. And he never knew...

Before I could stop myself, I burst into tears and, wheeling around, took off at a half run up the road. I could hear Meli calling after me, "Wait, wait, I didn't mean to..."

I had to get home. When I heard the loud beeping of a horn behind me, I veered off the road and, as the car slowed down, I jumped the ditch and began to run across a field of newly planted corn. A man's voice yelled, "Sibyl? Sibyl Witherspoon?" which made me race even faster up the gradual incline towards the escarpment. Fearing that it was Billy calling my name, I didn't look back but kept running until, dizzy and gasping for breath, I reached our property.

The rusty hinges of the gate allowed it to be opened only enough for me to squeeze through. As I was doing so, the faint sweet smell of Mama's perfume wafted past and I noted the lilac bushes on either side of the gate were about to blossom. I was struggling to straighten the leaning gatepost when Young Mueller drove by in his pickup truck. He whistled, calling out, "Need my help, Big City Girl?" I shook my head. "Well, never mind, I'll come around later to pick up the ointment for The Bride." I told him Gammer would not be back for a couple of days. He smiled, his wide thin mouth and pointed eye teeth reminding me, as always, of a snarling dog. "All the more reason for me to come," he said, and then winking, "you can invite me in for some refreshment."

Turning on my heels, I said emphatically, "Don't bother!" And then lying, I added, "I'm leaving tomorrow to go back to Toronto."

He called out something about tonight, but – pretending not to hear over the noise of the revving engine – I walked off as fast as I dared without showing my agitation. The lengthening shadows of the poplar trees that lined our lane blocked what remained of the sun's warmth and I shivered, crossing my arms over my chest. I could hear my bare feet squishing inside my wet canvas shoes and the bullfrogs in the pond were beginning their evening song.

I double locked both back and front doors. Making my way through the house (except for Mama's room of course), I checked to be sure every blind and curtain was tightly pulled. Wherever possible, I used clothespins to peg the edges of the material together. The constant drafts could create a gap. No one must be able to look in. To know that I am here. Not Meli or Billy. And especially not Young Mueller.

I was laying wood to make a fire when the phone rang. I dropped a log that knocked the kettle off the stove. I didn't answer it. Only afterwards did I think that perhaps it was Gammer calling. She could be in Toronto now and maybe she'd contacted Mrs. Janowski who would have informed her I had gone back to New Salem. The more I thought about it, the more I thought it could be true.

When the phone rang again a few minutes later, I had to risk answering. There were clicking sounds and then a woman's voice that I recognized immediately as Lou. She said she was calling from a payphone in the library lobby and only had enough change to pay for three minutes. She asked if everything was alright at home and when I hesitated she rushed on to ask if I would be back by next weekend. She couldn't get anyone else to take her shift and she didn't want to miss the chance of driving to Niagara Falls with some friends. I said I would let her know as soon as possible.

After responding with an enthusiastic "Great!" Lou started to talk about running into two of the guys we'd met in the pub and how they had asked after me and wanted...I never heard what because of clicking sounds and the phone went dead.

After that, I don't remember.

The urgent calling of crows has brought me to the kitchen window. Fearing that their ruckus is caused by Young Mueller cutting across the back field, I force myself to open the side of the blind a few inches and look out.

It's early evening. I can tell the unseasonal spring heat has dissipated because of the coolness of the glass when I press my cheek against the window. My head aches. So does my left arm, resting on the sill to recover from forming the words that keep pouring out like a river. By straining my eyes to the left, I can see the silhouette of Great-Grandfather's cross towering against the twilit sky. Except for the birds circling for a place to roost, there is no movement anywhere. If Young Mueller had disturbed them, he'd be knocking at the kitchen door by now.

I remain unmoving, staring at the blackened shape of the cross that had been hit by lightning sometime over the summer of Mama's disappearance. For the first time it occurs to me how formidable it looks, which is probably why the words *Black Madonna* pop into my brain. That was the title of one of the books displayed at Robarts as reading suggestions for Easter. Indeed, from this angle and distance, what remains of the cross does resemble a primitive sculpture, roughly hewn with an axe, of the Madonna with her head bent in sorrow – while the cross-bar, burned, could be a body she is holding.

The more I stare, the calmer and more protected I feel…like a pilgrim beholding a precious relic, I have become part of something bigger than me…part of something boundless and whole…and then I think of Gammer who always wears black and walks slowly with her head bowed…and, for the first time, I consider that the weight she carries could be grief for Mama – her dead child.

As I watch, more birds begin to circle around the cross. If Gammer were here she would wrap a shawl over her head, put on her rubber boots and, stomping across the yard and up the path through the vegetable garden, she'd shoo them away. The

Witherspoon cemetery with its white picket fence is her outdoor chapel, the sacred place where she can be found at the end of every summer day – weeding, watering, clipping grass, tending the profusion of flowers (considered a waste of time elsewhere on the property) and neatening the engraved slabs of cement that mark the eleven graves. There should be twelve, but Mama is missing because no body has ever been found to bury.

"I've always been more comfortable around the dead than the living," is how Gammer likes to tell of how Grandfather's casket had been laid on the long dining room table with her sitting there alone beside him, picking ants from the bowl of white peonies, when she heard a rustling from inside the casket. In a surge of joy that he had returned she had opened the lid. Out ran a mouse. "I felt my heart squeezed of blood," Gammer would say, "like water from a sponge, and after that it never beat in a steady fashion." Each time she told the story she made me promise to check her coffin before I closed the lid.

Rubbing my hand on the glass to remove the fog of my breath, I recall how, as a child, I would watch for Gammer's familiar wide-hipped shape plowing through the dusk. I think of the seven generations of Witherspoons that have lived here and now are watching us from the graveyard at the far end of the garden where the land tilts abruptly upwards towards the escarpment. Just as the geological periods forming the limestone ridge can be traced by the fossils embedded in the rock, our generations can be traced by the artifacts they leave behind. Of which Gammer, their curator, says little – a few passing comments such as, "You have your grandfather's upper lip," as she dusts his moustache cup, or, "Fetch me the lap desk where your great-aunt Martha kept her wooden hand," or, "That tortoise-shell comb you're about to use once belonged to your great-great-grandmother who died of a cold because she washed her hair in the winter."

It was Great-Great-Grandfather "Silverspoon" who bought the tall mahogany clock that has stood guard in the hall for over a hundred years. Once while Gammer was winding the pendulum, I asked if it were true that it stopped at the exact moment of his last exhalation and if she – "shhhh," Gammer interrupted, glancing up the stairs to the empty landing.

I am aware of the clock's silence pressing against my back as I try to keep my mind focused to stop from panicking that there will be a knock at the kitchen door, Young Mueller or Billy Parsons with Meli and the baby…or even worse, the three louts from the pub. No…no…Lou would not tell them where I live.

I am back sitting at the kitchen table. My eyes, like those of a night animal, have adjusted to the growing dark and – while concentrating on forming each letter with my left hand – I think of Gammer…trying, for the first time in my life, to understand what makes her silent and bitter as a gooseberry. Is it her failure to be able to express what she knows…or perhaps what she knows has no words? The only books she reads are about nature – the bird's flight, the hovering cloud, the lichen-covered stone, the trout jumping in the pond.

Usually when I ask Gammer how she can predict certain things she just shrugs. "I don't know," she says, "I just do." If I persist, she tells me that she's seen things when she's looked out of the corner of her eye into mirrors – a mirror, for Gammer, being any surface that casts a reflection. When I was young I would practice staring obliquely at windows and puddles and metal objects like tin pie plates or the copper bottoms of pans drying in the dish rack.

Of course, I was always careful not to look at myself. Perhaps that's why I turned myself into a mirror. "Homely as a fence stump," the village girls giggled as I passed. But it's something more than that. Just now, chilly from the growing cool of the spring evening, I got one of Gammer's knitted afghan throws from the parlour to wrap around my shoulders. As I was returning to the kitchen, I caught myself in the oval mirror at the end of the front hall and my heart leaped. For a split second I thought I was Gammer – the same wide face, the same hooked nose (only mine leans slightly left because of being broken) – and I heard myself saying, "There's an umbilical cord stronger than a ship's rope anchoring us Sibyls to this house."

How odd to find Gammer's words coming out of my mouth! For the first time I realize, not only do I recall almost every one of her comments, her sayings, but also she's the voice-over of almost every thought…guiding…judging…condemning…

Even more unnerving is that Gammer (who would not budge from her home) and I (who only wanted to escape) have exchanged places. Here I am in the House on the Hill and there she is in the Forbidden City. Without doubt, the reason she tried to reach me in the City was to tell me she and Aunt Aggie were coming. I couldn't have imagined it. But then I couldn't have imagined sitting at the kitchen table eating a tin of baby shrimp from the pantry. Or that I've been here for three days. Outside the house it feels like three weeks. Inside the house it feels like three hours. No matter that I escaped this place…I can never escape her…never escape…the house whispering, "Be long, be long"…in the bones of your ancestors…NO…

No, I won't go out again. I'll wait for Gammer to come home…home? Part of me can't believe I wrote that word. That part of me finds this place a prison where I am trapped by the past and the present. But the other part of me knows that this will always be my home and Gammer…Gammer is all I've got.

So I sit – frozen, unable to act – at the table while darkness blankets the kitchen. The heart of the house in its tall wooden box has stopped beating. My bones are heavy, the dead weight of this sprawling house pressing down on them. I can't turn on a light because Young Mueller could be lurking.

The glass eyes of the deer's head shine. The long pointed twigs of the oak scratch the kitchen window and the walls creak. The wind pushes through the loose-fitting joints. I should see about the scrabbling in the woodbox that I know to be mice. I should make myself something to eat. I should brush my teeth and wash my face and climb the stairs to my small back bedroom. Although I haven't slept for two nights, I can't make myself lie down on the lumpy old mattress stinking of my childhood terrors. I am afraid of the nightmare that won't go away but – like landscape lit by lightning – flashes deep in my brain.

And so I keep on…watching letters, industrious as a line of black ants as they march across the whiteness…listening for footsteps. As I'm listening I'm thinking that all this writing is also footsteps…a march of words opening the way to god knows where…

The Slant of Light

➳ DAY FOUR ➳

Another night, no sleep. Same as when I was a child. All that exists is here in the house. I never left. Without undressing, I throw myself down on the bed. It disappears, the trapdoor opening. I am falling. A scream tears out of me. It's out there in the pitch black of the house. I struggle out of bed. My feet on the floor, I am safe.

Downstairs in the front hall in the dark, I wrap Gammer's coat tightly around me and settle into the rocking chair by the kitchen stove. I rock, dozing a little, until the rising sun burnishes the pulled blind. As the glowing intensifies into a golden radiance, I think of the angel that came to Mary. Whatever news it brings I don't want to hear. I jump up and walk away, trembling at the thought of my flesh being invaded – by God…or…No! I cover my eyes with the palms of my hand as though the enemy is outside and not inside my brain.

All day I've been following my feet – their slow measured steps – counting each one out loud to stop the talking in my head. Twelve across the black-and-white tiles of the kitchen, stop, turn right, slide open the door, ten across the slanting pine floors of the dining room, stop, push open the door, three over the braided carpet in the vestibule, stop, turn right, push aside the heavy velvet curtain, thirteen across the even-more-slanting pine floor of the parlour (watch out for the buckling board by the fireplace), stop at the five stairs leading up to my cubbyhole den, turn right, then along the back corridor past the entrance of the pantry where Gammer scrubbed straight through the linoleum, stop, turn right, push through the squeaky swinging door to the kitchen.

Around and around. Past jars of canned food – to remind me to eat – lined up on the kitchen counter. Past the sleepless deer's head, the almost empty woodbox, the wicker knitting basket by the rocking chair. Past the mahogany dining room table where I run my finger along its polished top. Lemon oil. Past the Queen Anne sofa with its ancient silk brocade, the carved fireplace mantle with the oil lamp exactly in the centre. Over plaster dust fallen from the crack in the corridor ceiling and through the dangling loose ends of spider threads.

Around and around. Padding silently in my stocking feet. Circling like a wolf – the wolf that Rosie and I saw in a roadside zoo set up one summer on the edge of New Salem. That lean grey wolf. Thin legs. Matted fur. Tireless silent pacing, as though possessed, around and around the narrow cage. When I tossed a handful of popcorn through the bars – so casual was my cruelty – those burning yellow eyes for an instant stared right through me and I had the feeling I was that beast and an iron gate clanged shut. Caged. In my own body.

Then Rosie, who had been trying to get the wolf's attention by howling, made me laugh and the bad feeling dissolved… except at night sometimes I woke and in the pitch black I saw those phosphorous eyes – each time a little closer and larger – staring into the back of my skull…into the wilderness of my mind.

⁊ DAY FIVE ⁊

Gammer was to return. All night I've been waiting. All day I've been pacing from window to window. Must not sleep or will wake up the nightmare. Must not go outside or they will see me. I peek between the closed curtains. Why is Aunt Aggie's old black Chevy not coming up the road? Only a few cars pass. Young Mueller on his tractor looks over at the house but doesn't stop. A pickup truck slows down near our gate and Gammer's voice says, "Quick, hide," but then there is the roar of the motor as it speeds up again. After that, any movement outside – a bird in the leaves of a bush, a scurrying squirrel, the wind rippling the pond's surface – drains my blood.

When the shadows melt together and the gloom outside balances the gloom inside, I phone the craft store but only the machine answers. I consider phoning Meli but our chance encounter seems so long ago and far away that I tell myself I must have dozed off and dreamed it. Instead, I pace around the house to the count of one hundred and then try to call the craft store again. I repeat this same routine ten times. The moon is high and I know Gammer and Aunt Aggie will not be returning tonight.

All lights are switched off in the valley as sleep spreads from house to house. And yet here I am, unable to stop pacing. Unable to stop my fingers from reaching up every few minutes to touch my cheek. Do I expect to feel fur?

And why am I being watched? Not from outside but from inside.

"Gammer?"

My voice, a jagged white crack in the silence.

I know I am not alone. Any time, anywhere as I am pacing, especially at the turn in the stairs or outside her bedroom door, I grow aware of her odour, dry as burnt toast. Each time I pass her apron hanging on a hook by the back door I expect it to be filled. Each time I pass the dining room table I expect to find a message written in the dust.

And just now I thought it was her face at the end of the front hall. I couldn't look away. I couldn't stop from being pulled into it. I couldn't stop chanting inside my head *until I die, until I die, it's your face in the mirror, your tears when I crie, until I die, until I die, it's your face in the mirror, your tears when I crie…*

Gammer, please don't die. Don't let me die.

❧ DAY SIX ☙

I have not taken off my clothes since I arrived. They have become my outer flesh…their smell…their warmth…their security…and what does it matter? I don't go out. I don't even peek through the closed curtains or turn on the lights. I've stopped making a fire for tea so there's no smoke rising from the chimney. No one can tell that I am here. Except Gammer. I catch myself talking out loud to her. Listening to the words reverberate through the silence makes me wonder who is speaking them.

Just the same as now, watching these words materialize on the page, I wonder who is thinking them. I'm falling apart – parts of my body operating by themselves. Never have I been so disconnected. I watch myself watch the hand that holds the pen. Gammer's big paddle hand, numb with coldness. It doesn't seem part of me. I blow on her red swollen knuckles, her thick fingers to warm them. Then a rush of blackness sucks up my breath as I hear myself whispering, "Beware of the wind that comes in through a hole. Say your prayers and hold on to your soul."

I'm deeply cold…Gammer, I know what you always say, "A spot of hot tea will cure that."

The brown betty with the chipped spout is waiting in its usual place on the counter. The tea is kept in a yellow canister beside it. They are more connected to her than I am to my own hands. I wonder if inanimate things take on the life of those constantly touching them. Gammer would scold the canister when the top stuck in hot weather. I think I will try to heat water over a candle. Reaching for the tin box of matches, it jumps away and crashes on the linoleum...

Another day gone. Or could it be a week? The black phone in the hall snarls like a trapped animal when I reach out for it. The house is swallowing me whole. There's no time, yet I must wait...accept the dark rising like an ocean tide. The white linoleum tiles seem to float. The black ones are sinking. The metal stripping around the trapdoor has faded to a fine line. The brass ring handle looks like a heel print in the mud. When I walk – careful to step only on the white squares – I am wading through water. I must not sleep. I must not fall. The jagged dark is opening.

Gammer where are you? Gammer I'm afraid. Afraid I'll dream. Do we dream before we're born? Are we dreaming as we fall through the dark of our own birth?

❧ DAY SEVEN ❧

The dead of night. Silence like a black egg. I can't see. I struggle for breath. The dark so heavy. I feel where I am. My bottom on the chair. My feet on the floor. My hand holding the pen. A swooping sound like the spread wings of a huge bat. Gammer splitting open the night. On a broomstick propelled by its flaming straw.

"Sibyl," she hisses, "keep track."

"Track of what?"

From the bulging sack flung over her shoulder she dumps out shoes. I recognize a beige canvas shoe with a hole in the toe, a black winter boot that always pinched, two brown shoes with laces tied together, a rubber boot with a green sole that I wore fishing with Mama, a brown penny loafer with a cracked sole and broken heel that I loved because it was the same as what the other kids were wearing. More and more shoes tumble out. All of them mine. Even my bronzed baby shoe – the length of my thumb – and pink fuzzy bunny slippers tucked one inside the other that had been ordered from the Eaton's catalogue for my third birthday. And last, a white strapped sandal. It lies on top of the pile, fragile and personal as the skeleton of a fish.

I reach down and pick it up. This was my first sandal, bought on the day I began working at the library. It makes me feel strange. That person no longer exists. Still, how familiar the shoe is. The bottom of my foot is imprinted on the insole. As I'm turning it over and over in my hand, the shoe quivers as though gasping for air. Spasms of pity run through me. Shoes tell the story of the soul. Shoes tell the truth.

In one terrified movement I gather myself together. My feet on the floor. My bottom on the chair. My hand holding the pen. I can't see the words. The inner and the outer blackness are the same. Then I hear the sound again – not so much a wheezing as the hiss of Gammer's toothless whistling while she cleans the parlour.

"Gammer?"

I hold my breath, straining forward to listen.

"Gammer?"

It won't stop. That thin almost silent whistling. A ball of yarn is winding from present to past, and once again I am in my secret cave under the round table in the parlour. It's so hot. Mama's gone and my throat aches from not crying. Instead I'm teaching myself to whistle. Pucker and blow. Pucker and blow. The sound's never more than a hair crack from silence. Even a nine-year-old knows she can't whistle and cry at the same time.

The only sound the dull beating of a heart. I feel my bare feet moving across the cold linoleum. When did I take off my socks? All I know is what the soles of my feet are telling me. The Braille of grain in the wood and cracks in the tile. I'm walking towards a mouth, the trapdoor. That thin high crying again. Louder. Closer. Great-Gammer falling down the cellar stairs. I don't want to fall. There's a cold mouldy smell.

☞ DAY EIGHT ☞

I'm waking from a deep sleep, staring at words that are not lying still on the page. They pulse, they grow, one-celled animals coming out *until I be borne until I be borne* the end of my pen. Who *my hand on your mind* is thinking them? Not me. The kitchen table shakes with fear and, looking up, the blind window weeps. The weight of the house sits on my chest. The congealed breath of generations clogs my nostrils. I'm falling. God help me. Is this what happens *my life that you mourne* when you go mad? Is this what it meant when they said that Betty became possessed? That the Devil was living in her body? She couldn't let it out. I can't stay in. Quick! Split in two. Leave my body to protect itself.

But I must keep track. I must write. From a safe distance I will order the words on the page. I will construct something that has a beginning, middle, end, with my body the character and my mind the writer telling her what to do.

And so what must she do? First she must switch the pen from left to right hand. Then she must turn on the lights. All the lights. She must get rid of the dark where things take on a life of their own.

Slowly she stands up and moves to the light switch by the back door. The sudden brightness stabs her eyes. She covers her face with her hands, rocking back and forth as though in great pain. The bulb hanging from a cord in the middle of the kitchen is covered by a wicker shade. The dashes, circles, curlicues of light projected through the loosely woven rattan are transformed into hieroglyphics on the walls and ceiling. But she is not tempted to decipher the message. Instead, hesitantly, a blind woman being led, she makes her way from room to room.

Has there ever been a time when every light in the house, except for Mama's room, is switched on? The house is now alive. The cracks in the walls glower or smile. The uneven floorboards rise to greet her. Even without her touch doors open, curtains part. Every illuminated room is a new stage on which she plays herself. In the parlour, she bows to the massive intricately carved fireplace and then turns to retrieve a nickel she suddenly remembers hiding, when she was six, under the middle cushion of the sofa. In Gammer's room she forces herself to push through the disapproving air and turn on the lamp by the dresser. On the way out, without glancing at the pillow that still holds the shape of Gammer's head, she kneels to stroke the brown felt slippers as though they are kittens asleep on the bedside rug.

In the last room, after switching on the gooseneck lamp beside her own small bed, she rummages through the bureau drawers and picks out a nightgown. As she pulls off each item of clothes she winces slightly as though expecting it to be adhered to her skin. After sliding the white flannel nightgown over her head, she eases herself between the sheets. Finally, with a sigh, she lays her head gently on the pillow, her hair veiling her face.

❧ DAY NINE ❧

Night is fading. A brush stroke of light along the horizon turns the sky the colour of dishwater and slowly drowns the stars. The full moon in the west balances momentarily on the lines of the hydro towers as they march like giant Tinkertoy soldiers across the top of the far hills. In Madawaska Valley the shadows are struggling out of the earth and the farm dogs, turned predatory by the dark, are slinking home with blood on their jowls. A sudden breeze lifts the leaves of the maple trees lining the only street in New Salem and then rushes upland, ruffling the tail feathers of birds roosting on the giant burnt cross. In the dim light of dawn it seems a natural growth, as easy with its oddness as the old stone and timber house where every light has been switched on – except the northwest corner of the second floor. Mama's room.

In her own small back bedroom she lies in her narrow bed curled on her side like a shut drawer of a bureau. She does not know that, as the white of dawn turned to gold, she had been walking in her sleep through the grassy field beside the house, picking flowers bright as the rising sun. Hours pass. The sky, now blue with long straight streaks of clouds like horse tails, foretells bad weather and still she rests peacefully as the dead in the family graveyard.

It's not the steady rasp of Young Mueller's chainsaw in their bordering woods that jolts her awake but the long taut string of sound that she thinks must be Gammer whistling thinly through her badly fitting false teeth as she makes tea and packs her lunch for school. She wishes it could be a peanut butter sandwich like all the other kids' and not pickled eggs and flat bread that looks like a cow pad.

When she opens her eyes to the present moment, she cringes away from the unexpected brightness coming from the bedside lamp. Then she realizes the ceiling light, too, has been switched on, revealing the room as never before. The sickly grey colour of the walls, not painted in years, has the shock of dead flesh. Everything seems closer, more defined – the overweight pine bureau squatting in the corner, the ladderback chair with the sunken seat, the round rug braided from Great-Gammer's silk stockings. Three large fish eyes created by water stains on the ceiling stare down maliciously.

She hears the eerie whistling again and wonders if it could be an echoing from a dream. Still, the thought that Gammer has returned forces her out of bed. She makes her way down the long hall, pausing at Mama's bedroom door to stare at the red imprint of a hand. In the harshness of the ceiling light it seems to be a sign saying, "Stop, go no farther." But she does. It's the summer after Mama. She recalls how, tattooing the five-pointed star, she pressed the ballpoint pen so hard into her palm that the flesh opened. That was when she made the imprint of her bloody hand on Mama's bedroom door. The mark, soaking into the dried-out wood, has become indelible. When scrubbing proved to be unsuccessful, Gammer painted over the door but still, one by one, a ghostly hand was always there.

Her palm throbs with the memory. She presses her hand against the smaller red imprint and whispers, "The body never forgets."

After pressing the scarred palm to her lips, she descends the oak staircase to the foyer. Keeping outside the tent of light falling from the lamp on the table, she turns and walks through the doorway into the kitchen. She halts with surprise. There is no Gammer. The stove is cold.

She finds a handful of dandelions, yellow as sunshine, in a jam jar on the kitchen table. She wonders how they got there. Not seeing the grass stains on her nightgown or feeling the wetness around its hem, her mind jumps back to when she is four years old. She has just picked the dandelions in the grassy field beside the house. She can taste their bitter saw-toothed leaves that will be boiled and served with butter and salt at supper.

How plainly she can see Gammer and Mama sitting on a bench outside the summer kitchen, sorting the mushrooms in their overfilled laps. She supposes they must be talking because their bodies are leaning together. Above their heads, the evening star and the rising moon also lean towards each other in the early dusk.

She doesn't know why people speak at all. How can they listen and talk at once? She herself won't speak. She wanders about the field picking the golden manes of dandelions and listening to the long, slow, rolling motion of voices – so many of them – all making music together. So many languages – the rubbing wings of insects, the burrowing feet of groundhogs, the sad rustling of the dead twitch grass by the fence, the cooing of mourning doves in the jack pines. When the drumming of a woodpecker on the nearby post stops, she becomes aware that the rippling water sound of Mama's low voice is ruffled with worry.

"She'll soon be five years old. I've tried everything but she's just not interested. Do you think she could be...?" Mama touches her head with her forefinger.

"Absolutely not," Gammer's heavy hand slaps at the air, "she understands perfectly. She's plain lazy. Not like you who talked in sentences when you were two. She inherited more than..."

"Stop!" Mama hunches over, covering ears with her hands.

With burning cheeks – Gammer has a way of making words sting like sparks carried on the wind – she runs to where they sit on the bench. The rough wool of Mama's skirt whispers as she presses against it. She holds out the dandelions as a gift. Mama doesn't notice so she moves her lips and tongue together to create the sound *nosegay*.

Mama's hands fall away, her eyes shiny as wet pebbles from the pond. "Did you say *nosegay*?" she asks, and begins to laugh. Sibyl feels her own throat open, their sounds lifting like colourful balloons released into the warm spring breeze. Gammer joins them. One of the rare times the three of them have laughed together.

Wafting on the breeze, their cadences echo off the cliffs of the escarpment and then drift upwards to become a kind of music in the twilight. She will remember this moment. A kind of epiphany. The closest she will ever come to a religious experience.

Then Mama, taking the dandelions, says, "Where did you hear *nosegay*? The first word spoken by most children is *Mama* or *Papa*."

Still wrapped in the euphoria of their laughter, Sibyl dares to repeat under her breath the forbidden word – the one word she knows, without being told, can never be said out loud.

"Papa."

The word hangs in the air like a black hook.

Pressing harder against Mama's knees, she repeats:

"PAPA."

The explosion of her lips startles Mama.

"PAPA PAPA PAPA."

The sounds, loud and dangerous as machine-gun fire, won't stop.

Mama's hand presses hard on Sibyl's mouth. She smells the dank earthy mushrooms as her surprised teeth close on flesh. Mama cries out and jerks her hand away. Gammer stands up and stomps to the house muttering about her having a Devil big as a woodchuck inside.

Frightened by her own outburst, she buries her face in Mama's lap. They both begin to weep, Mama making high tight sounds like the yelping of a kicked puppy.

She is staring at the jam jar with its nosegay of dandelions, still wondering who picked them. Unaware of walking in her sleep, she thinks Gammer must have returned at daybreak and, not wanting to wake her by banging down the ash on the grate, has gone to forage for mushrooms, which would be plentiful because of the wet spring.

Not fully convinced, however, by her own reasoning, she tells herself she must go out and look for her. She eats a handful of stale baking-soda biscuits from the breadbox and, not taking time to dress, grabs Gammer's everyday coat from the hook by the back door. As she steps on the threshold, she hesitates, staring at the white porcelain knob. When she does reach out for it, she bows slightly as though shaking a frail venerable hand. She thinks of the thousands of times it has been grasped by Gammer, by Mama, by all her relatives. It's comforting to imagine the many hands that had been there before hers. Bending over, she kisses the cold porcelain knob just as she once kissed a book before returning it to the library shelf.

She pulls open the inner door and, taking a deep breath, presses down on the latch of the solid oak door. Only when she gives a sharp kick to the bottom does the warped door open with its usual groan, "Dooon't gooo." Even though the windows of the summer kitchen have a winter's worth of grime on them, she cringes, blinded by the intensity of the light. After being shut in the house for days with all the curtains closed, images from the external world appear as sharply coloured glass so thin it will break and cut her if she touches it.

Narrowing her eyes and focusing on the ground before her feet she steps outside. The noonday sun pouring down, hot as burning butter on her head, makes her wince. The vibrant air springing into her lungs causes her heart to race. She wants to turn back to the safety of the house, but the lingering odour of lichen and mushrooms and roots of marsh-marigold drying in the summer kitchen pulls her towards Gammer's slow-moving bulk, which she imagines is somewhere around the boggy edges of the pond.

She moves aimlessly with her head bowed, her arms folded across her chest, her eyes turned inward. As though the mirror she held up to others has now been turned to reflect herself, she is aware of how her own figure stands in dark relief against the throbbing green of the spring day...Gammer's threadbare coat folding around her...matted coils of hair hiding her face...her large bare feet shifting among dirt and pebbles. She could be any woman of any time – a hundred, a thousand, two thousand years ago. A woman who lives and walks alone.

As she wanders down the path, she startles a great blue heron on a dead tree. With wings flailing like a child having a tantrum, it lifts over her head and then, circling the half-acre pond, settles in the cattails on the far side. The water, flat and shiny as a sheet of steel, is always high this time of year because of underground springs. She follows the footprints along the muddy edge, trying to decide if they were made by a muskrat or a beaver. That is when she happens upon the old wood rowboat turned upside down among the tall reeds. She breaks off a brown hollow stalk and blows gently through the larger end. No sound. She blows harder and harder but the primitive reed pipe refuses to be played.

Dizzy now – the sky falling and the earth rising as though she had been whirling – she curls up on the overturned rowboat and tucks her bare feet under Gammer's coat. With her eyes closed, the mind slips away like the time.

Brought back by the distant whistle of the freight train, she is surprised to find the shadow of a willow tree has crept over her. She shivers a little. A slight breeze brings a tender, sad sweet scent – brings, too, the image of the lilac-cologne bottle on Mama's dressing table. She recalls how, shortly before the river took Mama, she was helping to pin up her hair when Mama pulled the gold stopper from the bottle. With a rare smile she dabbed some cologne behind each of their ears.

It was later the same summer that she poured the cologne down the sink and folded into the glass bottle the paper dolls she had cut from the mail-order catalogue. On the apron of the Mama doll she drew a red heart and on the curly blonde hair of baby Sally she put *x* and *o*. With a pen she printed COME HOME on the faces of Dick and Jane, while Spot the dog had small black circles for tears dropping from his eyes. As for Papa doll, who should have saved Mama, she tore off his arms and his one good leg and then threw him into the wood stove.

She sealed the gold stopper with paraffin wax and told herself to wake at dawn when Gammer would be foraging for whatever mushrooms and wild plants had escaped the drought. It was the first time she'd left the property without permission. The pale watery light of the rising sun slid down the shrivelled bushes and trees and pooled on the parched earth. Even this early she could feel the heat sucking her up but still she ran, without stopping, the whole mile to the river. Breaking through the undergrowth on the shore she found, instead of the swift flowing water of the Mad to carry the bottle with its message to Mama, a series of mud holes. In one of them, she discovered the putrid, partially buried carcass of a cow that had sunk too deep to struggle out. She understood that this meant there could never be any hope…for Mama or herself. So she buried the purple bottle under the lilac bush by the front gate and buried her emotions with it. Each spring the lilac bush smelled of Mama's cologne.

It suddenly occurs to her that the purple bottle is proof – concrete as the rowboat beneath her – of the love between her and Mama. She must unearth it.

She makes her way around the pond, head bowed, unaware of the innumerable Painted Lady butterflies as they dart and hover over the shimmering opal grey of the water. And, of course, walking down the lane, she is unaware of the unnamable shades of green as the enclosing poplars and pines weave themselves into the early afternoon sunshine.

When she gets to the road, a crow – unmoving as a forsaken rubber boot – watches from a gatepost as she hunkers down on all fours and crawls under the frothy blossoms of the lilac bush. She digs with her hands in one spot, and then another, like a dog that has forgotten where a bone is buried.

By the time she hears a car approaching it's too late to reach the security of the house. She attempts to crawl farther under the lilac bush. The postman stops his car and rolls down the window. As he is opening the mailbox to put in a letter, he glimpses her under the bush.

"Are you all right?"

She pretends not to hear but he repeats the question. Clearing her throat she mumbles about losing a letter.

"What did you say?"

He leans as if to open the truck door, giving her no choice but to part the branches and crawl out.

"Well, I'd be a monkey's uncle if it ain't Sibyl's granddaughter back from the Big City! Thought you were your granny scrambling for one of them fliers that blowed out of your mailbox. Nobody's seen hide nor hair of you in how long? Must be three years."

She remembers him. Mr. MacDonald. "Fast Mac" the villagers call him, because he is so slow – except for his tongue that never stops moving. While growing up she had considered him part of the mail truck – like the hood or the fender.

Staring at the puffy face and hand holding out a letter, it occurs to her how old and fat and hairless he has become, except for a few white tufts on the crown of his head. His features, washed away in only three short years, have left only his eyes, shrivelled into blue dots. To her it resembles more the head of a caterpillar poking out of his shirt. For a split second she wonders if he is metamorphosing backwards and if Gammer isn't making the same journey.

"How long did you say you've been home? Weeks go by and I don't stop here on the hill, especially now with the union slowdown in the city. Don't bother your granny since the only mail she gets besides seed catalogues are monthly cheques from the government and of course tax bills. Death and taxes you can't escape."

Fast Mac snickers and rubs his pudgy hands together. Shifting from one bare muddy foot to another, she mumbles under her breath.

"Guess you must've took the late bus. That explains why last night, when I got up – can't sleep through the night anymore – I saw all your windows lit up. Without my glasses I thought for a moment your house was on fire. Never known your granny to turn on a light. Even though her remedies keep the old-church-turned-store in business, she won't change her ways. Aggie Porter told me she tried to persuade her to buy an electric stove but she wouldn't hear of it. I don't blame her. Electricity is expensive this far from the city. A penny saved is a penny earned. Yup, that's what we were taught, your granny and me."

As Fast Mac is talking she begins to shiver and pulls the thin coat more tightly to her body. He continues without a pause, but his voice softens around the edges.

"Sure as shootin' she ain't going to approve of you walking around with bare feet. It's been hot as July which got the lilacs blooming early, but now the sun's gone under there's a chill in the air. My Myrtle got pneumonia last spring and was in bed a month. In the end it wasn't the antibiotics that worked but your granny's poultices, though I must admit they smelled stronger than cat piss."

She is drawn closer and closer to his voice – comforting as a cup of warm milk. She recognizes the odour of ham and dill pickle, the sandwich he ate for lunch. An envelope is waved under her nose.

"This one's for you. Same name as your granny but sure as the Pope's Catholic it ain't her getting a letter from the city police."

Her face contracts. Fast Mac peers up at the graveyard behind the house. "Holy Moly, what a racket them crows are making! Seen turkey vultures circling down from the escarpment this past week. You or your granny best check out the back pasture. May find a carcass of a sheep. Farmers around here are complaining of losing livestock. They say it's wolves. Me? I think it's their dogs that's gotten a taste of blood and go hunting when the moon's bright."

She stares at the envelope in her hand. She is not listening to Fast Mac who is watching the flock of crows.

"Speaking of the moon," he continues, scratching a black-fly bite behind his ear, "have you taken a look the last few nights? Never in my lifetime did I see one so large making its way up the sky. Needless to say, Myrtle, whose mother was half Huron, hasn't slept a wink. When I pointed to your house with the light coming through all them curtained windows she said it reminded her of a ship in full sail. Not that she's seen one except on the TV. It must've been the time of year brought it to mind. Other places get April showers bringing May flowers but here in the valley we get May ghosters. Thank the Lord the violence of them storms from the northeast don't last much more than an hour. Of course up here on the hill you get the full blast of all the weather."

It's Fast Mac's turn to shiver. "Lordy!" he exclaims, "that wind's sharp enough to skin a Turk." Struggling with arthritic fingers to zipper his jacket over his round belly, he mumbles, "If it's not too nosy, could I ask why, after decades of never switching on a light, not one but all the lights in the house on the hill have been turned on?" When he looks up, she has already started up the lane towards the house. He calls, "Give my regards to your granny. Ain't laid eyes on her in more than a week. Hope her ticker's not been acting up again. Aggie tells me it's been keeping her up at night."

She turns her head slightly and waves but keeps on walking.

As Fast Mac drives away he gives a friendly toot of goodbye on the truck's horn, but she does not respond. She is concentrating on her fingers that keep turning over and over the letter from the police department as though perfecting a magic trick. Each step she takes grows slower as though her body is winding down. Then, outside the back door, she stops dead as the clock in the hall. She can't go on. And she can't go back. She collapses on the wood bench where, for the past century, Witherspoons have rested between chores. Not long ago she had been sitting on another bench in the parkette outside the bus terminal, waiting for the morning bus that would bring her back to New Salem.

She had stretched out her legs and, with her head against the back of the bench, she was attempting to doze. Lids half-closed, she watched a woman with long legs and long blonde hair saunter past. The woman's trench coat was buckled tight to her small waist and the white material clung effortlessly as she sat down on the adjacent bench.

Her thoughts had drifted off. From a great distance, a voice that she did and did not recognize said something about her shoe. Opening her eyes, she was startled to find a man kneeling before her. His long tapered fingers were peeling away a wet Mars bar wrapper from the sole of her shoe with such care it could have been a layer of her skin. Although his face was hidden, she recognized both the hat with eagle feathers stuck in its brim and the long strangely cut coat made from animal hides. It belonged to the handsome panhandler who hung around the library entrance – the one Lou called Pan the Wild Man, the one who found her on the night she can't remember, the one who her mind finds repulsive but her body is pulled towards.

Brushing the dust from the chocolate wrapper and examining both sides, he delicately folded it into the bulging pocket of his coat. "God must be dead or not yet come," he sighed. "All these years of waiting, of collecting every scrap of paper in the streets, and not once has He sent a message." He sighed again, "I am so alone."

Shaking his head, the man stood up and their eyes met. She couldn't break his gaze. The more she looked the more beautiful his face became – as though he were lit from within by a dark

212

passionate longing. She thought of the eyes of Christ on the cover of a religious magazine that Mama kept in her dresser drawer. Except this holy face, less than a foot from hers, was lined with anguish as though he, too, had hung on the cross and sucked on the sponge soaked in vinegar.

He leaned in closer. She breathed in the rich earthy smell of his animal-hide coat mixed with something green and spicy. Behind her eyes appeared a branch ripped from one of Gammer's apple trees after a summer storm. He must have been peering into her brain because he began talking about the world shrinking to the size of an apple and the earth's crust, thin as an apple skin, being all that saved us from the liquid fire.

Spreading his arms, he cried out like a preacher, "Don't be afraid of the falling. Let yourself go. Go with the flow of burning lava. Don't be afraid. Follow your heart. Break apart. Break apart." As if obeying his words, his coat parted and she was only inches away from his muscular body.

She recoiled against the back of the park bench while at the same time he took a bright red apple out of his coat pocket and began to polish it on the cuff of his sleeve. Although she kept her eyes down, she was pulled towards the full rich sound of his words telling her that wherever there is a man and woman there is Adam and Eve, and wherever there is Adam and Eve there is the serpent, and wherever there is the serpent there is the forbidden fruit…

Leaning even closer, he whispered, "I see you under the thick lashes of your eyes, the bright coils of your hair. I see you exploding – exploding with life, with the need to know," and he handed her the apple.

When she hesitated in taking it, he sighed, "Please don't be afraid," and touched her arm ever so gently, but still it burned through her coat, her sweater, her skin.

"Don't let this crazy panhandler harass you." The woman in the white raincoat said in a loud shrill voice.

In a single motion, the man turned and doffed his wide-brimmed hat. "Here I am. Pan the Godman at your service."

The woman seemed to be stunned – not by his head, bald as an egg, but by the glistening blue-and-red tattoo of a serpent coiled around it. Tossing his hat on the ground, he bowed deeply to her and then began to dance – a polite gentle waltz – around the park bench on which she was sitting. He had the powerful grace of a lion, and as he swayed and turned his coat opened so the woman, too, could glimpse the rippling movements of his body.

At the same moment as the woman grabbed for the purse in her lap, the Panman pounced, landing in a crouched position at her feet.

"My lovely Luna," he whispered, "right here, right now, trace your fingertips over a god's naked head and feel the light."

The woman jumped to her feet, "You lunatic!"

"La lune, la lune," he sang out. "I am her servant, her consort here on earth. Oh the horror! The bliss! To be a god and man and animal."

"No, you're just an animal. A filthy feral dog!"

The Panman, who was still crouching before her, threw back his head as though he was about to laugh but instead let out a long high howl.

The woman's cheeks flamed. "Drunk or crazy, I don't care," she shouted. "I'm calling the cops."

As she charged across the parkette, he called, "Come back my Alabaster Aphrodite with your long curving bones and your long shining hair. Come to the Festival of Pan. Nature is dead and reason rules the world but the Great God is not dead. Mad, yes, yes, YES. A rock is a rock. A tree is a tree…"

He grew louder, more frantic. People rushing by on their way to work were turning to look. Wishing to flee, Sibyl stood awkwardly shifting her weight from foot to foot like a duck with pinioned wings.

He began pounding the sides of his head with his fists. "The only wilderness that remains is in here. I must open the gates. Let out the wild, the wild…"

A woman in a red coat stopped and pointed. A tall thin man with a briefcase turned as if to walk towards them. Sibyl picked the Panman's hat off the ground and handed it to him, saying, "Shhh, shhh," as though comforting a child.

His arms fell to his sides and he sighed. "You are my Earth Angel, my Heavenly Eve." As he spoke his eyes turned from deep brown to golden. She could not break away from his stare – so intense, so brilliant, that it entered her. She heard herself gasp.

"Don't be afraid," the Panman whispered as though she, alone, existed in the world. "Every day I've been worshipping you from afar. Catching sight of you…"

He stopped and, looking away, began rubbing his shaved head in the manner of Gammer polishing the lamp on the fireplace mantle. While Sibyl watched, half expecting to see the tattooed snake uncoil, he sighed, "You must think me mad." Then, with a shy smile, he added, "I am," and began to croon, "Oh earth angel, earth angel, please be mine, you turn my blood to hot mulled wine. Oh earth angel, earth angel, I am out of my head, you turn my body to freshly baked bread. Oh earth angel, earth angel, what can I do? I'm sad glad mad with love for you."

While he sang he swayed. And she swayed too. He reached out his hand to her and she took it. Then she was holding him and he was holding her. As their two bodies swaying together became two parts made whole, he whispered, "This meeting was planned as life on earth began. That is why the single-celled protozoa divided into two, why the fish crawled out of the sea and the bird grew a feather and soared over the green blankets of wilderness. That is why the monkey stood up and a toe became a thumb and a stick became a club and two sticks rubbed together became a fire. And that is why the same dumb instinctive reproduction of genes occurred over and over again. Yes, my perfect protoplast, chance or God has done nothing but prepare – through three-and-a-half billion years – for this moment."

They were cheek to cheek, heart to heart, pelvis to pelvis, dancing a stately waltz around the parkette to music only they could hear. And the boundaries of skin vanished and the molecules in the world around them became part of their swaying and swirling. They were the pigeons fluttering from their path, the empty wine bottle rolling in the gutter, the dog lifting its leg on the fire hydrant, the electricity pulsing through the wires above their heads, until, gasping for breath, she tore herself out of his arms.

Dizzy and dishevelled, she told the Panman she had to go home. "Home?" he said, "Home? Your skin is your home. Same as a grizzly bear or a mountain lion. Same as me. Oh my love, my love, you and I must be free – free as the wildest of beings or we will die."

Jerking away with bags of water for legs, she hauled herself across the parkette. She didn't look back when he called, "Let the dam break. Be mad. Be the maddest of nomads in no man's land."

Pushing through the revolving doors of the bus station she saw the woman in the white trench coat. "This is the person," the woman said to a police officer, "who witnessed that crazy man sexually harassing me. He harassed her…"

The officer interrupted, asking Sibyl to point out which man was responsible. She could still feel him rushing through her veins, smell his odour of wood smoke and wine, hear his words, "Be the maddest of nomads in no man's land." The woman shook Sibyl's arm. "What's wrong? Why are you protecting that panhandler? He's a sicko and should be put away."

"Is that him?" asked the officer. "The man wearing the hat with the feathers stuck in the brim?"

Sibyl nodded.

"Speak up," said the police officer.

"Yes," the word raked her throat coming out. She wiped her hand across her lips as though there could be blood.

When the officer asked for her name and address, she choked and coughed. "Now, now, don't be nervous," he said, awkwardly patting her back. "Our job is to protect you from those creeps."

Then he handed his pad and pen to her. "Just fill in the information on this complaint form and we'll do the rest."

A message over the loudspeaker announced that her bus was leaving from gate five. Thrusting the pad back into his hand, she whispered, "I have to go home. It's an emergency."

Seeing the bus nosing out of the station, she ran outside. The Panman reached for her arm as she passed. "Don't be afraid," he pleaded. But she was afraid – afraid because every cell in her body wanted to go to him.

"You're going to be arrested," she said, and ran to where the bus had stopped for a red light. As she pounded on the door she heard him call, "Dementia veritas. Dementia veritas. Don't be afraid."

Through the window of the bus she watched while the Panman – who was paying no attention to the police officer – took off his black hat and threw it up in the air. Silhouetted against the morning sun, its broad-brimmed shape became a bird.

❖ ❖

A sudden cacophony of sounds startles her into the present.

She is surprised to find that the sun has begun to sink beyond the far hills and, even as layers of luminous clouds fill the air, shadows are spreading over the valley. Looking up she sees crows and ravens squabbling for a roosting place on the charred cross – their soulless laughter mimicking the mad.

Before entering the house, she wipes her muddy feet on the mat, not noticing that they are bare. Using force to open the warped wood door, she is greeted by a cube of light that becomes the kitchen. The brightness gives finality to each object – the stuffed deer's head glaring down reproachfully, the slight sway of the empty rocking chair – but she, looking only at the black iron stove in the corner, moves as if hypnotized to where it sits, cold and sinister. Taking the envelope from the city police out of her pocket, she rips it open and reads "…currently being detained for observation. Do you wish to proceed…"

She strikes a match and ignites a corner of the letter. As it burns she has a feeling – an uncomfortable twisting and turning around of herself – that has no words.

Only when a flame licks her fingers does she drop the page into the stove. She crumples the envelope to put on top, lays some kindling, and watches to make sure that the fire will catch. As she waits, the sudden scraping of metal against wood caused by the evening breeze tugging at a loose screen forces her to turn. Although the kitchen blind is lowered, she realizes it is nearing night and the light through the curtained windows – transforming the house into Myrtle's ship under full sail – will draw the attention of the villagers.

And worse, Young Mueller will know she has not returned to the city. If she doesn't answer his knock, suppose he tries to force his way in? She rushes from room to room, from electric switch to electric switch. Only after the last light has been turned off, and she is standing in the gloom of the front hall, does she wonder about the desk lamp in her small study off the parlour. Pulling aside the heavy velvet curtain covering the parlour entrance, her body freezes like a night animal blinded by the glare of a headlight. She lunges forward and the light disappears, leaving her in a dark so dense and dazzling she can see nothing.

As her sight gradually returns she realizes what has happened. A crack in the drawn shades of the west-facing windows has allowed a narrow beam from the setting sun to shoot straight through the parlour, ricochet off the pewter lamp on the fireplace mantle and back across the room to momentarily blind her as she entered.

Watching the sunlight strike the shiny surface of the lamp, she recalls how the Panman had rubbed his bald head with the same circular motions as Gammer polishing the lamp. She feels his presence, violently alive, beside her. She hears him say, "You and I must be free," and she thinks of his truth, of his persecution, and in solidarity with him she knows what she must do...

With ease and speed she moves through the house gathering her instruments and laying them, precisely, beside the tub in the bathroom. Once she has removed her coat and nightgown, she feels vulnerable as a snail without its shell and quickly climbs into the bathtub and turns on the faucet. The cold water surprises her. She has forgotten that the water heater must first be switched on. Although her skin feels like it's growing a layer of ice, she begins.

She picks up the scissors. With one hand she grabs hold of a length of hair and with the other hand snips it off as close as possible to her scalp. Watching the strands fall into the water, she repeats this process until nothing remains to be cut. Then she lathers her head with soap and, chanting *dementia veritas dementia veritas*, carefully glides the razor around and around until her skull is bald as the outcropping of rock on the escarpment. Next she sticks her head under the faucet and turns on the water to wash away the soap.

Her long naked shape, gleaming in the darkness, rises out of the water. She dries herself and puts on a clean nightgown. She touches her head and rubs her palm around her shaved skull. She finds it soothing although it hurts where the razor has grazed her skin, especially the slightly rough patch on her left temple.

With Panman's catlike grace, she glides through the house to stand before the fireplace in the parlour. She nods, as if in agreement with what someone is saying, and picks up the box of matches next to the oil lamp on the mantle. When she cannot ignite the wick, she pulls on it until she reaches a length soaked in oil. She snips it close to the base with the scissors kept for that purpose in the matchbox. Then, with a touch of the flame from a struck match, she is engulfed in a halo of light.

Stepping back, she stares at the lamp – the oldest, most sacred possession of the house. With great care she curves both hands around the base and, lifting it up, kisses it. That's when she sees, in the circle left by the lamp in the dust, a large iron key with square teeth and long shank. It is the same one Mama used to open the hope chest on the morning of her tenth birthday. Shifting the lamp to her left hand, she picks up the key. The weight and balance of it in her palm makes her think of a small ancient instrument designed for intricate surgery.

This is where it has been hidden all these years. She recalls how each time Gammer finished polishing the lamp she would repeat, "Remember, Sibyl, it's always darkest under the lamp." It was one of her riddles that Sibyl felt referred to her father who, because he could never be mentioned, was implicated in everything that Gammer or Mama said. He was the absence that lay like a circle of darkness under her childhood. Now she could shed light upon it.

Dropping the key into the pocket of her nightgown, she holds the lamp high and crosses the parlour. In its living light, the walls and ceiling curve as though to protect her while even the smallest object creates a fantastic shadow. As she passes the grandfather clock in the hall, it sways and bows like a drunk guard. At Mama's door she does not bend to look through the keyhole but stares at the bloody imprint of her childhood hand that, in the lamplight, is beckoning. With the touch of her hand on the china knob, the door opens.

The faintly sweet odour of dead lilacs and dust draws her over the threshold. Shadows multiply, leaping back from the flame of the lamp dancing wildly in the draft created by the opening door. Wishing the glass shade had not been broken long years ago, she cups her hand around the flame.

Crossing the floor, she puts the lamp down and kneels before the Lebanon cedar chest – burnished to the colour of ebony by many polishings, but now grey with dust. She removes the key from her pocket and cautiously inserts it into the ornate lock. It won't turn. She attempts more force. Only by using the key as a wedge to pry the hope chest open is she finally able to raise the top enough to slip in her hand and then her arm. A dry dead smell grabs at her throat making her cough. She moves her hand around inside but can feel nothing. She reaches deeper. Her fingers touch something and she lifts out a large manila envelope. Inside she finds a thin square box, the kind that once held silk handkerchiefs, and removing its cover she sees a sheaf of parchment papers yellowed to the colour of weak tea. On top is an envelope.

Lowering herself to sit cross-legged on the floor, she holds the letter in the circle of lamplight and reads…

My child,

Tonight the star I have been following, the star that led me to your mother, rose huge and bright to announce that your soul, your life's star, has unfurled into the world. It's been two hundred and seventy nights of loneliness and longing since your unstoppable need to come into being. Two hundred and seventy nights of waiting and watching since the white light of your soul penetrated the black egg of your body. You, my dearest, are the only child of two only children. You, my darling, are the last descendent of two families entwined by a shameful event that took place three hundred years ago.

When I was young enough for our backyard to be Paradise, on hot summer afternoons my granny and I would sit in the shade of a huge magnolia tree. She loved to talk and, while sipping ice tea, would tell me cautionary tales that ran like sap through our family tree. The oldest and most repeated story told about one of our ancestors, Elizabeth Proctor, who was betrayed by her trusted maidservant during the frenzy of the Salem witch hunts. She made a point of telling me that it was in all the history books and a famous play had been written about it. She always began with, "In the same way that Jesus was betrayed by Judas…" and ended with, "Let this be a lesson to you, Johnnie. The closer you are to someone the more likely they will betray you."

Now, beloved child, as the last unfurling leaf on our tree of life, these enclosed letters belong to you. I discovered them in a scratched and dented tin hatbox in an attic crawl space that had not been entered since my ancestor built the house two hundred years ago. The ink used in writing the letters has so faded that I can make out

only an odd word and the date 1692. If you, too, find them unread-
able, I am sure that any number of museums collecting and pre-
serving historical documents would be pleased to receive them.
Remember though, history can only construct and deconstruct the
events of the past. It cannot resurrect the dead. That can only be
done by delving as deep as the darkest understanding of your self.

By the miracle of your birth, my child, I pray that you will
choose to keep, and to muse over, these letters passed down through
generations of our family.

I love your beautiful mama more than all the stars in the night
sky. I know she loves me too. And just as our ancestor was delivered
up, so I have proven false to your mama's trust. It is the barbwire I
wear like thorns around my heart.

Each time, bowing my head before the evening star, I ask that
I may suffer to the fullest.

Forever and ever,
Your Papa

"Papa," she whispers, kissing the letter. It is his only acknowl-
edgement of her. Carefully she folds the letter in the creases that
already exist and returns it to the envelope.

Then, untying the sheaf of papers, she lifts out the first page
– so brittle and fragile that the edges break under her touch –
and lays it on top of the hope chest. Next she turns up the flame
of the lamp as high as possible without letting it smoke.

For a long time she gazes intently at the indefinite markings.
She recognizes a scattering of letters and a few words, but nothing that makes sense. The inconstancy of the light gives the
paper the appearance of being unsteady, tremulous as a tiny pool
of water. This brings to her mind how she and Rosie practiced
the art of divining by dropping hot wax into a basin of water.

Neither of them could agree on what the amorphous shapes floating on the water told of their future.

She pores over the first letter, not moving, until the almost invisible writing reveals itself.

April 6th, 1692
After the waggon left for Jail

To my Mistress Elizabeth Proctor,

I be out on the stoop scraping plattes into the slop pail when I heerd the wheels clanging over the frozen mudd & dung of the barnyard. Shading my eyes from the sun I stood in the doorway to watch you & Mr. Proctor drive off. While I be staring at the back of your hooded cloak & his huge shoalders my week'r eye began drifting upwards so at the same time I be glimpsing tops of trees & blue skie.

Thats when th'Angels appeer'd at the edge of my sight. Thousands of them. Dancing acrosse the Heavens. Dancing like a path of sunlight across water.

I fell to my nees. Cover'd my face with my armes. But 'twas as tho I be seeing with my Soule. Befor me rised up a bull bigg'r than Gallows Hill with hornes the shape of new moons. Chained to his shoalder a mightie bird of prey be ripping at his flesh.

Then it all disappeer'd in a whirlwind of fethers & blood & I fellt words like handes of the Lord being laied upon my hed — Feer not, Mary, they saied, thou hast found favour with the Lord. Thru thee the unseen shall be seen. Thru thee the bound shall be freed.

Next I remember I be lieing on my back in a puddel from the overturn'd slop buckett & staring up at the skie thru chinks in the roof.

Rite awaie I know'd 'twas a Revelashun cuz of the dazzeling dark befor my eyes. Also I know'd, Mrs. Proctor, that the bull chained to the bird of prey be Mr. Proctor chained to you. Husband to wife. Erthe to Hell.

With my heart pounding hard as hoofs I pickt up my sopping skirt & ran outside. I want'd to warn Mr. Proctor to wait for the

Constabul. Not to take you by himself to Jail. Altho I ran all the waie to the gate the waggon be too farr downe the road for him to hear me calling.

After much thot & pray'r I hav decided, Mrs. Proctor, to tell you of my vishun. 'Tis a warning to you as much a promise to me. Take heed. Tho I am only eighteen and your servant I am speshull. The Lord has chosen me to reveel your witchcraft.

When my left eyeball comes unbound I hav seconde sight. I can see th'invisibel world bulging in from th'edges of thinges. You be scared of what I will find out. Thats why you beet me 'bout the hed saieing eyes must work together same as ox'n in a yoke. Thats why you tell everyone my eye be a signe of weeknesse in the hed and not to take serieusly what I be seeing.

But now I am not alonne. Them other girls hav cried out at you. Now they will beleev that when you be lifting your arme to beat me I truely didd see a brown growth like a nippel in your arm pitt. Abbie saies while you be in Jail it will be prick't with a needel & if there be no sensashun that proves 'tis a witches teat for suckeling imps & demons.

For a long time peepul have suspecked that magpie of yourn, Mrs. Proctor, be a demon helper. 'Tis unnatural for a wild bird to swoop out of nowhere & perch on a personnes shoalder.

My Soule shivers to think of it. The waie it glares with them round black eyes – lifeless as beeds sewn to the sides of its hed – while chatt'ring in your ear a languige without words. A languige only you understand.

In a few weeks or mor there will be a Heering to decide if the evidence against you warrants a trial at the Court of Oyer & Terminer. Altho I am one of those that your specter self torments Mr. Proctor will not allow me to go. He saies us girls be acting madd as March hares to get attenshun & if tied to our spinning wheels we will be cured fast enuff.

Since you both refused to attend the Heering for them oth'r three witches you did not see how we swoon'd & writh'd & howl'd when the accused be brot in. The magistrates called us bloodhounds of the Lord.

Soon everyone between Salem & Boston shall know who I am. Then the Governor himself shall listen to me. Even Mr. Proctor. Tho since you be accused of witchcraft he does not speek but lookes unutterabel thinges at me. Eech time I feel kikt in the head.

In truth & trust
I remain your servant
Mary Warren

April 9th, 1692

After Morning Prayers

To my mistress Elizabeth Proctor,

Now that Mr. Proctor be taking a pacquet of vitalls every daie to the Jailhouse 'tis eesy to slip in your letters. He warn'd me not to tell anyone – not even the littel ones – so he must hav brib'd the guard.

I hav much to saie & you best not laff like you alwaies donne when I spoke the truth to you. Speshully I hated how – if Mr. be 'round – you would roll your eyes & chuckel so it seem'd you be indulging me. And that soft hollow chuckelling, Mrs. Proctor, be like an echo of your magpie. 'Tis not a human sound.

Abbie agrees with me. She been here yesterdaie for tea & the haires on her armes stood up when she herd the magpies evil laffing in the branches of the bigge elm. Then when she seen it flie onto the back of Shep & start picking at the poor old dogge's open sores she cover'd her eyes & cried out that bird deserves to be hanged. Without a dowt, Mrs. Proctor, you will soon be hanged & I donn't want you crying out at me when meeting the Lord, face to face, for your Final Reckoning.

Since the Revelashun I no longer feer you. With the help of th'Almightie I shall stopp you from destroying Mr. Proctor. I know how much you feer him. His animal strength. His animal lawes. Being almost seven feet high he alwaies gettes his own waie. Peepul shake their head & saie he be more like Samson than Solomon.

I beleev them. I beleev he be the strong'st man next to God. Not alwaies good but then why should he be? God be not good. God be God. And you Mrs. Proctor? You be like Delilah. You want to find the secrett of his power. Thats why you be pacting with the Devil tho Mr. Proctor donn't beleev it. He beleevs only what he sees.

I remember the first time I seen your specter self. 'Twas last summer after you rode off to a Quilting Bee on the Meetinghouse Green. An xcuse, Mr. Proctor saied, for gathering heersaie from the other goodwives. Tho I had not left the farme for som months you told me to staie with the babee who be weak'nd by the Bloody Flux.

While heeting water in the bigg iron cauldron to wash its clouts & coverlettes my wand'ring left eye cawt somethinge moving. I thot your cloake hung by the open door be blowing in the wind. But no, Mrs. Proctor, 'twas your specter. Same as you but loos'r looking as tho your bones be made of jelly.

As you slid towards me I seen your eyes be emptie holes. Your face twist'd & white like it be burnt by acid. My holl'ring brot Mr. Proctor running from the house. As I throw'd myselfe into his armes I fellt you strangeling me. Your handes on my neck greesy & cold as intestines pull'd from a fresh kill'd goat.

Mr. Proctor must hav been standing on the hem of my skirt cuz when he tried to push me awaie he rippt it. I lost my balance & fell to the floor with him on top of me. Thats when your specter self crosst my legges with so much force they poppt out of joint & Mr. Proctor for all his strength could not uncrosse them. Not without breaking them he saied.

Even then he wouldn't beleev me. Even when I point'd to your specter standing beside him he saied 'twas his shadow. Threten'd to ram a hott pok'r down my throate if I diddn't stopp screeming your name.

Thats why now I be too scared to tell him 'bout the Revelashun. For sure he would wopp me. Perhaps send me awaie.

Later

After Cockshut

I be sitting near the winddowe listening for Mr. Proctors hors. The only sounds be the bull kikking at the slattes of his small stall & the calling of a whip-poor-will down by the creek. Makes me bone lonely to hear it.

Mr. Proctor saies its wisiling be an omen the frost has gon from the ground. Time to start plowing but he & the two old'st nev'r be here. They ride farr as Ipswich trying to gett persons to signe a petishun saieing you be a dilligent attend'r upon Gods Holy Ordinances.

Wonnt do no good, Mrs. Proctor. Again todaie th'Almightie reveel'd He be on my side by helping me find that strawe doll of yourn.

I be in the smoakhouse unhooking a legge of bacon for dinner when I seen it wedg'd in a crack between chimney & wall. 'Twas wearing clowthes made from Mr. Proctors shirt & the pin peercing the place between his legges be winded with haires so black & thick that I know they came from his hed. I recall at the Harvest Feest Daie you be fureus cuz of his flirty looks at the Widow Brown. You reminded him how one snip of your curv'd scissors fix'd the wandering of his favourite hound.

I wager you be practicing the Black Artes. I should show the strawe doll to Mr. Proctor & warn him where theres smoak theres fire. But it will do no good. He will giv my ears a box & saie to stop repeeting the village heersaie.

Perhaps thats why he wonnt lett me com to the Heering & see you xamined by them Magistrates. He hates their high-fal-lutin waies. Powder'd pigges in wigges he calls them.

He must be scared I will cry out in publick just like that starkel'd nitwitt daughter of Reverent Parris cried out on their slave & then fell into a fitt. Abbie tell'd me she laie on the floor gasping & writhing like a long white fish thrown up on the shore.

Since you be taken to jail, Mrs. Proctor, the wave of afflict'd girles growes bigg'r. They saie it be cuz erly April comes midwaie between winter & summer solstsis when the influence of the moon be the great'st.

Confess, Mrs. Proctor, Satan took you for his bride. The Lord shall forgive you. So shall I. So shall all of Salem – town & village.

Confess & they shant hang you. They knowe we be born damn'd. All of us lost from the Lord. Lost as leeves that loosn'd from a tree be blowing forever in the wind.

With trust & hope

Mary Warren

Bloodhound of the Lord

April 10th, 1692
Forenoon, Sitting on the stoop

To My Mistress,

The first warm breezes be coming from the West. Day &
Night I heer them shaking the willows from sleep & now the
budds be the sise of a mouses ear.

Your littel ones be on the creek bank cutting branches to feed
the bull. I can heer 'em laff abov the peep of froglings and the
faroff ringing of an axe. Must be Mr. Sheldon cleering land on
the other side of Gallows Hill.

Erly this morn while hanging out the wash I pegg'd my pet-
ticot to Mr. Proctors breeches. As I be watching them cling &
sway in the wind – dancing togeth'r as we nev'r can – I glim'st
out of the corner of my week eye flashes of hellgreen flames by
the back steppes. Turn'd out 'twas crocus leeves poking up from
dirty crusts of snowe.

As I pickt the wee purple blooms I thot of them sleeping
curl'd in their bulbs all winter. Then I thot of my heart sleeping
curl'd in my body. Waiting like these flow'rs donne for the
warmth of the sun. Waiting for Mr. Proctor.

Since you be in jail eech time I put my hand on my con-
shence it comes out black as pitch. I must confess I love Mr.
Proctor. Thats the truth. Last week I tell'd him when he looks at
me I go week as a rained-on bee. He laff'd & laff'd & ask'd me
if I tell'd you.

I donnt care, Mrs. Proctor, I knowe he loves me even tho he
donnt showe it. He cannt help him selfe. The Lord ordain'd it.
Diddnt He give me the gift of seeing the visibel & th'invisibel
meeting at th'edges of my sight? That be so I could reveel your
witchcraft.

Take heed Mrs. Proctor. 'Tis no sinne to cheet the Devil. Old
Hornie, Mr. Proctor calls him.

Yours truthfully

Mary Warren

Bloodhound of the Lord

April 11th, 1692
Spring Feest Daie

Dear Mrs. Proctor,

All night I toss't & turn'd like butter in a churn. Theres no relying on a starrie evening to giv one plesant dreems.

I woke to Mr. Proctors footsteppes on the stairs. Even in his stockings he qwakes the howse. That heavy menacing walk of his'n alwaies seems 'bout to gather into a rush.

This be the third morn Mr. Proctor has rode awaie befor the cock crow'd. So farr twentie-seven persons sign'd the petishun on your behalf. But nobodie from Salem village. They saie Mr. Proctor ownes 4 howses & 700 acres of the best lands & still he donn't paie his ministrie tax.

Two daies ago Reverent Parris stopp't him on the Village Green & saied to xpect a heavy fine. They argued & Mr. Proctor lost his temp'r. Poking the Reverent in the chest with his forefinger he saied no man whose eyebrows meet could be trust'd. Not even an ordain'd Minister.

After the Reverent yell'd that he be a devilish churlish uncivil dogge Mr. Proctor accus'd him of being mor interest'd in his salarie than in saving Soules.

Then the Reverent clasp't his handes togeth'r & throw'd back his hed crying O Lord protect us from blasfeemers. At that moment he be shat on from above by a big pidgin. Nobodie could stopp themselves from laffing.

Abbie who been there saied the Reverent grow'd green-looking as an erly apple & seem'd 'bout to vomitt. Todaie she tell'd me he plannes to file for sland'r. Being the Reverents neece she knowes all 'bout the goings-on at the Parsonage. And being best friends we tell eech oth'r everythinge.

Did you remember, Mrs. Proctor, this be the annual Spring Feest Daie to celebrate the end of our long winter & the incoming of shippes with salt & sugar & foreign news? They saie Governor Phipps return'd afer five yeares of perswading King James to giv our colony a new charter.

I am longing to go to the Meeting-Howse but Mr. Proctor saies the maddness of one be making many madd. He forbiddes me to take the littel ones.

Since you be gon they keep crying off & on. They paie me no heed. Mor like littel caged animales they eet what they will & sleep where they fall. They cann't be mising you, Mrs. Proctor, cuz you never be 'round. You staied all daie in front of the house overseeing the Taverne Room. Gossiping with the men.

I nev'r told you this but Abbie overherd Mrs. Parris saie you licents as a taverne keep'r might be revoked even tho the front roome be th'only Ordinarie to wet one's whisel between town & village.

Mrs. Proctor why donnt you paie attenshun to what peepul saie 'bout you? Speshully to what I saie. You never com to the Meeting-Howse with Mr. Proctor & me & the littel ones. On Lecture Daies you be too busy in the Ordinarie. To Labour be to pray you alwaies saied.

On the Sabbath you be too tired xcept it be a Feest Daie. Then you would gett gussied up in that wool'n cloak you order'd from Boston & them leather gloves with the pearl buttons.

There still be time to sav your Soule. Confess, Mrs. Proctor. Confess that the Devil holds you in the hollow of his hande. Confess befor his hande closes into a fist & you be broken to bits like a clod of erthe.

In truth &loyalty
Mary Warren
Bloodhound of the Lord

April 12th, 1692
After boiling up deer fat for candels

Dear Mrs. Proctor,

For over two winters I hav been living in your shadowe under the roof of a man who be neither my father nor my husband. Alwaies I be in the back of the house doing a wifes chores. Waiting for Mr. Proctor. Waiting since the daie I arriv'd & he lift'd me out of the waggon. Staring at me with them eyes – black & wild as any hunting animal – while my heart flippt-floppt like a scared bird in a cage.

Do you remember the first winter, Mrs. Proctor? In the evenings after th'Ordinarie closed & the littel ones been in bedde I would quilt on the bigg frame in the corner of the middelroom while Mr. Proctor & you sat in the warmth of th'inglenook. He in his deep chair whitteling them flee trappes we wear'd 'round our neckes. You in your rocker clucking over the book where the tavern ernings be recorded.

You wouldn't knowe how I used to stare at Mr. Proctor. Outlined in the crimson glowe of the fire he be so strong & solitarie & solem looking. Like the Angel who pour'd the Lords Seeds into Marys ear.

Do you remember the time, Mrs. Proctor, when you been clapperclawing about something that happen'd in the Taverne & he reach't over to tapp your nee. Elizabeth, he saied, you could talk the Devil out of a witches howse. You toss'd your hed & reply'd I already talked the Devil of a handsom man into the howse. Mr. Proctor shook your knee saieing, stop this comeupance or you will be wearing a scold's bridle but not on your hed. Then you both looked long at eech other & gone up to bedde.

You didnn't knowe Mrs. Proctor how that look splitt my heart in two. Just like one of them aspens behind the howse

236

splitting in the cold. Its dry crack echoing from tree to tree to tree.

Even after all this time when I heer his stamping outside the backe door – three times with eech boot to knock off the mudd or snowe – I cann no more stoppe my heart from pounding than a dogge upon his masters return cann stoppe his wagging tail.

Specially in winter when he has been hunting cuz then I gett to rubb polecatt oil into his feete to cure the rheumatisme. Who would guess with his face weather riven'd as a hilltop that his feete be so pink & smooth & warm. Like fresh skinn'd rabbits in my handes.

I wager you haven't seen the scarr – shaped like a wee clov'n hoof – on the outside of his left foot. Nobodie but me knowes he be born with six toes. His Mama birth'd alonne while hiding in a root cellar during an Indian raid. Feering they would saie she been diddel'd by a demon she bit off the xtra toe. Easie as chewing on a bit of chicken gristle she tell'd Mr. Proctor.

Mrs. Proctor, do you remember the Feest Daie last New Years? We be going to the Corys pigge roast but the sleigh been too full. I saied that I would ride ov'r with Mr. Proctor when he got backe from deer hunting.

Upon heering his hounds I closed the shutters & lit the candels. Then I took off my bonnet & lett out my haire. I knowe you warn'd me to keep my head cover'd cuz my haire be redd. You alwaies be saieing Judas had haire redd'r than fire.

But I donn't care. Mr. Proctor cann nev'r keep his eyes off me when my haire be sett free. This be specially true last News Year Feest. When he came in I be standing with my back to the fire. My haire falling 'round me soft & heavie & long like a shawl. All the time he be taking off his cloak & hat he stared at me. Ask't me what happen'd that my eyes had grow'd mor green than a catte stalking a mouse. I giv'd no reply. Just smil'd.

Soon as he sat in his chair by the hearth I nellt to pull off his bootes & stockings. Then hidd'n by my haire I slowly caresst his feet while I rubb'd in the warm oil. He paied no heed. The only sound been the crackel of the fire & the wethercock screeking as it turn'd on the roof.

Thinking how Mary show'd her love by kissing the feet of Jesus I began gently to run my tongue along his soles. And then to mouthe his toes as I snugell'd his feet like a newborn babee to my breasts.

I thot the moaning been the wind coming thru the keyhole of the doore but 'twas Mr. Proctor. Suddenly he giv'd a slite shudder & grabbing my haire yank'd back my hed. I remember how he kept mutt'ring so sweet an evil ov'r & ov'r as he be spitting in my face & then covering it with kisses. It fellt as tho a burning arrowe peerc'd my heart – melting it like hott wax into my bowelles. Darling, I wisper'd, pressing clos'r to him. He jumpt up. Kickt me awaie. I be scared cuz his face had gon white as leprosy. When I start'd crieing he pickt up the spinning wheel & smash'd it against the wall.

You be the gatewaie to Hell, he yell'd, charging out of the howse.

When I heerd his hors galloping awaie I be sertain he had gon to sign a warrant for my arrest as a harlott. I tried to pray for my sinne but when I closed my eyes I seen flammes. And the mor hot it grow'd the mor I want'd Mr. Proctor.

At sundowne he return'd with you & the littel ones. Tho he pretended nothinge had gon on I could feel his coal black eyes burning into me with all the pent up force of Lucifers last look at the Lord.

You nev'r notis'd but ever since that daie, Mrs. Proctor, I havnt been abel to look you in th'eyes for feer you would see how I yearn'd for him. But now that I hav been bless'd with

the Vishun I need not be feer breaking the Ten Commandments.

In my armes – with my lippes – I shall comfort Mr. Proctor.
Yea, tho he be made to walk thru vallies of dry bones & dust I
shall be with him. For the heart, Mrs. Proctor, the heart cannot
be divided from the flesh.

Yours truthfully
Mary Warren
Bloodhound of the Lord

April 14th, 1692
Moon on the rise

Dear Mrs. Proctor,

These past two daies I diddn't gett a minute to write. Besides my usual duties I steep'd peppermint leaves to make a Poshun Physick cuz the littel ones be taking a Cold.

I heer them now snuffeling in their sleep like piggelettes with their snouts in a troff of corn meal & lopper'd milk. Mr. Proctor be restless too. I heer him abov my hed thrashing about the bedde like the bull in his stall befor the Spring mating. Three more daies 'til your Heering, Mrs. Proctor. They saie you shall hang befor the first reeping of oats.

Since you be tak'n awaie Mr. Proctor wont staie alone with me in the same roome or even look at me when I ask him something. He alwaies hunches forward with his hed lower'd as tho about to charge. How powerful his emoshuns be. Like beests inside him. Fierce black beests pacing the cage of his loins.

Now that the Lords power has broke forth in me I cann make my own lawes. Thats why tonight I concock'd a Lov Poshun. 'Twas Tituba who taut me. At her Heering last week she confess't to being a witch. Must be you, Mrs. Proctor, who forc't her to sign the Black Book. Mr. Proctor saies 'tis a lie she made up so not to be hanged.

While waiting for th'ash to cool I thot to finish this lett'r so I cann hide it in the food pacquet Mr. Proctor will drop off at the Jail tomorrowe. He would whopp me for sure if he found out about the Lov Poshun. He would saie to leeve that crazie flim-flam for the Papists & Quak'rs.

However you knowe bett'r, Mrs. Proctor. You knowe my making of the Lov Poshun be not witch'ry cuz it comes out of lov. Perhaps I should not reveel so much. I alwaies be talking to you inside my hed but the wordes echo like they be in a empty cavern & I cann't think strait. When I write the wordes down it all comes cleer & I knowe I be doing the Lords Will.

Anywaie you cann't show these letters without divulging that you be getting illegal pacquets. Then peepul will turn against you & Mr. Proctor will get no mor signatures for his petishun.

Much later the same night

Unabel to sleep I trimm'd a candelwick so I cann add a note to this letter.

Befor going to bedde I went out for an armfull of wood to bank the fire. For the first time this Spring I cot the odoure of appel blossoms. In th'orchard the patches of moonlight sparkel'd like fresh fall'n snowe.

Out of the corner of my loose eye I glims't figures in greye capes dancing widdershins 'round th'orchard. I couldn't see any faces but your flatt feet giv'd you awaie Mrs. Proctor. Made you clumsie as a hoofbound mare. For sure it be a Witches Sabbat.

I start'd yelling as lowd as I could. Mr. Proctor came running with his muskett but when he seen where I point'd he cuff'd the side of my hed. 'Twas nothinge but mist, he saied, wafting in & out of the trees. Thats when I began to choak, Mrs. Proctor, as tho I be breathing in smoak & I know'd 'twas you smoth'ring me.

I must hav lost my senses cuz next I recall Mr. Proctor be lifting a candelstick to look at me as I laie on my bedde. Elizabeths right, he saied, your eyes be so week I am surpriz'd you can tell a tea pott from a chamber pott.

I paied no heed cuz at leest he be looking & speeking to me. While he scolded I could see abov the candels flamme a crease – deep'r than a frown – cutting downe the middel of his forhead. I know your spectral self put it there, Mrs. Proctor, same as you would put a branding iron to a prize bull to prove your ownership. Thats why I grabb'd his arme & pointing at his browe cried – Beware the mark from the Devils bride. But he jerk't awaie. Stomping out of the room he shot a look over his shoalder that almost destroy'd me. As tho it be me not you, Mrs. Proctor, who has becom the embodiement of Evil.

Tomorrow morn I shall visit your jailer & ask that irons be placed on your armes & legges to stoppe your specter from coming to torment me. Remember I have an eye that never sleeps.

Yours truthfully

Mary Warren

Bloodhound of the Lord

April 18th, 1692
Gloomie but no clowds

Dear Mrs. Proctor,

'Tis a qweer daie. The skie ting'd yellowe. The sun turning
the coloure of brass while wolves on the farr side of Blind Hole
Swampe howl as tho it be a full moon. You should see Mr.
Proctors dogges – tether'd to the gatepost – barking & straining
on their ropes when they heer them. Makes me laff to see them
lunging 'round & 'round on their hind legges. Like dwarves with
long pointy noses dancing the Maypole.

Soon as Mr. Proctor left this morn I rode into Town to speek
to the Jailor 'bout chaining you. He tell'd me at dawne you &
five oth'r accus'd women be tak'n by oxcart to the Boston Jail.
Seems th'outburst of witchcraft has ris'n to such a tidal wave
that the Salem Jail be filled. Since it be a daie ride to Boston I
am sure Mr. Proctor will not be bringing pacquets of food as
often. Fortunately the Jailor saied the condishuns be bett'r in a
larg'r jail.

When I return'd from town the littel ones tell'd me the
horses wonnt eet & the hennes be flapping 'bout refusing to laie.
John Junior saied the cowes in the back pasture be wandering in
circuls with their tongues lolling out in the most frightfull manner. He thinks it comes from a witches malice. The littel ones be
afraide. But not me. I am too blythsom.

This morn Mr. Proctor ate the Lov Poshun. I mix't it in his
porridge & then put on xtra creem & sugar. As usual he rode off
without looking or speeking to me. Dont matter cuz he only likes
talking to his hors & hounds anywaie. Tonight will be different.
I will witness the manifestashun of his lov. Thinking of it I cannt
stopp hugging myselfe & dancing 'round like them roped dogges.
Happiness be bursting out all over me. Same as Spring bursting

out of th'erthe. Same as the time Mr. Proctor slapp't my bottom while I be picking up the milk pailes. Called me his buxom bonnie maid.

I saw you watching us from the kitchen window, Mrs. Proctor, jellusy blooming like a flow'r garden in your face. While washing the supper dishes I herd you wisper to Mr. Proctor that I be a bad influens on the littel ones. When he ask'd why you saied I be turning into a gossip monger. You remind'd him that the root of my wickedness be my Granny who suffer'd the scold's bridle cuz of her tainted talking. I grow'd so angry heering your evil tongue I diddn't notis that I took the fork I be washing and stabbed it into my arme. Not till I seen the bloode.

Same daies later when I be visiting Abbie at the Parsonnage Reverent Parris seen the marks on my arme. He thot they came from your specter self biting me. I tried to tell him the truth, Mrs. Proctor, but he wouldn't listen. Saied I be too valuabel a witness to talk gibb'rish.

Since I am the first person to be inflict'd by you heds turn when I enter the Meeting Howse. Now peepul talk to my face. Not to my backe.

I am telling you this, Mrs. Proctor, so you cann understand that I would not be your servant if I be not orphan'd. I com from a proper family. I can read & write. Altho Pa died befor I be born I know'd his Grandpa been a Land Owner in Old England.

Later, after the quake
When it happen'd I be working in the herb garden cuz Tituba once tell'd me that plantes hav mor power if planted at th'houre when daie & night divide.

As I be poking holes to droppe in the seeds of coltsfoot & sweet cicely it turn'd so quiet I almost heer'd the worms creeping. Even the sparrows pecking in the hors dung stoppt titt'ring & every new leef on the willow by the stable door hung heavy & dull as a nail.

Thinking 'twas the stillness befor a storm I look'd up. Th'underheaven be cleer & dark purpel. All the breath seem'd suck'd out of th'aire so smoak from the citchin chimney rolled along the roofe.

Suddenly my wondering eye cot a slite movement in the woods at th'edge of the pasture. I thot 'twas the Devil com to tempt me but 'twas Mr. Proctor staring at me while branches sprout'd like antlers from behind his hed. Over his shoalder a ded boar be slung. Bloode dropping from its mouthe. Carefully Mr. Proctor laied it downe. All the time he be staring at me. His face pinch'd & white with some kind of inn'r agony.

As tho a giant hand be drawing us togeth'r we moved slowly acrosse the pasture till we be standing so close I fellt his breathe on my face. Then his lippes be on mine. His fingers digging into my armes. Thats when the ground trembell'd. A kind of shudder like the flesh of a cowe just as it be kill't.

I clung to Mr. Proctor while the hounds cring'd against us wimpering. The shaking grow'd worse & I thot for sure the ded be fighting among themselves. I closed my eyes & try'd to pray while Mr. Proctor held me so hard I heerd his heart pounding. Pounding fast as the hooves of the cowes stampeeding passt us to the barne.

Pressing my eyes mor tightly shutt I tried againe to pray. But Mr. Proctor be biting my throat. His handes under my skirt sqweezing my thighs. Spreding them apart as we tumbel'd downe. Beneath us the ground swell'd into waves as tho we laie on the deck of a shippe during a storme.

Suddenly clowthes be pull'd awaie. O the paine as he broke into my body. An Angel in flammes. Fire flowing out of his mouthe. Nev'r have I fellt mor alive. Our bodies burning togeth'r. Our Soules one.

Being outside all feeling I diddn't knowe wheth'r I be ded or alive. On erthe or in Heav'n.

When at last I open'd my eye I be lieing alonne in the long grass at th'edge of the pasture. The qwaking had stopp't but when I tried to get up I found my bones cold & heavy as chaines piled upon the ground. In the distance I could see Mr. Proctor moving in the direcshun of the howse. I could heer the wailing of the littel ones.

For som time I laie like a Zombi with my hed bury'd in Mr. Proctors stain'd coat. In the rich smell of the boars blood mixt with his sweat. Then as my mind cleer'd I recall'd the Revelashun. Now it becoming true.

I struggel'd to my nees to giv praise to th'Almightie. I donn't knowe how long I be praying but when I lifted my hed nothinge be moving xcept for a lone starre blinking abov the roofe & smoak rising from the citchin chimney. Rising strait as a pillar of stone.

As I walked back to the howse everythinge 'round me giv'd off a kind of rainbow glowe. Like I been the first that that Lord created. My body so bursting with Mr. Proctor's glory seeds that eech foot cried out Halelujah as I pick't it up & Amen as I plac'd it downe on the firm unmoving ground.

Donnt worry, Mrs. Proctor, no harm came to the littel ones. The only damage donne to the farme be brok'n winddowes caws'd by stones falling out of the chimney & the brass sundial in the garden that splitt in two. Mr. Proctor saies 'tis a sign that Eternity be all that matters. But I beleev that now our Soules be merg'd what importance can time hav?

Most truthfully yours
Mary Warren
Chos'n by the Lord

April 19th, 1692
Evening, waiting for Mr. Proctor

Dear Mrs. Proctor,

Everyone be wond'ring what it means that th'erthe only qwaked along the coast between Reading & Topsfield. The worst calamity occur'd in Salem Town where a childe be kill't by a falling tree. Beware, Mrs. Proctor, cuz they saie the next quake will run south thru Boston.

Reverent Parris call'd for an all daie religious service. The whole village turn'd out. Even Mr. Proctor. Seems people like animals flock together when they be afraide.

The Meeting-Howse been crowded & hot. Stank of feer like a tub of rancid butter. Tho the Reverent preeched for two houres in the morning & three houres in th'afternoon not once did the Tithingman hav to wacke the back of that wiggeling Porter boy with his staff or tie a foxtail on th'end of it to tickel the face of dozing ole Goodwife Nurse.

During the dinner break at Ingersolls Taverne everyone be dismal. Shaking heds & talking lowe they agree'd nothinge could be mor awefull then th'erthe crumbelling to peeses beneath their feet. 'Tis wors, they saied, than the news from a travelling tink'r that 15 hundred Iroquois & French be discover'd on our back borders.

Reverent Parris warn'd us from the pulpitt that an ertheqwake has portenshus significance. Diddn't it occur when Christ died on the Crosse & againe when He be Resurrect'd? They saie an ertheqwake be caws'd by the Hand of the Lord striking the Heavenly Bells. The sound vibrating thru th'aire be what makes th'erthe shake. And yesterdaie at sundowne I knowe as sure as I be sitting right nowe in your rocker, Mrs. Proctor, that them Heavenly Bells strike for Mr. Proctor & me.

Altho we been in the same company all daie not a look or a word passt between us. Nonetheless there be a kind of force drawing us together. At the socialls between sermons we would be pull'd 'round peepul till we stood backe to backe. But if by chance we turn'd & brush'd shoalders we would be flung apart. Then slowly drawn together againe.

'Tis well after cockshut & Mr. Proctor hasn't return'd. I hope the moon be brite enuff to light his waie. He stay'd behind at the Meeting-Howse to join a gath'ring of Select Men. They will decide if the village militia needs mor ammunishun in case of an Indian attack.

It seems everyone in Salem be too panick't 'bout th'erthe-qwake to consern themselves. Everyone but me. What do I care if theres solid ground beneath my feet? Mr. Proctors my world. All else be fleeting. Just like the shadowes I be watching flick'r along the citchin wall when the fire flares.

The littel ones be in bedde. I cannt sleep. I be sitting here in your rocker, Mrs. Proctor, thinking 'bout what will happen at your Heering. In the morn I must reveel to Mr. Proctor how the Lord chose me to sav hime from your Evil Arts. He must allow me to giv witness.

While planning my wordes I be ripping apart & remaking that bodice of yourn with the French lace. You tell'd me you would nev'r wear it againe when Mrs. Putnam after a Service saied you be putting on so much wate you look 'bout as combly as a cowe in a cage.

Do you remember that daie Mrs. Proctor? When a Quak'r man be lock't in stocks on the Meeting-Howse Green & Reverent Parris preech'd from a fameus book that saied if th'invisibel world cannt be prov'n we shall hav no Christ but a light within. The Quak'rs, the Reverent tell'd us, be blasfemus Sadducces cuz they donnt beleev th'invisibel world be real & feelabel to the flesh.

Since you be gon I have much time to think. If I could just laie out all the thinges that hav happen'd to me just like I be laieing out these peeses of your bodice then perhaps I could make somethinge of it.

The thot keeps coming that I cann prove the real invisibel world cuz my wand'ring eye gives me a second sight. Wish't I could perswade Mr. Proctor but whenever I try to speek to him my tongue goes limp.

The fires dying downe. 'Tis almost dawne. 'Twas only yesterdaie the very ground on which we stood stirr'd & heev'd to bear witness to our bless'd consummashun.

Most truthfully
Mary Warren

May 10th, 1692
Daie of th'Heering

Dear Mrs. Proctor,

These past weeks there been not an houre to write. Mr. Proctor only coms home to sleep. I be doing all the indoor & outdoor chores. The plantings not neer compleet cuz the littel'st ones be clinging to me & crying all the time. Myself? I cannot hold down food or sleep.

Last night I must hav dozed off in your rocker Mrs. Proctor. When I open'd my eyes the winddowe panes had faded from black to greye. Your demon bird be hopping up & downe on the sill & flapping its winges like a fether duster being shak'n cleen. When I open'd the winddowe to shoo it awaie it dared me with them cold shiny eyes befor rising over the barne roof. High'r & high'r till it disappear'd into a pink bank of clowd.

I be lighting a candel when I heer'd Mr. Proctor coming downe the staires. My hande shook as I held it up to show him the waie. He still moved slow as a sleepwalker with his hande over his heart as tho he had somethinge to hide or a hurt.

I stared at his face. It be blank & white & wax'n looking as the candel in my hande. The crease cutting even deep'r into his browe.

I want'd to ask him why he be pushing me out of his life these past weeks but it seem'd an invisibel noose be titening 'round my neck so I splutter'd & coff'd & couldnt let out the wordes. He stoppt at the bottom of the staires. Staring at me but not seeing. Staring strait thru me to the wall behind. In feer I lower'd my eyes.

We stood silent & unmoving. The first raies of the sun streem'd thru the winddowe into a poole on the floore. The logges sang in the hearthe. A cock crow'd & then another much clos'r. Still we stood. On the floore between the fire & the sunlight I watch't our shaddowes slipping in & out of eech other. Slipping in the waie th'unseen world slippes thru our lives. In the waie our Soules slippt thru our bones to be merg'd into one by the Lord. O why then can our bodies not follow?

Without a word Mr. Proctor walk'd passt me. The candel in my hande flick'rd out. I want'd to tell him that now his glory seeds hav taken root it wonn't be eesy for him to snuff out his lov for me. Again the noose titen'd sqweezing my throat so I start'd to coff.

Without a worde Mr. Proctor turn'd & left. The slamme of the door set your cloak swaying on its hook & a cold wind blowing thru my bones.

I open'd the door & ran out calling to Mr. Proctor that he must take me with him to the Heering. When I tried to seez his armes he push'd me awaie saieing he would rather take a dogge with rabbies. Push'd so hard I tripp't over th'endd of my skirt & fell to my nees.

I staied there holding my bellee & watching him walk towards the barne. How slowe he be moving. His hed downe. His shoalders bunch't. 'Tis strange, Mrs. Proctor, but when he be close theres somethinge enormus 'bout him. Somethinge too bigg to see. As he walk'd awaie he came mor cleer. Seem'd like I be looking at him for the first time. He has grown old since you be gon. The pow'r of his body leeking out as tho it be a sack of corn meal with a hole chew'd in the bottom by a mouse.

Forenoon, after gath'ring fiddleheds

Not wanting to think of you or the Heering, Mrs. Proctor, I decided to go downe to the creek & look for fiddleheds to serv with the boars hed I be cooking for supper tonight.

On the muddy path thru the woods I found prints that I recogniz'd be the soles of Mr. Proctors boots. Carefully I placed my foot in eech of his steppes. How deep & sure & even they be. How I lov the ground he treads. Lov seeing what he seen. The dogwood blooming twinklee as starres at dusk. The wild turkeys mating in the undergrowth. 'Twas here last Fall that Mr. Proctor shot a sixty pound turkey sitting on the fork of a beech tree. It be so heavy, he saied, when it struck the ground it splitt open. Gobs of yellow tallow rolling Out.

In the heel of one of his footprints my wand'ring eye catch't a littel pool of water. Gold & shimm'ring in the sunlight. At first I thot 'twas a mottelly stone plashing into it. Then bending downe I seen it be a toad. Signe of a demon lurking near. I grabb'd it & tear'd off its back legges eesy as if it been a tiny cook't phesant. Then I throw'd them over my left shoalder saieing very lowd – Protect me in the name of ArchAngels Michael & Gabriel.

Mr. Proctor would smack me for this. He beleevs it be evil to kill anythinge 'cept for food. Even if it be an imp or a demon. Com to think 'tis a wond'r Mr. Proctor nev'r has whoppt me like them other farmers whopp their maids. He just stares at me.

As I follow'd Mr. Proctors boot marks deep'r into the woods it grow'd glooming & dank as a cellar with vines thick as thighs creeping along the ground or flinging themselves to gripp the top of giant trees. I know'd as long as I follow'd in his steppes I would never be lost but I grow'd afraide picturing a savage behind every tree – a child of Satan with paint'd face & naked body slith'ring in bear grease. Mor & mor it seem'd a nightmare.

Forgetting 'bout Mr. Proctors footprints I start'd to run. Thats when I came upon a small cleering blankett'd in mayflowers. You knowe them wee pink blossoms, Mrs. Proctor. You been the one who tell'd me they brot a message of hope to our forefathers after their first dizasterus winter.

Tucker'd out from running I throw'd myself downe on the flow'ry bed. I must hav doz'd for the next I know'd my eyes be forc'd open by a frightful screech. Thats when my loos eye glimpst a clump of matt'd browne haire on a fork't branch of pine. Looking hard I made out what seem'd bits of dry'd blood & brain & skinne. Suddenly something rised up & I screem'd. As it clatter'd thru the branches I start'd laffing & crying cuz I realized it be a bird & what I thot be an Indian scalpe 'twas only a nest of twigges & mudd.

And the bird, Mrs. Proctor? The bird been that magpie of yourn. It follow'd along while I be gath'ring the fiddelheds among the roots & moss of the creek bank. I couldnt see it but I heerd its chortling. So lowe and fullsom I could hav sworn you be laffing at me.

Later, Suppertime

The boars hed – stuff't in the French fashion with stale bred & butter & basil & minc't chestnut – be roasting for houres. When I open the oven doore its brisselly pink snout be steeming same as the spout of a tea ketel.

Soon its bulging eyes will turn the grey'sh white of hard boil'd egges & the meat cann be carv'd. The last time I be serving one of the cheeks to Mr. Proctor he pull'd me to him by th'apronne stringes & pinch'd my bottom wisp'ring that these be the cheeks he desir'd. 'Twas over a year ago but I still remember how he throw'd back his hed & laff'd. Th'edges of his teeth gleeming.

Right now I wish I could remember how you made that rich gravie Mrs. Proctor. I think the Madeira be what turn'd it red & thick as ox blood. Mr. Proctor loves to sopp up the drippings with bred. Carefully licks th'end of eech finger. How he loves to eet. I lov to watch him. His mouthe opening so wide that once – to tees the littel ones – he put a whole appel in it.

While waiting for Mr. Proctor to return from your Heering the littel ones be settel'd 'round the citchin tabel copying out the Ten Commandments on their slate boards. Thats when Annie ask't what covet meant. Gazing up at me with them black greedie beed eyes. Just like yours, Mrs. Proctor.

Later, After the Constabul

While writting th'abov I heerd the grumbel of cart wheels. I thot Mr. Proctor be back at last. But 'twas Constabul Williams asking for a cup of tea. Abbie thinks he has the face of an old hors cuz of his bigge long nose & sunken cheeks & high forhed. He be taking the Reverents daughter to staie with her uncle in Town. Littel Betty be the first in the village to becom possessed &, they saie, after the Devil had his waie with her she be drows'd as a mouse dragg'd in by the catte.

As the Constabul carry'd her into th'ingelnook I notis'd how meg'r she look'd. How her butyful blonde haire has turn'd pale & thin as watery milk. Soon as he putt her on the settee she start'd screeming Mama Mama while her eyes be fix't on the boars hed keeping warm on a platt'r in the hearth. The draft when I open'd the doore must hav blow'd the embers into flammes & nowe the boars eyes be melting & sliding slowly downe its cheeks.

It brot to mind them white sticky blobbs of snails I used to gath'r from inside the rainbarrels & boil into a porridge. The littel ones hated it but it stopp't the ricketts. The only waie Constabul Williams & I could stopp Betty from screeming be to pull a pillow casing like a hangmans hood over her hed.

Soon as she quiet'd downe I ask't the Constabul if he had any news of your Heering, Mrs. Proctor. He shook his hed but saied if it be the same as oth'r witchcraft Heerings the Meeting-Howse would be pack'd as a barrell of herrings.

It seems Reverent Parris has been consern'd for sometime that th'afflicted wouldn't take th'stand. Most be maid servants, he tell'd the Constabul, ov'rawed by th'crowd & speshully the presiding Magistrates cuz they be fameus men from Boston. Thats why befor your Heering the Reverent made sure eech of the torment'd giv'd sworn statements to the Constabul.

I already know'd, Mrs. Proctor, 'bout the one sign'd by Abbie claiming your specter flied thru a keyhole & offer'd her a pockett of gold sovereigns to becom a handmaiden of the Devil. But I diddn't knowe you also torment'd Titubas husband. The Constabul tell'd me John Indian has swear'd twice that he woke to find your specter standing naked by his bedde. He claim'd it had the same body as you, Mrs. Proctor, but with no skinne. And when you tried to laie on him he saied it fellt like raw red meat.

While the Constabul be getting ready to leeve – wrapping the simp'ring littel Betty in the folds of his bigge black cloak – I ask't him if the date of your hanging be set at your Trial or afterwards by the Governor. The Constabul look'd at me aslant saieing by lawe a woman with a babee in her bellee couldn't be hang'd.

Not a worde mor did I saie to him – not even goodbye – but I knowe you be lieing, Mrs. Proctor. Trieing to gain time so Mr. Proctor cann take the petishun to the Governor & ask for a repreeve. If only Mr. Proctor would com home. Why has he been so long at your Heering? And this forboding deep inside me. Why be it spreding – shade upon shade – like th'aire thats dark-'ning outside the winddowe.

Som later
Not to you Mrs. Proctor
This be different

I sit & stare into the fire. My mind dissembeling. No more will I be waiting for Mr. Proctor. No mor will I be writting to you Mrs. Proctor. So much has happen'd. I must make som order in my hed by putting downe worde for worde what John Indian tell'd me when he stopp't for a dram of whiskey on his waie back from the Heering.

He start'd saieing he been the first to take the stand when they call'd for witnesses to your witchcraft & 'twas while he be giving testimony that he seen your specter sitting on a cross-beem. He point'd it out to the Magistrates & then it swoop't t'attack the girles. Been awesom, he saied, to see Annie crawling on all fours & biting the ankels of the Magistrates. Mercie choaking on the floore cuz her throate be puff't as tho a fist be inside it.

Then John Indian tell'd me how the crowd screem'd & push't up to the pulpitt. Sweating body press't so close to sweating body that when a goodwife faint'd there be no room for her to fall. No waie to remove her from the Meeting-Howse till after your last test which be the repeeting of the Lords Prayer.

And then John Indian tell'd me when you saied Hollow'd be Thy Name instead of Hallow'd be Thy Name the crowd began screeming Witch Witch.

I wond'r how it fellt, Mrs. Proctor, having the peepul straining forward to tear at your clowthes while the Magistrates begg'd for order & Mr. Proctor suddenly be at your side. I cann pictur him standing there with his hed lower'd – like he be 'bout to charge – & the fureus damn-the-world look on his face. I can pictur him pointing at th'afflicted & yelling Bitch Witches they make Devils of us all. The girls, John Indian saied, began blatt'ring like hennes that sens a wolf behind the barne. It been him that had to stand up & name Mr. Proctor for what they saie he be – the most dredfull wizard this side of Boston.

'Twas while John Indian be telling those wordes that my mind start'd dissembeling. Everythinge 'round me changing. Not cuz my week eye be rolling but cuz the citchin dwindel'd as tho I be falling asleep. The walls – even the howse itself – fading. My body no longer me. I dreem'd it into being.

And I must be dreeming still for I cann see John Indian sitting on the stook in th'ingelnook. A dirty-looking dried-up littel man searching for lice in his haire while he be talking & talking. Saieing how Abbie stood up & tell'd the court that one night Mr. Proctor flied with the wind downe the chimney of the Parsonage. That he spred his specter self ov'r her. On & on he be talking. His rasping voyce. I cann feel it cutting thru me like a sawe thru wood as he saies Mr. & Mrs. Proctor be tak'n togeth'r to the Boston Jail to await trial. I can hear myselfe saieing Abbie my best friend while watching him fold into a muddy greye cloak & skuttel out into the night. And I can still hear myselfe saieing Abbie my best friend while list'ning to the fading sounds of his waggon wheels…list'ning to the gusts of wind & rain following behind him like the wheels of fate turning & turning.

Mor late

With every gust the fire flares up & the sealskin dressing trunk be chang'd into a hump't sea monster sliding acrosse th'floor. The four turkey-work't chaires with the bowed legges becom dwarfs dancing a jig.

In the flick'ring spurts of flamme the picture of yourselfe Mrs. Proctor abov the mantel stirrs & comes alive. Eyes blinking & following me 'bout the roome. Sometimes she speeks the same as you to tell me taint a babee inside me but the Devil himself bigge as a woodchuck. Tonight be the witches Sabbath & soon they shall com to steel the littel ones so their fleshe cann be eet'n at the midnight feest.

While I sit rocking & praying I heer a swishing sound like wind outside the howse but I knowe it be broomsticks sweeping th'aire. The weth'rcock turning on the roof screeks kill kill kill & somethinge blasts down the chimney snuffing out the fire. Not even th'afterglowe of embers.

It be so dark I cannt see my hand in front of my face. There be nothing 'round me but aire blowing. It nuzzels my neck. Pulls up my skirt. Cold fingers pinching my thighs & forcing them apart. It presses into all my openings. Thrusts deep'r. I want to wake up. I want to crie out but cannt. My eye like a scared bird flies up into my skull. Into a place immens & silent & curv'd. Like the night skie with starres the coloure of blood.

Now I knowe eternity. Now my Soule has chang'd places with my body & everywhere be God. The wind be His Breathe rushing thru my seven openings. His Shaddowe so bright be Mr. Proctor letting go his bones & slipping inside me. I can see him like the moon floating thru my darkness. He be a thousand times clos'r than my own skinne. Than my own breathe.

What I do care if we be witches or Gods Chos'n. If I be asleep or awake. Mr. Proctor be the Light within me & togeth'r we take the shape of Heav'n. Now & eternally our child makes us one.

Blessed be the Lord
Mary Proctor

The letter is yanked from under her fingertips.

A gust of wind has blown open the casement window and snuffed the lamp. Something's here. In this room. There's a thudding against the walls, a crashing of objects. Sibyl crouches, covering her head with her arms. Above her…breathing… ragged…fast. Like the beating of wings and then a swooshing past her ears and a thump.

In the silence that follows she listens to the squeaking of the loosened window hinge, the distant rumbling of thunder, the barking of a dog…answered by another much closer. She lifts her head slightly and strains to make out a small sprawling shape. Rocking back and forth on her haunches, she stares at the skewed head with its gaping beak and bright unblinking eye.

She reaches out and runs her fingertips along the black iridescent feathers. The body shudders while the head flops in a way that could only mean a broken neck. She sees the glimmer of bone protruding from where the wing joins the bloodstained breast, hears the soft fluttering of fear and pain. She rises and, moving unsteadily, gathers up the convulsing creature and swaddles it tightly in the curtain torn from the window by the wind. With the back of Mama's wooden hairbrush, she beats it until motionless.

Knowing that a wild bird in the house foretells of a death in the family, she decides it must be buried quickly, before the storm hits – especially if it's a ghoster. With the bloody bundle under her arm, she hurries down the stairs and out the back door to the summer kitchen where she slips on rubber boots and a yellow rain poncho over her nightgown. Grabbing a spade, she heads up the path towards the graveyard.

So intent is she on burying the crow she pays no attention to the splatter of raindrops on her shorn head or the wind tugging at her clothes. Even as the storm blows in from the northeast, blackening the moonlit clouds, she does not turn back. Only the constant flicker of lightning reveals the path before her.

At the entrance to the graveyard she grips the limp bundle more tightly under her arm and, with the spade as a kind of white cane, feels her way between the engraved slabs of cement. She almost reaches the foot of the cross when she stumbles over something and falls to her knees. Putridness assaults her. Grabs her throat. Feeling around for the dropped bundle, her fingers close on what seems a smooth flat pebble. In the next flash of light she finds herself holding the button on Gammer's tattered blue gardening jacket. A fallen scarecrow, she thinks, to keep the crows from roosting. A loud clap of thunder is followed almost immediately by another brighter flash and now she sees the fleshless face, hollow pits for eyes…

Her body – a spooked horse that has thrown its rider – bolts.

And the wind cries God O God O God as it blows through her. And it rains harder. And she runs faster. Terrified of falling. Terrified that some crack will open between the dead and the living. But she keeps running. Foot in front of foot. She herself alone. Eclipsed by the dead.

She crashes down on her side. She cries out – pain and fright exploding from her lips – but it's ripped away by the onslaught of the storm. The rain, turning to hail, slashes her skin. The wind pelts her with dirt. Making herself small as possible, she covers her face with her hands. Still it is there – the image of the flesh-eaten skull – as though etched with a burning knife into her brain.

At first she is unaware of the nose sniffing around her feet. She squints into the storm. A creature the size of a small black bear whimpers and attempts to lick her face. "Good dog," she whispers, "good dog."

A jagged stroke of blinding light brings her to standing. A crack of thunder shakes the ground, pebbles rattling down the incline. The dog leans against her, trembling. She puts her hand on his big head and murmurs, "It's all right. It's all right."

She attempts to tighten the hood of the poncho and turns her back to the driving rain. With the next flash that rips open the night, she recognizes the stony north field backing onto the escarpment. She has come here many times to pick blueberries. She takes a tentative step. Her ankle throbs but she can walk, the dog holding close to her leg, each step measured as a pallbearer because of the pain.

By the time she reaches the stunted apple trees and vegetable garden behind the house the fury has died out of the storm, but this does not stop the dog from squeezing through the back door while she is opening it. Immediately he shakes himself, spraying her with water as she struggles out of the poncho and rubber boots.

Limping around the kitchen, she waves her arms over her head until she locates the cord to the ceiling light. Only after she has pulled it a few times does she realize the electricity is out. "It happens sometimes with a storm as violent as a ghoster," she says to the dog as he thumps his tail on the linoleum.

The emergency candles and matches are kept in the drawer of the kitchen table. Eyes adjusting to the blackness, she finds them easily, but has difficulty striking a light because of the spasms of cold and shock running through her body.

As soon as she has changed into dry clothes, she kindles the fire in the stove. The dog sighs and collapses with a thud in front of the crackling flames. Water streams from his long fur pools on the linoleum, filling the room with a boggy odour of skunk cabbage. Easing easing herself into the rocker beside him, Sibyl hears a loud banging and realizes it's the casement window in

Mama's room that had been blown open by the blasting wind. As she is hopping on one foot up the stairs, a rush of air from the open window snuffs out the flame of her candle. She stands there until her eyes adjust to the darkness and then, holding the varnished oak rail, she makes it up the steps. Once in Mama's bedroom she closes and latches the window.

She lights the oil lamp that had been snuffed while she was reading the letters. With its wavering halo illuminating the room, she begins to gather the ancient parchment papers that had been tossed about by the wind. She hears an almost imperceptible sound – thin and intense as the blade of a knife scraping across cold metal. She hears it again. Louder. One continuous note that seems to be coming from the window. She looks over to where the rain is trickling down the glass. Like tears of a lonely world. But she isn't crying. Her eyes are dry.

Then she feels a tiny breath of air on her face. Holding up the lamp, she goes to the window and sees by its quavering flame that a crack in the glass pane leads to a tiny hole in the corner. She realizes the wind blowing through has been the cause of the high eerie sound that reminded her of Gammer's toothless whistling. Wondering if the tiny hole was created by a boy shooting a pellet gun, she reaches up to touch it.

That's when she glimpses a sudden movement outside in the dark. A face floating in the shiny-wet black glass. A face featureless as the moon in a daytime sky. A living skull.

She jumps back. Then it comes to her. The lamp in her hand has transformed the window into a murky mirror.

She stares at this ghost of herself as though scrutinizing an alien baby to which she has given birth. Slowly she turns her shaved head this way and that. It is not smooth and translucent as she had supposed it to be, but streaked with dirt and patches missed by the razor. Then she sees a tiny crimson patch on her left temple. She reaches up and touches the rough bit of flesh. The mark is the shape of a flame. Was it there at her birth? Mama and Gammer would have seen it. Surely they would have warned her. Told her she carried the sign – the sign that the soul of her ancestor had housed itself in her body.

She rocks back and forth, one hand on top of the other pressing down on her navel. We all come out of the flesh of each other. Links in an endless chain.

How many days has she been in New Salem? It could be eight or eighteen. Time has become elastic…one continuous day held together by the repetition of domestic duties. Gammer is dead. She knows that. But she believes if she does nothing, tells no one, then she will not have to acknowledge that reality. It need not be final.

She busies herself to exhaustion, falls asleep for a few hours and then starts again, welcoming as a distraction the pain of her swollen bruised ankle. Her first task has been to putty the tiny round hole in the corner of the windowpane in Mama's bedroom. After that she begins to fluff the pillows, straighten the scatter rugs and dust the windowsills.

Once Mama was gone, she had seen the room only through the keyhole of the closed door. Nothing had changed. It was a shrine rigorously attended by Gammer who kept the smallest most insignificant things exactly as they had been. Six hairpins lay in a row beside a silver dollar on the dressing table. A folded sock with a hole in the toe waited to be darned on top of the bureau while the invoice from the Eaton's catalogue for her nightlight – her birthday gift on that last day – had been tossed on the small chair by the bed.

Since it is May, the neatening of the room gradually grows into the ritual of spring cleaning. Sibyl washes and irons the curtains, turns the mattress, polishes the wood floor, pulls out the furniture so as to wipe down the walls, ties a damp rag on the end of a broom to rid the corners of the ceiling of spiderwebs… but she does not open the drawers of the bureau or the door to Mama's clothes closet.

With the expansion of time she repeats the ritual, moving her pail, mop, broom, washrags and feather duster from room to room. By keeping constantly busy she's not conscious of herself, and the thoughts running through her brain are as unconnected to her as the air running in and out of her lungs.

In the dining room she mends tiny tears in the brocade on the chairs and washes with care the delicate china cups and saucers belonging to generations of Witherspoon women. In the front parlour she teeters on the top rung of the stepladder to wash the moulding around the top of the walls and the cornice in the centre of the ceiling. The rite of spring for the mahogany floor-to-ceiling fireplace – declared by Gammer to be "the envy of the county" – demands the intricate use of a toothbrush for the ornately carved mantle. The same is true for the wedding-cake trim on the oversized sideboard.

In the pantry, while wiping down the shelves, she discovers a mouse nest behind the jars of preserved food. Woven into the straw and horsehair stuffing pulled from the chesterfield are shreds of paper with parts of words on them. She pieces bits together and makes out the childlike printing of "Sibyl," "forgive," and "going." Although she recognizes the handwriting as similar to that on the labels of Gammer's glass jars, she throws the pieces of paper, along with the nest, into the wood stove.

Even with the larder so well stocked, eating would not have occurred to her except – because Good Dog has to be fed – she chokes down a few mouthfuls to keep him company. In the morning she makes porridge, and in the evening she opens and shares a can of food. Whether it is mushroom soup, smoked oysters or tinned ham, Good Dog gulps it down and whines for more.

During this time the phone rings twice, but of course she doesn't answer it because the outside world would impinge upon her, and THAT she cannot allow. Alone, with the protection of the house, everything can be the way it always has been...and soon, she will hear Gammer stamping the mud off her shoes on the back door mat.

The only time she leaves the house is to air out the comforters and blankets on the clothesline or to fetch logs from the woodpile beside the back stoop. She's always careful to go out very early or very late in the day when there is no chance of Aunt Aggie driving up the lane. One morning when she opens the kitchen door she finds a basket of food with a note from Fast Mac instructing her to leave the empty picnic hamper by the mailbox. She shares the roast chicken and a bit of the apple pie with Good Dog who looks up at her with pleading hopeful eyes, his tail whisking gently against the kitchen linoleum.

She has become accustomed to his big, barrel-shaped body following her around all day. At regular intervals he patrols the halls of the house. Galumphing along on paws that look as if they have been dipped in white paint, he stops to sniff at every closed door and, when he thinks she isn't looking, lifts his leg on the upstairs newel post. Not only does Good Dog growl at every tiny sound, he also pounces at anything that moves – a curtain swaying slightly in a draft is ripped from its rod, the leg of a wooden rocking chair when she sits in it is grabbed and yanked as though it is the pant leg of an intruder.

Most of all, he protects her from the intrusion of thoughts. He stares up at her, his dark inquisitive eyes dancing with light, and then, with a sigh, drops a shovel-sized head onto her lap as though offering a gift. She kisses him between the ears, breathing in his gritty warm smell of burnt sausage. Good Dog loves to nap stretched out in front of the wood stove. Sometimes she lies beside him, pulling burrs and thistles out of his black matted fur. Other times she lies with her head on his neck knowing she can sleep because he guards her dreams.

Every evening, when it grows so dark that his white paws seem to be moving without him across the floor, he whines at the kitchen door. Putting him out for the night, she hears crows and ravens squabbling for a place to roost on the cross, but she doesn't dare look up towards the graveyard. Instead, she stands before the fireplace mantle in the parlour and, after drawing the sign of the cross on the pewter base of the oil lamp with her forefinger, strikes a match and ignites its wick. Then in the halo of light, she says a prayer of thanks to the generations of women who have polished the lamp. Sometimes she senses that they are present – that they are holding hands in a circle around her – their love eternal as the hills enclosing Madawaska Valley.

Picking up the photo of Mama in its silver frame, she stares at the beloved face locked in time. She recalls her tenth birthday and how Mama, hugging her fiercely, had said she would always be with her and even if she were to die she would never leave, but live in the family's ancient lamp like a genie. With a slight smile, Sibyl lightly kisses the photo and returns it to the mantle. Then she settles into the sofa, with Great-Gammer's knitted throw tucked around her legs, and stares into the pulsing flame of the lamp while the old house sighs and grumbles, adjusting from the warmth of the days to the damp coolness of the late spring evenings.

Now and again, she runs the palm of her hand over the downy growth on her head, over the rough raised patch of skin, imagining that the shape resembles a rosebud, or a ladybug, or a feather from a robin's breast, or a flame – and if it is a flame, is that necessarily a sign of her ancestor's soul being housed in her body?

Still, she cannot stop herself from thinking, "But nothing is the same," and feeling a shiver run up her spine…though she dares not consider what these words mean.

As Above
So Below

⇜ LAST DAY ⇝

Only thirteen pages remain in the journal. I will make an effort to be precise.

Good Dog had not returned for his morning bowl of food. Wondering where he could be, I opened my bedroom curtains to look out, and was surprised to see the sky hidden by black waves of cloud, so low they appeared to be the ocean breaking over the top of the escarpment. My first thought was I must quickly bring in the blankets from the line. As I crossed the room I felt a violent shaking and heard a roar louder than a train coming through the house. At the same time, roof shingles, boards, fence posts flew by the window. The air thickened with leaves and dust. Then a huge blast like the fist of the Almighty smashed the glass. In slow motion I watched it splinter, the shards scattering like invisible flower petals.

It happened so fast. Picking up my journal from the bedside table, I headed down the stairs, clinging to the banister while the plaster fell around me in chunks. Small objects were whizzing past my ears, biting like bullets into the walls. In the front hall the wind grew worse, ripping away my clothes, my breath. And I knew where I had to go…where I would be safe. The place that had been sealed for generations. The place I feared the most.

Struggling to reach the cellar, I was lifted so high off the ground that my head hit the ceiling and then I was smashed down on my knees on the kitchen linoleum. The walls started to break apart and the floors to contort.

I grabbed the brass handle. A strength that was not me, but ran through my arm like a river, splintered the buckling wood and popped the rusty nails. The trapdoor was open just enough for me to squeeze through. My feet on the rungs of the ladder. The door slamming down. And then falling. The long dream of falling. Nothing between me and the bottomless hole. Me and death. I was retreating thousands of years into the earth. My lifeless body felt nothing. And out of nothing came darkness. And the darkness grew warm, cradling me.

I understood. Understood it all. My mind became a blank page.

I recall next the sensation of returning from a long journey, struggling to open my eyes, vision thick, but in the darkness above there was a crack of light, a rectangle the shape of a door. I saw my feet sticking up. Embedded in earth I was alive. Back in my body. I wiggled my fingers and toes. Slid my hurting head from side to side. Yes, I could move. And my mouth opened and a sound rolled out and hung – long and bright as a red silk ribbon – in the dirt-choked air above me. And then the trapdoor was flung open, dirt and pebbles tumbled down.

Blinded by light I gradually made out a dazzling blue rectangle and then a man's head appeared like a giant face on a billboard. It was Fast Mac silhouetted against the sky. "Holy Hell!" he gasped.

I can imagine how grotesque I looked – bald, smeared with earth, bloody from the flying glass. He reached down and helped me up the ladder, pulling me by the wrist over the rungs that had given way under my weight.

I didn't have to ask what happened. Fast Mac couldn't stop talking about how he wasn't much for church going, only high days and holidays, especially when they had to drive all the way to Bancroft, but Myrtle liked Pentecostal Sunday with its celebration of the outpouring of the Holy Spirit on the Apostles and the choir wearing red gowns rather than the usual black. Afterwards, he said, they'd been driving back on the main road through the valley when Myrtle pointed out a strange-shaped grey cloud hanging low in the distance. Since blue sky was all around he figured a barn had caught fire, but Myrtle disagreed, saying there was no burning wood smell.

When they arrived home she told Fast Mac that she was going to roast two chickens, one for the Witherspoons, so Fast Mac started up to the house on the hill for the picnic basket that was sure to be left by the front gate. He was driving along the upper road, so preoccupied with watching Mr. Parry's Holstein cows stampeding across the fields as though being chased by a pack of invisible wolves, that he didn't notice how the wind had steadily increased and the air darkened. It was the sound like a low-flying plane that made him look up and he saw the cloud had moved closer and lower. Its huge rolling boiling form was so alive, said Fast Mac, he thought the Holy Ghost was descending out of the heavens. And since he couldn't throw himself down on his knees, he pulled over to the side of the road and threw himself down on the floor of his car.

Within seconds it seemed to Fast Mac that he was inside a steel barrel on which a hundred drummers were beating, and he found his car engulfed by hail the size of turnips. When it stopped a few minutes later, he saw dust and dirt and debris flying everywhere and heard a roaring so terrifying that he thought this can't be the Holy Ghost but The Beast from the Apocalypse coming to take him and, although he tried to pray, all he could remember was, "The Lord is my shepherd, I shall not want."

While Fast Mac watched, the whirling shapeless grey mass tore through the strip of scrub woods, wove across Mr. Miller's pasture, sucking up a lone sheep, fence posts and a small shed. Only when it passed a hundred metres in front of him did he recognize what was happening. In horror he watched it veer directly south and descend upon our house, the Witherspoon home, of generations...

All the time Fast Mac was carrying on, he had been leaning over me, gently wiping the mud and blood from my face with the end of his shirt. Now he stopped and demonstrated with his hands how the roof of our house lifted and then the walls exploded, stuff going up and spinning...

Suddenly, as if to bring an unruly child under control, he smacked his own forehead with the palm of his hand and said, "Holy Moly, I'm forgetting your granny."

He kneeled and peered into the cellar. "She's not down there."

I shook my head.

"Where is she?"

"Gone." My mouth formed the word but no sound came out.

Fast Mac patted my arm. "Don't worry, I'm sure she's all right."

I shook my head. Strained to speak.

Fast Mac kept on patting my arm. "Take it easy, now. Don't try to move. The fall knocked the breath out of you, and that bump on your head don't help much. A good thing I was close by. Your cry scared the bejesus out of me! So I found the trapdoor."

While Fast Mac was talking, he removed his jacket and, wrapping it around my shaking body, gently laid me down on a blanket taken from his truck. I closed my eyes. I heard him say something about looking for Gammer but I was too tired to speak. His jacket was as warm and comforting as Good Dog and reeked like him, too.

"Don't you worry," Fast Mac said, "After such a long wet spring sure as shootin' your granny's mushrooming in them crevice caves."

He gave my cheek an affectionate pinch. "I can't imagine your granny approves of your haircut. You looked like a shorn lamb. Hope you don't belong to one of those new-fangled religions. The Good Lord gives hair for a reason you know. And He specially blessed the Witherspoons. You should be proud of your crowning glory. Like your granny and mama. My Myrtle always said if the Good Lord had given her hair half as beautiful she wouldn't ever cut it."

Vaguely I felt him slide something soft under my head and tell me he was going for help but it could take some time since the road was blocked by blown-down poles and power lines. "I've left you a bottle of Coke and half a ham sandwich I had in the truck so you just stay put and rest and don't go walking around in this mess with no shoes."

How strange it was to stare up at the sky – now the bluest of blue – where the kitchen ceiling should be. The back of our house was gone – even the towering oak tree that had protected us all these years, bending its enormous branches over the roof. The only part that remained was its trunk, twisted off like a wrung-out rag, a few feet above the ground.

Putting on Fast Mac's jacket, I slipped my journal that I'd been clutching all this time into his pocket, and began to pick my way through the helter-skelter of splintered timbers, warped door frames, chunks of plaster, wiring, floorboards and metal piping. I had to constantly watch where I stepped. Whenever I lifted my eyes to look around it seemed I was peering through the wrong end of binoculars. Everything was small and far away. Still, I recognized the rocking chair minus a back, the parlour sofa lying upside down in the vegetable garden, a drawer from

275

my dresser with the socks and shirts still neatly folded (how weird!), the cracked top of the dining room table in the raspberry bushes, the bathtub up-ended like a rearing horse in the rubble that used to be the garden shed, a pillow – no, the lifeless body of a lamb – wedged like a child's cuddly toy in the fork of an apple tree.

Then, underneath the crumpled braided rug that once lay beside my bed, I discovered a clump of pale mauve violets, tiny delicate blooms close to the ground. I remember Mama saying they were a manifestation of the fairy spirits that guarded the graves. The bones of my relatives were safe in the earth. Not like Gammer.

Kneeling in the debris, I brushed the plaster dust from the faces of the violets. Then, as I was loosening the ground around their roots, I exposed an earthworm. This translucent strip of flesh, folding and unfolding in terror, knew nothing of what had occurred.

Repeating "All we need to know, is from the earth we come, and to the earth we go" (Gammer's favourite retort to my childhood questions), I covered the worm with dirt. That's when I glimpsed her shoe underneath a broken cupboard door, one of the old black Oxfords with no laces and a ripped tongue that she wore for gardening. Swallowing hard to keep down the sudden wave of emotion, I cradled the shoe in my arms. Running my fingertips over the shape imprinted by her foot inside the shoe, I discovered something wedged into the toe. Taking out what seemed, at first, to be a marble, I realized it was a glass eye from the deer's head that hung in the kitchen.

I stared in amazement. By what mad whirligig of chance had the glass eye landed in Gammer's shoe? If I were a child I would believe the fairy spirits of the graveyard had placed it there. If I were Gammer I would believe it to be a sign. But a sign of what?

Was it a warning like mouse turds in the flour bin, or a blessing like a falling star at dusk?

As I stood rolling the glass eye between my thumb and forefinger I looked up towards the crevice caves (I knew, of course, that Gammer wasn't there) and a turkey vulture caught my eye. Watching it turn lazy circles in the empty blue sky, I found it almost impossible to accept that there had been a tornado a few hours earlier.

Over my childhood years I had often witnessed a vulture gliding high above Madawaska Valley. Always it gave me pause knowing that, no matter how graceful it appeared in the air with metre-long wings spread like an angel's, on the ground it was an ugly creature with a featherless head and an ungainly body.

The vulture was joined by another, and another, and still another, in a gradually expanding circle – soaring and sliding, swaying from side to side, hovering, dipping and veering – they seemed more than anything else to be folk dancing.

Birds like these had eaten Gammer's flesh. She was now part of them. The thought didn't repulse me. Rather, I felt my heart suddenly lift, straining as though it, too, would soar away. Gammer! Gammer! I flung out my arms imagining the joy of her, who had kept her feet so solidly on the ground, floating in the warm air currents above the escarpment – the umbilical cord that moored her to the house, broken. She was free...free.

Putting the glass eye in Fast Mac's jacket pocket, I slipped on the shoe. Shortly afterwards I found a man's rubber boot with the name _Linwood_ in black marker pen on the inside, pulled it on, and began to wander in larger and larger circles around the place where the great burned cross had loomed over our lives. Now it had gone, but its shape remained as a displacement of air – similar to presences I'd seen out of the corner of my eye as a child.

Here and there I stopped to dig in the debris. With the concentration of a dog digging for a lost bone, I unearthed the top of the brown betty teapot, Great-Grandfather's moustache cup with its handle broken, a copper hair clip, the silver frame that once held Mama's photograph, a souvenir teaspoon from Niagara Falls sent to Gammer by a distant cousin, a wooden egg used for darning the toe or heel of stockings and, most surprising, from under a smashed door frame, Gammer's dentures, which she had always kept beside her bed in a glass of water.

As my circling grew into an ever-widening dream – a searching for something that I couldn't remember – I was finding the odds and ends that had trickled down the long history of our family. Since these little things had survived to become all I had in the world, I cleaned each one and placed it in Gammer's wicker basket, which I had found on the weedy shore of the pond. Each was a reminder of some daily ritual connecting me and my dead ancestors.

Scavenging through the sumac and brush that bordered our land, I discovered the patchwork quilt, made from the clothes Papa had left behind, tangled around a barbwire fence. I ripped off a corner square containing an intricate five-pointed star, remembering how – snip by meticulous snip, stitch by tiny even stitch – Mama had transformed her fury and grief. And how, over the years, I had doodled thousands of these images on every imaginable surface. I sensed that I would never make another.

In the neighbouring pasture, frightened sheep remained huddled in the far corner, except for a black-faced young ram pulling the ancient straw stuffing out of our Queen Anne chair. Broken parts and pieces of our house were everywhere. However, as though in preparation for a lawn sale, in the middle of the grass stood – upright and on all four legs – our kitchen table with an aluminum milk jug on top.

Searching around for other unbroken items, I picked up the wooden spoon that used to hang beside the stove and which still smelled of all the soups and stews it had stirred. It seemed simple and innocent enough – its hollow the size of a baby's palm. Only as I was deciding if I should add it to my full basket did I recall Gammer beating me with it so fiercely.

Suddenly tired, I sat down on a clump of twitch grass. A rabbit bounded out of the bushes along the pasture's edge, chased by Good Dog who, seeing me, joyfully slavered over my face. I hugged his rain-barrel body and let him lead me across the meadow until I spied the lap desk half-hidden among a tall patch of clover and purple vetch.

The lid was cracked, but the inside black leather surface tooled with gold looked the same and so did the pens and almost empty bottle of ink. As I was rifling through the many papers I discovered a bulky envelope containing letters I had written to Gammer from the city. There were fifteen, progressively shorter and more perfunctory, until the last, dated January 18th of this year, which spoke only of the weather. Each letter was worn along the creases, Gammer's callused arthritic fingers moving slowly from word to word as she struggled to read. Yet she had written to me every week for three years, and I – desperate to break loose from her – had not even opened the envelopes before tossing them into the top drawer of the bureau.

How embarrassing it must have been for Gammer to admit she couldn't write. Yet, she must have dictated hundreds of pages – to whom I don't know, any more than I know what was said in them.

Before closing the lap desk, I eased out an envelope that had slipped into the crack at the far back of the compartment. Printed in childish capital letters was, "PLEASE GIVE TO MY

GRANDDAUGHTER SIBYL ELIZABETH WITHERSPOON AFTER MY DEATH."

It is no easy task to write as I have not the schooling of you or your mama and look for words in the dictionary. It takes much time but I do not trust another especially Aggie for what I am about to say. I have gone downhill fast with pain in my heart and cannot find peace. I ask forgiveness for burning our ancestor's diary given to you by your mama before her passing. I take many secrets with me. Better that way. Forgive the wrong I have done you. It was love always. God speed you safe home.

As I read, I started heaving but no tears came, only a thin squealing as though my throat were a dried-out pump. Good Dog, who had been sitting beside me, lifted his head and, pursing his lips into a lopsided O, began to howl.

I felt a cry, painful as a cramp, gather deep inside me and I threw back my head, opened my mouth and joined him in a sound with no edges, no ending, expressing what I'd never been able to say – a long-throated howl of regret for my last angry words to Gammer. For now there could be no reconciliation. For now everything and everyone was gone, leaving me utterly alone.

As suddenly as our howling had begun, it stopped. I took a deep breath. The black-faced young ram had run over to join the sheep and they all stared at us from the far corner of the pasture. Good Dog stood for a moment staring back. Then, lifting his head to sniff the air, he turned and headed along an old sheep path to a stream trickling across the bottom of the field. Stopping to lift his leg on a lichen-covered stone and then splashing through the shallow water, he looked around to make sure I was coming.

As we followed the turn of the stream down the gradual slope, Good Dog flushed out birds from the thickets while I stuffed handfuls of juicy wild strawberries into my mouth.

Perhaps the leaves flickering in the gentle breeze and the constant murmuring of the water are what made it seem as though I were outside time...or was I inside time? Like Good Dog? Yes, I was in Good Dog time...free of my mind...

Not until I saw the mantle from our mahogany fireplace, which had landed on the flat marshland close to the river, did the memory of the destruction flood over me. The wicker basket became unbearably heavy. Collapsing on a small grassy mound, I must have fallen asleep, for I was wandering through the airless gloom of the house, neatening each closed room, picking up and putting right.

Good Dog's barks and growls roused me. I could see him thrashing in the shallows where the stream ran into the river. Concerned that he had cornered a muskrat or a beaver, I was stepping carefully through the mud when I saw – unbelievable as a pot of gold at the end of the rainbow – the hope chest nestled in the reeds and bulrushes a few feet from the water's edge.

Here I am, once again sitting on this soft green mound of grass and moss, and I have finally caught up with what happened since falling (can it be only hours ago?) into the root cellar.

Only a few blank pages remain to be filled. So many words pointing the way to a place deep inside where I hadn't wanted to go. A place I never dreamed I would go. A place I prayed not to go. Was I mad? Hysterical? Possessed? I don't know. A feeling swept over me, swallowing me up even as I was wrestling with it. Gone now. Disappeared. Like the tornado.

Looking across to the far ridge, I can follow how the tornado mowed through the valley erratically – veering, skipping sideways, chopping, jumping over the river to head up the hill behind me. I long to turn. To see what I left behind. But if I look homeward, the tears flooding my veins will harden my heart to salt. I will believe like my Puritan ancestors that God is punishing our family and me for our sins.

So here I am – unable to go back and not ready to go forward – comforted by these final words flowing from my pen. And, of course, by Good Dog, who has tired of chasing whatever moves in this boggy lowland where stream meets river. He sleeps with his big head in my lap, unconcerned that I am using him as a desk to write on. The air has grown cooler and the remains of the sun are a brilliant smudge above the western hills. By a trick of the last fading rays, the surface of the river has been transformed to wavering molten gold.

As I watch the colour dim, the first star appears in the deep purple of the sky. God's eye, I say out loud. In my pocket is the glass eye of the stuffed deer's head that I found in Gammer's shoe. As I am rolling it between my thumb and forefinger, I suddenly understand. It is a sign from Gammer. The umbilical cord that looped around my neck in the womb, and choked me even after I was born, has been loosened by her death. I am free as she is free. What need have I of belongings? I belong to myself… my feet to follow…my eyes to see…

The distant whistle of the evening freight train tells me it must be eight o'clock. Good Dog runs up to me, whining. "What is it?" I ask. He lifts his muzzle, nose quivering, and I, too, catch the scent of roast chicken. I tell him not to worry. Fast Mac is sure to invite us home for dinner. I rummage through the wicker basket. Perhaps Myrtle would like the silver sugar bowl with the filigree design. It has only a small dent.

I am stiff and cold. Every inch of my bruised flesh aches. Taking the torn piece of patchwork quilt from the basket, I fold it into a head scarf as I hear the sound of a tractor and men's voices. Good Dog rushes off to greet them. I will follow, but first I must make my way to where the hope chest is caught in the bulrushes and reeds on the river's edge. Running my fingers over the word LIVE carved into the front, I will push the chest out into the current so it can begin its journey to deeper waters. So, right here, I say goodbye. God speed you safe home.

ACKNOWLEDGEMENTS

I would like to thank Stephanie Keating who was my guiding light, tirelessly reading draft after draft.

I would also like to thank Helane Levine Keating, Arlene Lampert and Ingrid Style for their thoughtful feedback and enthusiasm that never faltered, Jean Greenberg for her meticulous attention to the text, Chris Keating for his endurance.

I owe much gratitude to Barry Callaghan for his support and editorial insight during the many years it took to complete this book.

I am indebted to the many historians whose work helped me in writing the 17th century sections: in particular, John Demos for *Entertaining Satan*, Marion Starkey for *The Devil in Massachusetts*, Paul Boyer and Stephen Nissenbaum for *Salem Possessed* and John Foxe for *Foxe's Book of Martyrs*.

Finally, I thank the Ontario Arts Council and the Leighton Studios at The Banff Centre for the Arts who assisted with finances and facilities.